Working My Way Back to You

by

Doreen Alsen

Lobster Cove Series

Working My Way Back to You

COPYRIGHT © 2015 by Doreen Alsen

Cover Art by *Tina Lynn Stout*

The Wild Rose Press, Inc.
PO Box 708
Adams Basin, NY 14410-0708
Visit us at www.thewildrosepress.com

Publishing History
First Champagne Rose Edition, 2015
Print ISBN 978-1-62830-733-7
Digital ISBN 978-1-62830-734-4

Lobster Cove Series
Published in the United States of America

"She isn't here. Don't say anything else." She disappeared behind the door.

A tiny blonde, Jenna squeezed the bridge of her nose looking like Tinkerbelle trying to stave off a migraine. "I wouldn't dream of doing anything different."

"You are totally made of awesome," Beth said from behind the door. "I owe you."

Jenna sighed. "I'll put it on your tab."

"And that's why I adore you."

"You adore me because I sign your paychecks." The door to the shop opened. "Shut up," Jenna said, *sotto voce*. "May I help you?" she said, in a very hearty voice, to the new arrival in the shop.

"Yeah, I'm looking for someone named Beth." Jeff glanced around the store. "I know this looks weird, but Maggie and Sally told me she works here."

Jenna cleared her throat. "Beth isn't here right now." Big pause. "Do you want to leave her a message?"

Beth trembled waiting for Jeff to answer Jenna. "When she comes back, tell her Jeff Myers was here asking about her. Here's my card so she knows how to get in touch with me."

"You got it."

"Thanks."

Beth waited until the store door opened and closed.

Jenna yelled, "Ollie, Ollie, oxen free! Come out, come out wherever you are!"

Beth inched out of the storeroom. "Thank you so much."

Jenna crossed her arms under her chest. "Okay. Who is that guy and why is he wearing my coffee?"

Dedications

To Jackson, my best buddy, who kept me company
while I worked on this book.

~*~

A great big thank you to the
Ithaca Genre Fiction Critique Group
and to the other authors of the Lobster Cove series.

~*~

And, as always, to Eberhard, Emilia, and Louisa.

Prologue

"Pull over, I'm gonna be sick again!"

Jeff Myers turned his car through the heavy snow onto the side of the road, and Beth threw open the passenger side door and tossed her cookies for the fifth time during their trip.

He undid his seatbelt and reached over to pat her back and pull her hair out of the way, while she hacked out rusty sounding, shuddering sobs. "Shhhhh," he whispered, desperate to help her and not having the first clue how.

Loaded with guilt, tears welled in his eyes. It was his damn fault Beth was puking up her guts.

Frigid air blew snow in the open door and it swirled around them. Miserably cold, eyes burning from driving at night in the worst blizzard of the century, terrified of being caught and arrested, Jeff only wanted to get to Lobster Cove, Maine where he could take care of Beth.

She pulled her head back into the car, leaned against the seat and closed her eyes. Her normally rosy skin had turned so pale and waxy. He ran his hand down her hair. "Want some water?"

She nodded. "I'm so sorry. This must be so gross for you," she croaked.

He turned the cap of the water bottle and handed it to her. "No way. I'm sorry you're going through this."

All because of me, he thought. All because of me.

She rubbed her lips together, licked them, then took a small careful sip of her water. She sighed. "Where are we?"

They'd been driving for hours in a raging blizzard, running from their hometown of Addington, Massachusetts to Lobster Cove, where his best friend's family had a summer home.

High school sweethearts, totally in love, Beth was pregnant and Jeff was the daddy. Beth's father went crazy over it and tried to have Jeff arrested for statutory rape. Jeff nearly hyperventilated at the thought of going to jail.

So, left with no choice, they were on the run, eloping and getting married as soon as they could find a justice of the peace. He would not let Beth's father keep them apart.

They'd been on the road, in whiteout conditions, for what felt like forever, but they were finally just outside of Lobster Cove.

"We're here, I think. All we have to do is find Tim's house."

She gifted him with a watery smile. "Good."

"We'll pick up some food and wait until tomorrow to get married." He leaned over and kissed her on the tip of her nose. "I love you, Bethy. I'm going to take care of you and the baby." He hoped.

To tell the truth, he was scared shitless. Scared of going to jail, scared of getting married, scared of having a baby.

Totally terrified.

She bit her lower lip. "You don't think Tim and Katie told on us?"

"Not Tim. But I don't know about Katie. She's your friend, not mine."

"She might." Beth frowned and rubbed her stomach. "If she gets worried."

"Well, let's hope she doesn't." He checked the GPS, put the car in gear, and tried to pull off the shoulder. He could barely see the road for the snow. The car wheels spun and whined, but he managed to get back on the road. "We'll be there soon." He rested his right hand on the gearshift.

Beth covered his hand with her small, cold one. "Good."

They didn't talk much as they drove on into town. Just about everything was closed because of the storm, but they found a grocery store on First Street where they picked up some food, including Saltines and ginger ale for Beth.

Tim's house appeared all boarded up for the winter, but Tim had given Jeff the key for the one door not covered with weathered pine. They trudged through the deep snow and let themselves in the dark, cold cottage. They found some flashlights right where Tim said they'd be. Because of the dark, Jeff couldn't see if the fireplace was good to use, so he didn't dare try to light one. The two of them cuddled under a mountain of blankets.

Beth dropped right off to sleep, her head on his chest while he held her in his arms. He drifted off, only to wake to the sound of someone banging on the door. "Jeff Myers! Open up, son! We're the police."

Chapter One

"Jeff, can I have a minute?"

Jeff Myers stopped in the high school hallway and turned to see Principal Julia Stewart behind him. "Sure! You can have two."

She laughed. "I just wanted to check in and see how it's going. How you're settling in."

He smiled. "It's going great! The kids are putting one hundred per cent into it and I think the Lobster Cove Sharks will have a winning season if they keep this up."

The petite blonde nodded. "Good. Look, I want to talk to you about the proposal you gave me for that football clinic you want to do next summer. Make an appointment with Beth Anderson to set up a meeting."

"Absolutely." Jeff rubbed his hands together. "I'll do it right away."

"Good." She gave him a smile and walked away.

Jeff felt a huge grin spread across his face. Here he was, his first teaching and coaching job in one of the prettiest towns in the nation, Lobster Cove, Maine.

The last time he'd been in Lobster Cove he'd been on his way to elope with his pregnant girlfriend. It had been smack dab in the middle of winter in a blinding snowstorm. He shoved thoughts of Beth to the back of his mind, where they belonged.

Now he was here teaching Physical Education at

the high school and coaching football, a dream gig. Football had saved his sanity back when his life was going to hell. Now, he could pay it forward and help kids find the joy in the game and in what they could do with hard work and dedication.

He just really liked working with kids.

His stomach grumbled, so he needed to grab something to eat before he ran to his next thing, sign-ups for the Lobster Cove youth football team. He knew just where to go.

Maggie's Diner. Where he always went.

He sucked at cooking.

Thankfully, Maggie and Jill, the owners, had a lobster burger with his name on it.

****

"Oh, you've got to see this guy, Beth. He is wicked hot." Sally Pelletier, one of the waitresses at Maggie's Diner, fanned herself with a menu. "Sex on a stick. Hottie McHotterson hot."

Beth Rawson laughed. "Oh, really?"

"My hand to God, yes." She tossed back her head. "Paige and Avery say all the girls are totally crushing on him. Watching football practice has become everyone's favorite way to goof off after school." She leaned over the counter. "They say he's a dead ringer for Channing Tatum," she confided.

"With him taking over the rec. department's youth football program I hear there're going to be a lot more kids joining so their moms can go watch practice," Maggie Harris, the diner's owner chimed in.

"I'll keep that in mind," Beth said.

"You should sign Danny up," Sally told her.

Let her son play football? No way. "Maybe," Beth

5

fudged. "I'll check into it." Not.

"Here's your iced coffees, one regular, one just cream." Sally put Beth's order on the counter. "Tell Jenna we said hey."

"Will do." As Beth picked up the go-cups, the bell to the diner's front door jangled. She turned quickly.

And ran smack into one of the hardest bodies she'd ever met.

Really. Like a wall.

The cold coffee and ice poured out of the crushed cups, all over Beth's hands. She jumped back as they landed on the floor, spilling more coffee on slacks and shoes. "Oh my God, I'm so sorry!" She looked up at her victim.

Her stomach dropped to her feet. That handsome face she never thought she'd see again.

Jeff Myers was standing right in front of her.

Her son Danny's father.

The father he didn't know about.

Which made Danny and Jeff even, because Jeff didn't know about his son either.

In the flesh, all 6 feet, 2 gorgeous inches of him. Dripping with the icy liquid she'd just dumped on him. "Oh no," she gasped.

He looked at her like he was seeing a ghost. "Beth?"

No time to be a hero. She pushed past him and skedaddled out of the diner as fast as her Minnetonka booties would take her.

****

Jeff didn't know what to be more shocked about, being drenched with coffee or seeing an exact replica of Beth Pritchard's face. It had to be her. No one else in the world had blue eyes as beautiful as hers. And those freckles.

Unless being back in Lobster Cove had turned him insane and made him imagine seeing Beth everywhere.

The hair on the back of his neck stood up and tingled.

First he had to deal with Sally and Maggie fussing at him.

Oh, and the fact that he'd been doused with coffee.

"Oh no, Mr. Myers! I'm so sorry." Both Maggie and Sally barreled toward him carrying rolls of paper towels.

He pulled his shirt away from his abs. "S'okay." He'd have to detour to his apartment before he went to sign-ups. "Who was that?"

Sally scrunched her eyebrows together as she swabbed at his button-down shirt with paper towels. "Beth?" She shook her head. "She's usually not so—"

"Clumsy?" he asked. Actually? All he heard was the name Beth. Saw the brown hair. Saw that sweet, sweet face.

His Bethy had been a bit of a klutz. He'd teased her about it all the time.

"Are you hurt?" Maggie handed him a cold, wet towel.

He lied. "I'm good." He wanted to get out of there to follow her.

"No, you're not good." Maggie was all business as she cleaned him up.

Sally swabbed a little more south. "Did you chill anything vital?"

"I'm okay. You might want to check that lady's hands." He shifted to get a little bit away from Sally.

"I'm sure she's fine." Sally rubbed against his lower belly with more enthusiasm. "She'll be okay."

But was she Beth? His Beth? He had to know.

"Where do you think she went?" He checked out their confused expressions.

Maggie took charge. "She works for Jenna Sanborn at Happy Thoughts, just a couple of doors down. What can we make for you? You did come in here to get food."

Dripping coffee not withstanding, he ordered. "I came for a lobster burger, of course." He gave them a grin that belied the fact he'd just been gob-smacked. "I need one, Maggie. No one makes them like you."

Maggie sniffed. "No one else makes them, period."

True. They were one of a kind. Large pieces of lobster tail and claw, little bites of sweet red pepper, and lime-marinated hot jalapenos held together by some sour cream and crispy Panko bread crumbs. Even better when they had some fresh tomalley to top it.

"Yours will be on the house tonight, Jeff," Maggie said. "I've got tomalley. Want some on it?"

"You know I do." A true New Englander, he loved the soft green lobster liver mixed with the coral-colored roe. "And a bottle of Moxie, please." He turned and looked out the front window. "Where did you say this Beth works?"

"Happy Thoughts," Sally said. "The brand new sewing shop three doors down."

Chapter Two

"Hide me." Beth scrambled into Happy Thoughts, the everything-you'll-ever-need-for-any-kind-of-sewing shop. Her boss, Jenna Sanborn, raised her eyebrows. "I thought you went to get us some coffee."

"That was the plan. I ran into a problem." She dashed into the storeroom then peeked her head out. "If a guy comes in looking for a Beth Pritchard, tell him you don't know where she is right now."

"There's a story here, and I'm sure I want to hear about it later."

"Beth Pritchard," Beth hissed. "She isn't here. Don't say anything else." She disappeared behind the door.

A tiny blonde, Jenna squeezed the bridge of her nose looking like Tinkerbelle trying to stave off a migraine. "I wouldn't dream of doing anything different."

"You are totally made of awesome," Beth said from behind the door. "I owe you."

Jenna sighed. "I'll put it on your tab."

"And that's why I adore you."

"You adore me because I sign your paychecks." The door to the shop opened. "Shut up," Jenna said, *sotto voce*. "May I help you?" she said, in a very hearty voice, to the new arrival in the shop.

"Yeah, I'm looking for someone named Beth." Jeff

glanced around the store. "I know this looks weird, but Maggie and Sally told me she works here."

Jenna cleared her throat. "Beth isn't here right now." Big pause. "Do you want to leave her a message?"

Beth trembled waiting for Jeff to answer Jenna. "When she comes back, tell her Jeff Myers was here asking about her. Here's my card so she knows how to get in touch with me."

"You got it."

"Thanks."

Beth waited until the store door opened and closed.

Jenna yelled, "Ollie, Ollie, oxen free! Come out, come out wherever you are!"

Beth inched out of the storeroom. "Thank you so much."

Jenna crossed her arms under her chest. "Okay. Who is that guy and why is he wearing my coffee?"

Beth hurried to the window to make sure Jeff was gone. "It's a long story."

"I'm getting that."

Beth turned to face Jenna. "I am so screwed."

"Why don't you tell Aunt Jenna all about it." She leaned on the glass counter.

Beth burst into tears.

"Oh, God. What did that rat bastard do to you?"

"It's not what he did to me. It's what I did to him." Her breath shuddered in and out.

"Okay." Jenna's tone brooked no disobedience. "Spill, girlfriend." She handed Beth a tissue.

Beth took the tissue and blew her nose with a loud, prolonged honk. "No."

"Why did I know you'd say that?" Jenna lifted her

eyes toward the sky. "If I threaten to fire you, will you tell me?"

Beth blew her nose again. "Maybe."

"Reconsider that answer, sweetie."

"Okay, okay, I will." Beth looked at her feet. "But not right now. I do have one request."

Jenna nodded. "Shoot."

"My last name is Pritchard. And I don't have a child."

Jenna blinked several times. "That's two things." She shook her head like she needed to clear it. "Except for the fact that your last name is Rawson and you do have a kid." Jenna had a clear WTF look on her face.

"I can't say anything right now. Just please don't ask me any more questions until I'm ready to answer them. I promise it'll be soon."

"Better be," Jenna muttered. "I can keep a secret." She grinned at her.

"Thank you." Beth grabbed another tissue and blew her nose.

"I'll find out sooner or later no matter what you say or don't say." She leveled her eyes at Beth, the intensity making Beth squirm in her sensible but oh-so-cute shoes.

"Please, Jenna. I've got excellent reasons, but I can't talk about it right now."

"Okay." She shook her finger. "Remember that I am not a patient person. God, I need some coffee."

Beth sighed. "I can go to Bea's if you want."

"I'll go. You stay here and mind the store."

"Whatever you say, boss."

"I love the way you say that." Jenna grimaced. "You're lucky I like you."

"I know, I know." Beth heaved a huge breath. "I'm the luckiest woman on earth."

As Jenna left, Beth reflected on her luck.

She'd been pretty damn lucky. Even though it hadn't seemed so ten years ago.

How could Jeff marry the woman who called the police on him, knowing he could get arrested. The woman who ruined their lives.

What a jerk! Her blood pressure spiked just remembering how devastated she felt when she found out he'd married her. It still made her irate.

Now that Jeff and Katie lived in Lobster Cove, Beth would have to find a way to tell him about Danny.

Katie could take a flying leap, the traitor. Beth clenched her teeth. No way did she want her playing mommy to Danny.

She'd figure it out. She had to.

****

Jeff looked out over the park watching the kids run around. Just like puppies, they tumbled and dove onto each other. The chilly breeze held a hint of the coming season, falling leaves, the bite and tang from the sea. Perfect football weather.

"I want to sign up for the team."

He looked at the kid standing in front of him. Cute kid. Messy brown hair, a Lobster Cove Sharks sweatshirt over grass-stained jeans and kicks that were coming untied. Typical ten-year-old boy. "That's great! Where're your parents?"

The kid scuffed the toe of his sneaker in the sand. "My mom's at work. I don't have a dad."

Jeff knew how that felt. He'd grown up without one too. His high school football coach was the closest thing he'd had to a father. Jeff's brows smashed together across his forehead. "Is there anyone here with you, an adult who's responsible for you?"

He jerked his head toward a woman who'd just registered another boy. "Mrs. Parks is taking me home."

"I can't let you sign on your own, without a parent."

"Danny?" Mrs. Parks and her son Ben came up behind the kid.

Danny. Okay.

Jeff tapped his pen against the clipboard he held. "Danny wants to join the team, Mrs. Parks. He says you can do that."

"Oh, no," she said. "I'm just keeping him at my house until his mom can get him." She looked down at Danny. "You know your mom doesn't want you to play football. C'mon, we have to go." Smiling at Jeff, she put one hand on Danny's shoulder and one on Ben's to guide them away. "Thank you, Mr. Myers."

"Call me Coach," Jeff said. "I'll see you and Ben tomorrow afternoon."

They walked in the direction of the parking lot. Danny dragged his feet, head bowed, shoulders slumped forward. Before he got to the car, he looked back at Jeff, sighed and gave him a little wave.

Poor thing.

The kid wanted to play football. He should be able to play football. He'd ask Mrs. Parks tomorrow who Danny's mother was and go and talk to her himself.

Chapter Three

"Mom, I want to sign up for football," Danny said as Beth put his dinner down in front of him. "And quit piano lessons."

"Danny, we've talked about this." Beth got her own plate and sat across the table. "You're too talented. You can't quit your piano lessons."

He poked his fork into the macaroni and cheese and pushed the noodles around. "But Ben is gonna be on the team and I want to play, too."

"I think it'll just be too much." Beth put her napkin in her lap. "With homework and piano practice, you're already plenty busy." Not to mention the ruin of any kind of music career if he permanently injured his hands.

"But I really want to be on the team." He stabbed at his carrots. "It'll be fun and the coach is really nice."

"You need a lot of equipment to play football. That might cost more than we can afford right now." She'd taken the job at Happy Thoughts because the economy was hell on people trying to afford piano lessons. Fortunately Jenna had needed a little help to get her brand new business off the ground.

"I can do stuff to make some money." Danny's eyes lit up. "I can mow lawns for people and I can be a dog walker. People need someone to walk their dogs all the time."

Beth resisted the urge to close her eyes. Danny wanted a dog more than anything else in the whole world. Given Beth's work schedule it would be unfair to bring a dog into the mix. She'd lost her appetite, but forked up a piece of chicken to set a good example. "That's really sweet of you to offer, buddy, but I don't think so."

Danny heaved a huge sigh. "I really want to play football, Mom." He looked at her with swimming eyes. "Please. All you have to do is talk to Coach Myers and I can play."

She lost the ability to breathe for a second. Coach Myers?

Oh, no, no, no, no, no.

Beth set down her fork very carefully. "I'll think about it." She plastered a smile across her face. "What else went on today at school? How'd you do on that math test?"

"Okay." Danny shrugged. "It wasn't hard."

She managed to keep the conversation away from football and Coach Myers for the rest of the evening. Danny helped her load the dishwasher and did his homework at the kitchen table while she took care of cleaning the rest of the dinner debris and polishing the stove and counters.

She pretended to read a book while he practiced piano. Danny really had the gift. The Bach Two-Part Invention got better every time she heard it and he was getting a good start on the first movement of the Mozart sonata. She'd worried it might be too hard for him, but he was digging in and finding the music in it as he learned the notes, rhythms and fingerings.

He got a little bit of reading time after his bath,

then bed. It made for a lot of activities to fit in already. Football would be just one more thing.

How long would it take for Jeff to see that he was Danny's father?

About a half an hour after Danny went to bed, the phone rang. "Hello?"

"Hey, Beth," Anita Parks said. "Hope I'm not calling too late."

"No, not at all." Beth frowned. "What's up?"

"I wanted to talk to you about Danny playing football on the rec team with Ben."

"Okay." Not. "I'm afraid football is too violent."

"It's flag football. They don't let them tackle each other at this level."

"Well…"

"It would make both boys so happy. Ben wants to, but not without Danny. I know you can't get there to drop them off and pick them up. I don't mind doing the driving at all."

"I don't know," she fretted, her heart heavy.

"You should have seen him today. He wanted to be a part of all the fun. Ben really wants Danny to join with him. If you let him, it'll so be doing me a favor."

She couldn't argue with that. Anita already did Beth so many favors she would never, ever catch up. "What's involved?"

"All you have to do is give me permission to sign him up and it'll all be taken care of. I called Coach Myers up to find out if I could be your proxy and he said he didn't think there'd be a problem."

"You talked to him about me?" Her voice squeaked.

"Well, yeah. I had to. Is that a problem?"

Beth took a breath. As far as Lobster Cove knew, Danny's mother was Beth Rawson, not Beth Pritchard. No way Jeff should put two and two together based on that. "No, of course not." She swallowed. "I guess it's okay. I don't see how it's a favor to you, but if you say so, I'm happy to let it happen."

"Fabulous!" Anita laughed. "The boys will have so much fun. Pack some sweats and stuff in a bag for Danny tomorrow and we'll figure out the rest later. Coach said we didn't have to worry about equipment quite yet. And Beth..." Anita's voice got softer, like she didn't want anyone else to hear, "He's so handsome. Movie star handsome. Channing Tatum handsome."

Twice today with the Channing Tatum comparison! Beth thought Jeff was way, way more handsome than Channing Tatum. "Well, I imagine his wife enjoys having such a good-looking husband." Traitor Katie, the Queen of the Skanks.

"His wife? I don't think he's married. He wasn't wearing a ring, but then a lot of guys don't. Anyway, thanks. The boys will have so much fun. G'night!"

"Yeah. Good night." Beth hung up the phone, closed her eyes and tried to come to grips with the fact that at some point she'd not only have to deal with Jeff directly, but also she'd run into Katie.

Maybe she'd get an answer as to why Jeff married her after she betrayed them both so badly.

Jeff hadn't aged much at all. He still wore his brown hair military short, still had the same mouthwatering athlete's body only bigger and more muscular. Why did he still have to look so good? She hoped Katie had gained a million pounds and

17

contracted some kind of flesh-eating disease that left her disfigured.

How could he have married her? It just boggled her mind. Beth turned off the light and sat in the dark. Life had been going along fine since her father died and she'd finally gotten control of her life.

All hell was going to break loose and there was no help for it. She had to find a way to tell Jeff and Danny about each other and get some answers of her own.

****

Jeff was eighteen again, wrapped around Beth in the backseat of his mother's Volvo. He caressed her soft skin, kissed her sweet mouth, and lost himself in first love. He couldn't remember the last time he'd been so happy.

A strident noise pulled him out of the dream.

A dream he didn't want to leave. He was back with Beth, back when he knew what love was. He bolted awake and grabbed for the phone next to his ear. "Myers."

"Jeff, it's me."

Katie. He'd recognize that pissed-off tone anywhere.

Especially as he'd just woken from the sound of Beth's voice in his head. "What do you want?"

Katie sighed. "The support check isn't enough."

The hell it wasn't. "It's what our lawyers agreed on."

"We've had some extra expenses. Cookie was promoted to the next level of her dance class and made the competition team. She needs to get the costumes and some other things."

Well, hell. "How much?"

"With traveling fees along with the costumes and shoes and the increased tuition," Katie hesitated, "about $700.00."

"Are you kidding me? What are the shoes made of—solid gold?"

"No, but she needs shoes in several colors, to go with the different outfits, and then there are the traveling fees and the hotel fees. I'm not making anything up."

And he was the Easter Bunny.

"The fact is," Katie continued in that snotty tone he hated, "Cookie is a talented dancer and she needs this. Of course, if money is more important than your daughter—"

Ah, there was the Katie he knew and didn't love. "I want receipts."

A yelp of outrage assaulted his ears. "You bastard. You actually think I'd cheat you?"

"My lawyer told me to get documentation for every check I send you. Matter of fact, why don't you send the receipts directly to my lawyer."

"I'm not a cheat, you—"

"Or give them to your lawyer to give to mine. I don't care. As long as it's to the letter of the law."

"Cookie wants to talk to you."

"Jesus, Katie. It's eleven at night. Why is a six-year-old still up on a school night?"

"She wanted to talk to her daddy." Katie's voice dripped saccharine. "Unless you don't have time to talk to your daughter."

He gave up. "Of course I want to talk to her. Put her on the phone."

There were some fumbling noises. "Hi, Daddy."

His daughter yawned.

"You're up late, Cookie."

"Mama told me she was calling you and I wanted to talk to you."

"You can call me anytime. You don't need to stay up late until your mom can call me on her schedule."

"I'm on the competition team, Daddy. If we're good enough, we'll go to the Big E next August."

The Big E was a six-state fair held in Springfield, Massachusetts. All the New England states were competing and with exhibits. It was huge.

Bigger than huge.

"That's great, Cookie girl! I hope you guys make the cut."

"When can I come see you, Daddy?"

More guilt. Yay. "That's up to your mom, of course." Dammit. Since he'd moved out of state, Katie controlled when and where Jeff saw his daughter.

"You can come here to see me, Daddy." Jeff heard the pout and petulance in her voice.

Another damn. "Don't worry, princess. I'll get to Addington as soon as I can. It's hard starting a new job."

"S'okay. Mom wants to talk to you again."

"Okay. I love you, Cookie girl." He did with his whole heart.

She yawned again into the phone. "I love you, Daddy."

There were some muffled sounds as the phone passed from Cookie to Katie. "We need to put a deposit on the costumes by next Monday. Is that a problem?"

As if she cared. "A deposit?" Thank heaven he didn't have to cough the full shot right away. "No, it's not a problem." At least not much of one. He'd figure it out. "You be sure to send me some pictures."

"I wouldn't have to if you made the effort to come visit."

"The new job is taking a lot of my time. I'm not the highest man on the totem pole here."

"They should make some accommodations for you to visit your daughter."

"Maybe you should be thankful I finally have a job that gives you all the things you want."

"All I ever wanted was you." Katie sniffed.

If he didn't know better, he'd have thought she was crying. But he did know better. Been there, done that, got the T-shirt. "Well, that didn't work out for either of us, did it?"

"And we know why that happened," she said in a bile-laced tone. "There were three of us in that marriage. You, me and Saint Beth."

Jeff would not talk about Beth again with Katie. He most certainly wasn't telling her he thought he'd found her here in Lobster Cove. "Is there anything else? I'm tired and I've got a long day tomorrow."

Silence. His favorite tone of Katie's voice.

"That's it. I'll be looking for your check."

"Of course you will. I'll put it in the mail tomorrow along with the usual documentation."

"Fine."

"Is that all?" he asked.

"Yes. Good night." Katie's voice was tight right before she snapped off the phone.

He could count on three things. Death, taxes, and Katie being a bitch.

Chapter Four

Jenna crossed her arms underneath her breasts. "So spill. I'm running out of patience." She handed Beth one of the blueberry muffins she'd brought in from Sweet Bea's.

"Thanks." Beth really wasn't hungry but took the muffin anyway. "I'm sorry."

"Forget sorry." Jenna laughed. "Be loquacious. As in, talk a lot. Don't leave out a single detail."

There were many times Beth wished she could forget every detail of her past. But she couldn't lie to Jenna.

"Jeff Myers is Danny's father."

Jenna's jaw dropped open. "Get outta here!"

"It's true. We went to high school together back in Massachusetts, were childhood sweethearts, like as in shy, musical geek falling head over heels for the gorgeous quarterback of the football team." Beth shrugged. "Long story short, I got pregnant." She swallowed. "My father hit the roof, like totally lost it."

"Was Jeff one of those jerk jocks that take advantage of you?"

"Oh no, nothing like that. We were really in love, both of us. Anyway, like I said, my father went ballistic."

"Well, can you blame him?" Jenna broke off the top of her muffin. "I can only imagine what Bran would do if we had a daughter and some jock got her pregnant."

"It was really bad. Really bad. He went insane." She picked up the glass of iced tea she had at her side. "Tried to have Jeff arrested for rape. Jeff and I ran away so it wouldn't happen." She took a sip of tea. "We ended up right here in Lobster Cove in the middle of a huge blizzard."

"Yikes." Jenna put her hand on Beth's arm. "What happened next?"

"My supposed best friend, his current wife, the biggest skank in the universe, told on us, like actually called the Lobster Cove police and my father so we got hauled back to Addington. My father packed up me and my mom and made sure we disappeared. He got super paranoid about Jeff finding where we were and moved us all over the place."

"How'd she know where you were going?"

"One of Jeff's friend's family had a summer cottage here. We were going to stay there until we could find a justice of the peace and get married."

"Oh, honey. I'm so sorry."

Beth nodded. "Here's the thing. My father wanted me to give Danny up for adoption but I couldn't do it. I begged him to let me keep him."

"Obviously he let you."

"But with a price. I had to change my last name to Rawson and give Danny that name, too. I could never let Jeff know about Danny or have any contact with him at all."

Jenna shook her head, broke off a hunk of muffin, and popped it into her mouth. "Damn, this is good." She swallowed. "Aren't your parents dead?"

"Yeah. I was going to do the right thing, find Jeff and tell him about Danny."

"What stopped you? I mean, I'm guessing he still doesn't know—hence all the secrecy."

Beth shook her head. "I looked him up on Facebook. His status said he was married"—she scowled—"to Skankarella—who called the police on us, remember?" She sniffed. "Bitch. Call me petty, but I just couldn't make myself share my son with her." Shrugging, she said, "Plus I was so mad he married the one person who split us apart and ruined my life, who almost got him sent to jail, I decided he was too stupid to deserve to know Danny. So I kept quiet."

Jenna frowned. "You'll have to tell him at some point. Lobster Cove is a really small town. You need to give him the news before he finds out on his own."

"I know, I know. I just don't know how I'm going to find the courage to share my son with the two of them." She took another sip of tea to cool her temper down. "But there's more."

Jenna groaned. "Of course there is. Do I want to know?" She shook her head. "What am I asking? Of course I want to know."

"My father wouldn't let Danny know he was created outside of marriage, so he made up a husband for me and a father for Danny. For his whole life Danny's believed his father died a hero in Afghanistan before he was born."

"Holy petunia."

"For real. How can I tell my son I've lied to him for his whole life? He's going to hate me."

"You're his mother, he's not going to hate you. I imagine he'll be mad for a while, but he loves you.

24

He'll come around."

"But what if Jeff sues for custody? He's married and has a good job. I'm a single mother, working all these pick up jobs to take care of us. I don't have the money to hire a lawyer." Beth ran her hands over her face. "I've let it go on so long. I don't know what to do."

"Don't get ahead of yourself and borrow trouble. I haven't heard anything about a wife, but if anyone can find out, it's Sally at the diner. I'll schmooze her to find out what she knows." Jenna stood. "Why don't you go talk to Father Zack? I know the two of you are close. Maybe he can help you come up with a plan."

Beth pursed her lips. "That's probably a good idea. I've got a meeting with him tomorrow about some extra music for mass on Sunday. I'll ask him then."

"Good." The big antique clock on the wall chimed five o'clock. "Closing time. We did pretty well today." Jenna smiled as she went to the store's door, turned the lock and flipped the Open sign to Closed. "You've got a lot of friends here and they're strangers in town. Don't forget that."

Beth got up and took the plate with her untouched muffin to the little kitchen off the storeroom. Sure, she had friends now. They'd most likely all hate her by the time word of her secret got out.

Chapter Five

Jeff's Junior Sharks ran laps. A mixed bag of abilities, as usual, but they were enthusiastic. Most of them had some experience playing football, but there were a couple who'd never been on a team before.

That was okay. He loved introducing kids to the game.

One kid in particular caught his eye. That kid from yesterday, Danny Rawson, had shown up today with permission from his mom to be on the team.

The kid could run. He turned out to be super-fast and agile. Jeff couldn't wait to see what the kid could do when shown how to throw the ball.

Some of the kids were slowing down. He blew his whistle. The kids looked at him.

"Walk it off and take a water break!" Some kids were visibly relieved. Not this Danny kid. He looked disappointed, like he wanted to keep running, but he followed orders. Jeff remembered the feeling. Back in the day he couldn't stand still even if his life had depended on it. He never walked when he could run, never sat when he could stand, always had to be on the move.

He walked over to the kid. "Hey, Danny. You're a pretty fast runner."

Danny grinned. "I like to run."

"I could tell." He cleared his throat. Somehow a

lump had formed in there. The kid just got to him. "So, you got your mom to let you join the team."

"Mrs. Parks did that. First Mom said no because she wants me to play the piano and I don't want to." Danny looked up at him with happy eyes. "Mom said I got a lot going on and that we can't afford the equipment, but then she said yes. I told her I'd do some stuff to get the money for the equipment but she said she didn't care. She'd figure it out." He wrinkled his nose. "She works a lot of jobs because my dad died in Afghanistan and sometimes she says money is tight."

Jeff resolved that Danny would get his equipment for free. "I'm sorry you lost your dad." However, he was curious. "What would you do to get the money?"

"Lots of things. Mowing lawns, cleaning garages, walking dogs." He rubbed his grimy hand over his mouth. "I really want to walk dogs."

"Like dogs, huh?" Jeff didn't want to speculate about how many germs were on the hand Danny swiped across his face. "Me, too."

"I really want a dog, but we're not home enough to take care of one. Mom says maybe someday."

Jeff smiled. The kid was a pistol.

He noticed a couple of boys pushing each other around over by the bench.

Okay, break time over. He blew the whistle. "Everyone come over here and grab a ball. We're going to learn to pass!"

****

"Hey, Beth! Thanks for coming in special for this." Father Zack beamed at Beth.

Larger than life, Father Zack had a full head of gray hair as well as a bushy gray beard. Today he wore one of his favorite tie-dye shirts over a pair of jeans and running shoes.

He was a great boss. If you were good at your job, he pretty much left you alone to do it.

The youth of St. Joseph's Catholic Church loved him.

"Happy to do it. What's up?" Beth's stomach might as well have been filled with a flock of hummingbirds, their long, pointy, beaky things poking her. Confession might be good for the soul but it was hell on the gut.

"The twenty-first is the International Day of Peace. I think we need to make sure all the music is about bringing about peace next Sunday."

Beth sighed inwardly. The choir was so going to bitch about music changes they hadn't practiced. "No problem. Do you have any songs in mind?"

"I thought you'd never ask." Father Zack opened a file on his desk, took a paper out of it then handed her the paper. "Everyone should know these."

Of course they did. Every single one of them was a hippie cliché. She grimaced inside.

Father Zack hadn't quite left the sixties behind.

Could have an up side. Maybe the choir would keep quiet for once and not complain about having to learn new music. "I'm sure there'll be no problem."

"Great." He leaned forward on the desk, planted his elbows on top of it. "I really appreciate your flexibility about the music. I know it's a problem that I'm so last minute."

"Well, that was true, but, I knew the twenty-first is world peace day. I should have been on the ball."

Zack studied her. "You okay?"

She shook her head. "No. I'm nowhere near okay."

"Want to tell ol' Father Zack about it?"

"No, not really." She met his gaze. "But I need some advice."

"Shoot."

Beth told him the whole story. He listened and didn't say a word until she finished.

"Lucy, you got some 'splainin' to do." Father Zack picked up his pen and drummed it on his desk blotter.

She hung her head. "I have to tell Danny and Jeff, but I just don't know how to do it."

"Here's an idea. You just sit face-to-face with them and tell them the truth."

"Easier said than done," Beth muttered.

"Duh."

A laugh tickled the back of her throat. "Seriously. What do I do? How do I do it without making them hate me?"

"I don't know."

"Plus, how do I share my child with Katie? Oh, God." Beth wrapped her arms around her middle. "I can't do it."

Zack waited until she had calmed herself. She appreciated that about him.

"Cross that bridge when you come to it," Father Zack advised.

"I've lied to everyone in town. How do I come back from that?"

"I don't know. I guess it's uncharted territory." He leaned back in his chair. "I've got my faith in you.

She wished she had that same faith. "From your mouth to God's ears, Father." She made the sign of the cross. "From your mouth to God's ears."

Chapter Six

Jeff took a deep breath as he stood outside the Happy Thoughts door. He needed to know once and for all if the Beth who worked here was his Beth. He grabbed the door handle and pushed his way in.

The little blonde Tinkerbelle clone stood behind the cash register. He barely noticed her. His gaze focused on the slender dark haired woman putting cards of buttons on a display. "Beth."

She turned at the sound of his voice, blue eyes wide, rose-colored lips open. She'd been a pretty girl ten years ago, but the woman standing in front of him was beautiful. She still wore her long brown hair up in a ponytail. He remembered slipping off the elastic so he could run his fingers through the soft silky strands.

His heart clanged like a church bell on Christmas Eve. Beth. His Beth.

"I knew it was you," he whispered.

"Jeff." She clasped her hands in front of her. "Long time, no see."

He crossed to her and wrapped her in his arms. Inhaling deeply, he rested his cheek on the top of her head. "You just disappeared. Where did you go?"

Beth pulled away and took a step back. "All over. My father didn't let us stay in one place very long." She hesitated. "He's dead now. My father. My mother, too."

He grabbed her hands. "What about the baby?"

Beth looked at the floor. It was several heartbeats before she looked up. "A girl. We made sure she went to a good home."

The blonde behind the counter coughed like she was hacking up a lung. "Excuse me."

"I'm so sorry. I've always had this dream that…well, never mind. It must have hurt."

"My father didn't give me much choice."

He nodded. "Listen, can I take you out to dinner sometime?" He just blurted it out.

A glacier of ice slid across Beth's gaze. "Will your wife be joining us?"

Damn. "You know about me and Katie?"

"I found out, yes. How dare you ask me out while you're married to…her?"

Didn't take an advanced degree in physics to figure out Beth had some hard feelings about that. "Katie and I got divorced a year ago. She still lives in Addington." He fought the urge to touch her since it looked like she didn't want him to. "With our daughter Cookie."

"You have a daughter with Katie?"

"Yes. She's the light of my life." A thought blinked across his brain as his stomach clenched. "Are you married?"

"No."

"Dating?"

"Look, Jeff, I don't think dinner would be a good idea. There's no point in rehashing the past."

"Then we can talk about the now. I can't believe both of us ended up back here. I'm coaching football at the high school. I've got to call Coach Mike and Mrs. Coach and tell them I found you."

She raised one eyebrow. "Mrs. Coach?"

"You don't know? Of course you don't. Mike married Andi Nelson. Well, she's Andi Kelly now. We kind of got into the habit of calling her Mrs. Coach. She really took your leaving hard."

Beth brought a hand to her mouth. "I miss her so much. Are they happy?"

Jeff wished she'd missed him, too. "Deliriously. Come on, Bethy. Come to dinner with me. I'll catch you up with all the news." He didn't care if he had to beg. "Please."

She shook her head. "I don't think so, Jeff."

"I'm going to keep after you, you know. I'm pretty stubborn when it comes to getting what I want."

"The answer's not going to change. I'm sorry."

He grinned. "We'll just have to see about that." Though it was difficult to do, he turned around and left the store. But he'd be back. He didn't give up without a fight

****

"Oh my everlovin' God! How could you say no to hunka-hunka burnin' love there?" Jenna fanned herself.

Beth braced herself against the button display because her legs didn't want to work any more. All her circuits had fried. "I can't breathe."

"I know the feeling." Jenna came out from behind the counter and pulled Beth into a little gold brocade covered chair. "Why won't you go to dinner with him?"

"I can't! Not until I figure out how to tell him about Danny. And he has a daughter with Katie, a daughter who is the light of his freaking life. How could he?"

"At least Skankarella is now his ex-wife," Jenna pointed out.

"He still married her! And had a child with her!" She'd stopped trembling and could breathe again.

"Go to dinner with him and ask."

"That would be so humiliating. No way. It's best I stay away from him.

"I'd do it sooner rather than later, especially since Danny's on his football team." She folded her arms over her chest. "That whopper you told about having a baby girl and giving her up for adoption wasn't your finest moment."

"He hadn't told me he and Katie were divorced at that point."

Jenna shot her a pointed glance.

Beth's shoulders slumped. "I know, I know. I let jealousy get the better of me."

Jenna squeezed her shoulder. "Let's get back to work." She winked. "Those button cards won't go on display by themselves."

Beth nodded, thankful for the busy work. "Yes, ma'am."

She had to admit Jeff still had a hold on her. Just being in the same room with him made her heart race like Secretariat. God, what a mess!

Chapter Seven

"Mom, can we go to Shucker's Booktique to look for the new *Adventures of The Refractor comic?*"

Beth stopped stirring pancake batter to look at Danny. "Sure thing, baby. I need to pick up the latest Scarlette LaFlamme novel."

He pretended to gag.

"Hey, I like romance novels. I don't make fun of The Refractor."

"That's because The Refractor's totally dope!"

Beth and Danny loved Saturdays. They slept in and she made him pancakes and spent the day with him doing whatever he wanted.

That would change in a couple of weekends when the Junior Sharks had their first football game, which she'd still had to figure out a good reason to miss.

Danny's grin was worth a million bucks. Beth wouldn't trade it for anything in the world. She hated making him sad, which she would if she didn't go to the game. That's all there was to it.

In the meantime, "Go wash your hands. Pancakes are up in a minute."

"Thanks, Mom!" He ran off.

She couldn't ignore the reality waiting down the line. She had to come clean. Which meant Katie would be in Danny's life. She didn't trust Skanky Katie with Danny.

With anything.

End of story.

Jeff was still an unknown factor. Would he favor his daughter over Danny? She had no freaking idea. She hadn't slept in what felt like forever. She'd spent the past couple nights sitting in his bedroom watching her boy sleep.

The aroma of scorched chocolate chips pulled her back into Saturday morning. She dumped the ruined pancakes into the sink. After that she opened the oven warming the other pancakes. "Danny! Pancakes are up."

She smiled as he ran into the kitchen.

"Mom, you're the best!" He hopped onto a chair. "I love you."

Beth sat in the chair across from Danny. "I love you, baby boy. So much."

He looked up and grinned, his mouth full of chocolate chip pancakes. "I love you this much!" He spread his hands apart as far as they could go.

Oh, her boy. Her beautiful, lovely boy whose world was about to be blown apart. "I love you, more. "Across all dimensions."

The promise Dr. Pierce Powers and Princess Arabella gave to each other, teammates to The Refractor, the most awesome of the awesomest super-heroes.

Danny attacked another pancake, squirting Bosco all over it. He over-shot and got some on the table. "Thanks for letting me join the football team. Coach Myers is so cool!"

She nodded, her head feeling like it was encased in concrete. "I'm happy you like it so much."

"I do, Mom!" He now had chocolate smeared on his face. "I love football across all dimensions!"

Beth was afraid of that.

****

"How was your weekend?" Jenna asked Beth on Monday morning.

"Good. Quiet." Beth walked into Happy Thoughts and started to take off her jacket. "How was yours and, whoa! Bran must have bought every single rose at Flowers in Bloom!" Four huge cut glass vases filled with blush colored roses sat on the check out counter. "They smell heavenly!"

"They're not from Bran," Jenna said. "They're for you." She paused. "From Jeff."

"Jeff?" Beth squeaked. "Jeff Myers?"

"The one and only." Jenna held out the card to Beth. "Seriously, who else? I read it, of course."

"Of course." She took the small, stiff rectangle from Jenna. Her hands shook a bit. "'Can't believe I found you. Have dinner with me. Please. Even if it's just for old time's sake. Love, Jeff'."

Oh, Lordy. She gaped at the card. "What am I going to do?"

"Have dinner with him, perhaps?" Jenna shrugged. "One dinner doesn't necessarily rekindle an old flame."

"It's just not a good idea."

"I don't think he's going to give up until you share a meal with him. Go ahead, do it." She grinned. "Take a walk on the wild side."

"No, I can't. I just can't." Beth couldn't, however, resist going behind the counter and burying her nose in one of the huge bouquets and lightly tracing one soft petal with her finger. She couldn't remember the last time someone had sent her flowers.

Actually, if you didn't count Danny's construction paper tulips from last Mother's Day's Sunday school project, no one had ever given her flowers. Not even her parents when she was in the hospital after giving birth to Danny.

"His cell number is on the back of the card," Jenna said. "You should at least call him to say thank you."

True. To not do so would be incredibly rude. "I'll do it later when he's not likely to be teaching."

****

Jeff walked into his boss's office. Julia Stewart looked up. "Great job last Friday night, Coach! Have a seat." She gestured to the chairs in front of her desk.

"Thanks! The kids did all the work." He grinned. "I just yelled at them from the sidelines."

"I'd say you did a little bit more than that. So, I got the proposed budget for your football clinic. I'm surprised you think you can get Buck and Brock Nelson to donate their time. They're NFL stars."

Jeff laughed. Julia loved her sports. "I've got connections. My high school coach married their sister."

"Ah. How handy. If that's true, I don't know how I can say no. I'd love to meet them."

"Absolutely. They're great guys and really good with kids."

"I think with them guaranteed to come, we can get food donated from local restaurants." She laughed and narrowed her eyes. "You know how much I love getting the town involved with the school." She waved a hand. "It takes a village and all that."

"It's a great town to raise a family." Jeff wished

Katie would relent and let Cookie spend a weekend with him. She wouldn't have to do a thing except help his Cookie pack her suitcase.

He dreaded telling Katie that Beth lived in Lobster Cove. She would have a meltdown that would make Chernobyl look like a Cub Scout campfire. He'd learned early on to never mention Beth's name. Ever. And even more, not to wonder where his child with Beth lived.

A daughter. Beth had given their daughter up for adoption. Cookie had a sister out there in the world.

Katie was not going to be thrilled.

"Earth to Jeff," Julia said. "Hello."

"Sorry. I had a couple of thoughts about asking for donations."

"Don't pay it any mind. I'll talk to the district bookkeeper and we'll take care of that. Then we need to have a chat regarding presenting this to the parents, but I don't think we'll get too much trouble." She shook her head. "It's not like we're trying to start a daycare or something."

"I heard about that. I don't know how anyone could oppose a daycare center." He shrugged. "It takes all kinds, I guess."

Julia stood and held her hand out to Jeff. "We'll get this done. It's a great idea and opportunity for our small town kids."

He stood as well, and shook her hand. "Thanks for your support."

"Thank you for your initiative."

"I really want this."

"I can tell. You've got my support and I know we can make this happen. Next August?"

"Next August for sure."

"Keep me posted." She looked at her watch. "Got a meeting. Let me know about any progress."

"Will do."

He left Julia's office wondering if Beth had gotten the roses yet. Maybe he should stop into Happy Thoughts between practices.

Or not. Maybe the next move should be up to Beth.

He had to find out where she'd been all those years and about the family who'd adopted their daughter. He wouldn't let himself be distracted from that goal.

He'd get the whole story if it killed him.

Chapter Eight

After a week of gourmet chocolates, teddy bears (he still couldn't wrap his mind around that he went to Build A Bear without Cookie), and more flowers than he knew existed, Jeff still waited with his phone in his back pocket, set on vibrate.

He knew Beth. She'd have to say thank you sooner or later.

For once he prayed for patience. He'd waited forever and now he'd found her, he could afford to wait a little bit more.

Okay, that sounded a whole lot sappy. If he ever said it to another guy, they'd give him all kinds of crap, like ask if he was on his period or some other shit.

He didn't care. Beth was back in his world. He'd do everything he could to keep her there.

With him.

By hook or by crook.

Beth Pritchard was his first love. Now when he saw her again, he had a sneaking suspicion she was his last love. It was clear to him that giving up their daughter had killed her spirit. He wanted to make her whole again. To bring her back to the girl he'd loved and known so well before their lives were blown apart by her father and he could help her heal. He would help her. They'd help each other.

They could be together again. Happy. Most of all,

they could be grownups, making their own choices.

Free.

Well, as far as Katie would let him be free. She had the ultimate bargaining chip. Cookie.

He could not do anything to give Katie grounds to keep his daughter from him. He subscribed to the doctrine of "When in doubt do both." He'd find a way to have both Cookie and Beth in his life.

Misery—profound and soul deep—settled over him. Beth had had to give away their daughter and deal with it on her own. How could he ask her to accept and love his daughter with Katie?

His brain hurt.

He rubbed his hand across his chest. His heart hurt worse.

****

"Good night, Danny." Beth leaned down and gave her son a kiss on his forehead. "Sweet dreams."

Danny yawned so hard his jaw cracked. "G'night Mom."

The upside of the whole football thing? He was too tired to complain about his bedtime.

Beth went into the kitchen and turned on the kettle to make some tea.

Chamomile. Definitely chamomile.

She put the cellphone on the counter by the stove and stared at it, like it might have some answers for her.

It didn't.

Why was she surprised?

Tea made, she took a tiny sip then carried the cup and saucer to the kitchen table. Pulling the florist card from her jean's pocket she turned it over to where Jeff had written his number.

She had to call him. Jenna had really read her the riot act about not doing it yet. Since Beth couldn't bring Jeff's gifts home, Happy Thoughts was running out of room to keep them and Jenna wanted them gone.

As of yesterday.

She looked back at the counter, sighed, and picked up her phone. After she thumbed it on, she punched in Jeff's number before she lost her nerve.

Maybe she'd get lucky and it would go straight to voicemail. The phone rang once, twice, maybe she'd catch a break and—

"Myers."

She closed her eyes and took a breath. "Jeff, it's me. Beth."

"Beth." She could practically hear the smile in his voice. "To what do I owe this phone call?"

"You know very well why I'm calling. I really need to thank you but you've got to stop sending all these gifts to the shop."

"I will on one condition. Have dinner with me."

She sighed and threw caution to the wind. Maybe she'd finally get some closure about him and Skankarella. "Okay."

"Yessss!" He sounded like one of his football players who had just spiked a touchdown in the end zone. "When? This weekend? Saturday? Can't do Friday because of the game. Or, here's a thought. Come to the game, we'll go for a drink after."

"I don't think Friday will work. Saturday might." Beth hesitated. Jenna had already told her she'd watch Danny. "Let me check my calendar." She had no social life, hence no calendar. She wouldn't be surprised if her eyes weren't turning brown with all the fertilizer she was throwing around. "It looks like I'm free."

"Awesome. Where do you live so I can pick you up?"

No hope in hell that was going to happen. "I'd rather use my car and meet you at the restaurant."

"Really? Let me pick you up."

"It's not a date, Jeff. It's dinner. Just dinner between two old friends catching up." More bull. The lies piled one on top of the other.

"I don't like it, but I'll take you any way I can get you. Where do you want to go? Don't say Maggie's. I eat there at least once a day. How about Cliffside Restaurant?"

Wow! "That's pretty pricey."

"We never went on a real date. It's about time I fixed that."

Longing for a real date, out in the open—one that didn't end up in the backseat of a car—swamped her. She closed her eyes and gave in. "Sure, that sounds great."

"Awesome! Is seven good?"

"Perfect." Beth bit her lip. "I'll see you then."

"Looking forward to it. You have no idea how much."

"Good night, Jeff."

"Sweet dreams. I know mine will be because I'll be dreaming of you."

Her cheeks heated. "Good night, Jeff," she repeated then ended the call.

The thing? She wouldn't probably dream about Jeff.

She'd definitely dream about Jeff.

Chapter Nine

"Praise the Lord and can I have an Amen! I'm so proud of you!" Jenna thumped Beth on the back with all the finesse of an orangutan. "Where are you going?"

"Cliffside. Though I don't think I own anything I can wear there."

"If any occasion calls for a new dress, dinner with an old flame at the Cliffside Restaurant is it."

"I can't afford a new dress."

"If that's a hint for a raise, sorry. The store's got to show a profit first." Jenna smiled. "You need to splurge, Beth. Buy something sexy and slinky."

"Stating the obvious here. I'm not exactly the sexy, slinky type."

"What did you wear on your last date?"

"Ummmm. Jeff was my last date. As in ten years ago. "I lied to my father and said I was sleeping over at Skankarella's, which I eventually did. I wore jeans, an Addington Minutemen sweatshirt and he had his hands under it about five minutes after we struggled over onto the backseat of his mother's Volvo wagon."

"You're totally kidding me, right?"

"'Fraid not. I'm really not that interesting."

"Actually, I'm thinking you're getting more and more interesting by the minute." Jenna brightened. "Hey! You can sew like a demon. Why don't you make a new dress for your, uh, non-date." She flipped her hand. "Your term, not mine." Jenna rolled her eyes. "Face facts, Cinderella. It's a date."

"Jenna! I don't have time to make a new dress by Saturday!"

"I'll help! And of course you can use one of the machines here." Jenna rubbed her hands together. "This is my best idea ever! If it looks good we can show a sample and people will drool over it and ask us to make them one."

The door to the store opened and in walked Jenna's handsome fiancé Bran Cudahy. "I take that back. My best idea ever was to hook up with this guy." Jenna launched herself at her very handsome husband and kissed him thoroughly.

"What'd I do to deserve this?" he asked, his voice very husky.

"Just you being you!" Jenna inclined her head toward Beth. "Guess who has a date Saturday night?" She pointed at Beth with both forefingers. "That girl."

Beth wanted to drop through the floor. "Oh for the love of God, Jenna, please stop."

Bran grinned. "He better treat you right or else he answers to me." His grin got wider. "Don't forget I'm a computer genius. I can create a nightmare credit report he'll never be able to fix."

Beth's cheeks heated. "Please stop. This is just a dinner between two old friends."

Jenna snorted.

"Seriously, if you two are done embarrassing me I would be okay with that." Beth skewered them both with a glare. "Just sayin'."

Jenna made the my-lips-are-zipped gesture across her mouth.

Bran snorted. It sounded a lot like Jenna's.

Much like people who start to look like their dogs.

Beth shook her head. Jenna and Bran were good to her. She may have not gone on a lot of dates, well, any dates at all, but she had good friends.

They were named Jenna Sanborn and Bran Cudahy.

Forget Jeff Myers. Jenna and Bran both had her back.

****

Jeff looked at his caller ID and groaned. Katie.

Yay. Only not.

"Myers."

"So I was at The End Zone the other night and heard that Beth Pritchard is in Lobster Cove."

"That's right." And…what? He shook his head to clear his ears to make sure he heard her right. "Why were you at The End Zone? You hate it there."

"Are you seeing her?"

"Who?"

She made that noise she always did when he pissed her off.

He smiled, happy with his victory and then went in for the kill. "She lives here and I'm not blind." At her sharp intake of breath which he knew signaled a harangue, let the devil on his left shoulder to answer the question. "It's none of your business who I see."

"It is if you ever want to see Cookie again. Speaking of which. Does Beth still have your kid or did she get rid of it?"

"Jesus, Katie." He pushed the left shoulder devil off with the back of his hand. "She gave our baby up for adoption. A girl."

"That's what she told you?"

"I believe her. Somewhere in the world, Cookie has a sister."

Silence. "And you believe her?"

"Why would she lie?" He didn't understand. Katie had been Beth's best friend. Katie's jealousy of Beth just truly twisted his mind into knots.

"To get to you." Was Katie spitting? "How romantic! The two of you bonding over a child you'll never know. Poor pitiful Beth, poor pitiful Jeff for falling for her act."

Every muscle in his body tightened and his teeth ground against each other with enough force to turn them into bloody stumps. "You are way out of line. I've never heard you be so cruel." And he'd heard her be cruel a lot. "Were you ever her friend?"

"Oh yes, I'm totally a cruel bitch for questioning the motives of someone who kept a huge secret from you for years." She gusted a sigh that crackled in his ear. "Please."

Jeff felt the hand not holding the phone fist painfully. "Why did you call?"

"To let you know that I won't ever let Cookie stay with you as long as Beth is in the picture. Your choice."

"You don't get any say in whether they meet or not. And, if she's anything like I remember, she would never try to usurp your place with Cookie." He didn't dare tell Katie he didn't want to hurt Beth, who had given up their daughter, by making her deal with Cookie before either of them were ready.

Cookie was precious.

So was Beth.

Katie? Not so much.

"And I just saw a pig fly." She gave a very nasty sounding laugh. "Do you think I'm a fool?"

No, I think you're a paranoid bitch. "The Beth I knew, the Beth you knew, would never make trouble and if we start dating, which I'm hoping we will, she'll understand that we have to go slowly with Cookie."

"Jeff." Katie sighed with great drama. "Face it. I'm not letting you have Cookie in Lobster Cove while Beth is there."

"I'll take you to court."

"Go ahead." She laughed. "I'll win. I always do, because my father isn't a nut job like Beth's. He's the lawyer who's going to win me sole custody of Cookie. You want a relationship with Beth? Go for it. You'll never see your daughter again."

****

Beth fumbled as she tried to put the key into the ignition. "What the hell am I doing?" she muttered. This is not my life. Nothing about this is real.

She'd left Danny with a babysitter for the first time in his life. Here she was, hiring a babysitter for her child while she had dinner with his father. She bit back the urge to cackle like a mad woman.

She hadn't been able to eat all day. The closer her date with Jeff came, the more her nerves jittered like beetles on their backs trying to turn over. She'd almost poked her eye out with a mascara wand.

What would they talk about? He'd want to know all about her life. She should just come clean.

Maybe she would. She certainly should. Except that she was a total coward.

Hate was a mild description of the emotion she felt about herself. Never mind. Move forward. Always look forward and never look back.

Never, ever, ever again.

That Beth didn't exist anymore.

After a short ride to the harbor, Beth pointed her car into a space in the Cliffside's graveled parking lot. A soft wind blew, teasing her hair, which she wore long, not in the usual ponytail. If she'd used a curling iron, no one else needed to know.

The scent of salt rode on the air along with something charged that demanded her attention. She looked up.

Jeff stood under the dark green awning over the entrance of the restaurant. He wore a light gray suit, with a darker charcoal shirt underneath it. He'd even put on a tie. He looked way more sophisticated than the boy she remembered.

His smile and the light in his hazel flecked eyes nearly brought her to her knees. Her heart skipped a beat. She could barely breathe. So handsome. As always.

She was really glad she'd taken Jenna's advice and put together a new dress and a pair of sexy heels. Mascara incident notwithstanding, she thought she looked pretty good.

It always helped when you went on a date to not poke your eye out with the mascara wand.

He walked toward her. "Beth." He took her hands. "I can't believe you're here with me." Leaning in, he kissed her cheek. "You are so beautiful."

The way he looked at her made her feel way beyond beautiful. "Thank you." She licked her lips. "You're pretty cute yourself."

He chuckled. "I don't clean up too bad. But you."

His eyes lit with fire. "You're made of magic." He caressed her cheek. "Let's go in."

If he kept dazzling her tonight, she'd be a puddle at his feet before the end of the first course.

Speaking of dazzled, she'd never been in the Cliffside Restaurant and she'd never seen its like. Crisp white linen cloths covered tables standing on rich polished hardwood floors. The sound of actual sterling silver clinking against fine china plates competed with the sound of muted classical music. "Oh, Jeff. This is amazing."

"Yeah, I know, right? Ever been any place like this before?" He lightly touched the small of her back as the maître d' led them to their table. Jeff held out a chair for her then took the seat across from her.

A waiter, dressed in black pants and an immaculate white shirt, with a white towel draped over his arm, came up to their table. "Good evening, I'm Pierre and I'll be your waiter this evening. May I start you off with a cocktail?"

Beth had never gone out and had a cocktail. "I don't know what to order." Lord, how embarrassing.

"Do you like fruity drinks?" Jeff asked.

"I guess."

"Please bring the lady a Bellini and I'll have a Dewars on the rocks."

"Right away, sir." Pierre left and Beth was alone with Jeff.

She looked out the window. "The view is breathtaking." The sun had just started to set, spreading the sky with peach, magenta, tangerine and true fuchsia streaks.

"It is." Jeff was looking at Beth, however, not out

the window.

"I don't know what to say when you tell me things like that."

"You better get used to it because I'm going to say *things like that* a lot." Jeff presented his hand palm-up across the table.

In spite of herself, Beth laid her hand palm-down on his and he closed his fingers around it. She just couldn't resist.

"I'm serious about dating you, Beth. We didn't get our chance ten years ago and we owe it to ourselves to see where this goes."

She swallowed. "Jeff there are things you don't know about me, things I'm not very proud of. And I've got Texas-sized issues to talk to you about."

"Same thing goes for me." He rubbed his thumb along her knuckles. "Let's put that aside and enjoy the evening."

Beth sighed, feeling a little lightheaded. "I can do that."

****

Jeff had never seen Beth dressed up for a date; back in high school they had to hide from her father. Tonight though, she wore a deep blue silky dress, not overtly sexy, but it hugged her in all the right places and made those big blue eyes glow. And those high heels. He'd just about swallowed his tongue when he watched her walk across the parking lot.

"I want to know everything about you. Did you finish school?"

"No."

"Never? Not even to get your diploma?"

"My father wouldn't let me. He homeschooled me

and I got my diploma that way." She took a sip of her drink. "Thanks for the Bellini. It's delicious."

"I'm glad you like it. What about college and your music? Remember those plans we made, me going to Boston College on a football scholarship and you going to New England Conservatory to train to be a concert pianist?"

Her smile seemed sad and her eyes misted over. She looked away. "I do remember. But there was no college for me. My mother got sick and my father needed me to stay home and take care of her."

She'd lost so much, Jeff realized as he rubbed his hand over his heart. No high school graduation, no college where she could pursue her musical gift. And she'd had to give away their child. He'd make it up to her or die trying. "Do you still play the piano?"

"Oh, yes." Her eyes lit up. "Every day, but not for myself. I've got a full studio of piano students. I like teaching."

"So do I! I love working with kids, not just the high school kids. I've got this youth team made up of these ten- and eleven-year-olds."

She cleared her throat. "Really."

"They're great. I got this one kid named Danny. The kid is a natural. Throws like a champ, runs like the wind."

Beth coughed and grabbed her water glass. "Sorry. Something got caught in my throat."

She looked a little pale. "You okay?"

She nodded.

"Anyway, this kid is the real deal. I'd like to talk to his mom, but another parent brings him along with her own son. She even signed him up. I've never met the mother, which is something I need to do. That kind of talent is rare."

"It's great to have a student like that."

"Yeah. Mrs. Coach's brothers are coming to do a clinic next summer and I want them to meet him, just to see if my opinion is right. Do you have any students like that? Kids who just love the piano and have the gift?"

Beth stared down at her hands, then looked up. "I do. One. So much potential. He could go a long way if he doesn't get distracted."

He lifted his glass. "Here's to talented kids!"

She clinked hers against his. "To talented kids." Beth smiled but it lacked the warmth he'd seen earlier.

He wondered why.

****

"Let's take a walk around the harbor." Jeff wanted to make sure this evening lasted longer. "I think I need to walk off some of those calories."

"Surely, you don't need to worry about what you eat."

"Well, I do."

"Tonight was lovely, Jeff. You have no idea how special it was."

"I like the sound of that." He grabbed hold of her elbow. "Come on. Take a walk with me."

She looked at her watch. "A short one."

They walked along in silence. Jeff's skin prickled with the urge to kiss her.

"I can't believe you spent that much money on a bottle of wine." Beth shook her head.

"It was good, wasn't it?" The sommelier talked them into a bottle of a 2012 Mosel Riesling Kabinett from the Reichsgraf von Kesselstadt estate in Germany.

Not that he knew much about wine. Craft beer, yes. German wine, not so much.

"Let's walk over to the cliff. Warmer than usual in September, a light salt-laden breeze wound itself around them. Halyards pinged against the masts of the sailboats, the bell buoys clanged out warnings about shallow waters. Lights from the houses all around flicked on, one by one, dotting the landscape and the stars sparkled in the darkening late evening sky.

"It was delicious. Everything was." Beth put her hand on his arm. "You have no idea how special this is to me. A night full of firsts."

He gathered her into his arms. "It doesn't have to stop here. Like I said, I really want to explore what we could have."

She turned those big blue eyes to his face. "I'm not the person you think I am."

"I'm looking forward to learning about the person you are. All I ask is that you give us a chance, Beth. We owe ourselves that much."

"I want that, I really do, but there are things you should know."

Jeff came to a quick decision, even though it might de-rail things with Beth. "In the interest of full disclosure, Katie found out you're here and she's not happy."

"Katie?"

"She says she won't let Cookie visit me here if you're in the picture."

"What?"

"It won't last. She'll get over it. She just really likes to…well, never mind what Katie likes."

"What?" Beth shook her head and pulled herself out of his embrace. "That's crazy!"

"She gets that way sometimes. But I'm not letting her tell me who I can and can't be with. I really want to be with you. I just wanted to be honest with you up front."

"She actually thinks I'm a danger to your daughter?"

"She's a little self-involved. She's always sensed I never got over you."

Beth shook her head. Her body stiffened, her eyes furious. "She thinks I'm a danger to your daughter. That's ridiculous!"

"Not you. Your father."

"My father's dead!" Beth sputtered as the wind danced around them a little faster.

"I know. She'll see how ridiculous she's being. That's why I brought it up. That and I don't want any secrets between us."

A shadow flitted across her face. He couldn't read it. "I don't want to be the reason you can't see your little girl. I won't be the reason."

"You won't. It's all on Katie."

"I have to think about it."

"There's nothing to think about." He pulled her back in close and kissed the top of her head. "Don't let what I've just told you get in the way of what we might have. I just needed to tell you the truth before this went any further." He felt her tremble. "Shhhh, Beth, baby, give us a chance."

"I don't know if I can. I've got a huge problem with you marrying Katie."

"It was a stupid thing to do, I know. I don't know

what I was thinking. Please don't let it stand between us."

She shrugged. "I can try."

"Thank you. Now, I've been waiting for this all night."

He kissed her. Her lips were soft and supple and she responded, opening her mouth and welcoming him in. She blossomed for him as he deepened the kiss to taste her, to see if she still tasted as sweet as he remembered.

She did.

She whimpered then wrapped her arms around his neck and pressed her body against his. His body celebrated when he pulled her in tight. The last time he'd held her close she was a girl, but he wasn't holding a girl in his arms. He wasn't kissing a girl. Beth was all woman, warm and soft and oh so sexy.

His woman.

They came up for air and Jeff was about to dive right back in, but Beth looked at him, her eyes big and bewildered.

"What's wrong?" She ducked her head but he took a finger and lifted her chin. "Talk to me, Beth."

She shuddered. "I haven't kissed another man in ten years. It's a little overwhelming."

Say what? His ears buzzed. "Beth, what are you saying?"

"You're the only man I've ever kissed," she whispered. "The only man I've ever wanted to kiss."

That couldn't be true. She was too good and too beautiful for it to be true. "How can that be?"

"It just is."

He kissed her again with all he was worth. Not as

the boy he'd been, but as a man, one who knew what he wanted and how to get it. She pressed so closely to him, she had to feel how much she affected him.

She clung for a moment then pulled away, her breathing ragged. "Jeff."

His own breathing was none too smooth. "Beth."

"There are things we need to work out."

"Not from where I'm standing."

"I need to think about this." Shadows cloaked her eyes.

"Don't think too long. I'll start sending things to Happy Thoughts again. I ran into Bran and he told me Jenna was running out of space to keep 'em all. Um…why didn't you take them home?"

She stilled. It looked like she wrestled with a million demons. "I don't know. Afraid of bringing up all those feelings from the past, I guess." She glanced quickly to the left.

For the first time, he felt uneasy. He decided to ignore it. Beth just didn't lie and keep secrets. She was just a very shy, private person.

Maybe.

It didn't compute. Something was off.

He didn't care. He had Beth back in his arms and for the moment, nothing else mattered.

She said she had things to tell him, but knowing Beth, they could wait. She was such a good person. How bad could her secrets be?

Chapter Ten

Jenna pounced on Beth the minute she entered the store. "So, how was the date?"

"It was wonderful," Beth sighed. "The Cliffside was so elegant and Jeff was, well, so handsome and sweet." And I fell in love with him in one fell swoop. "Thanks for talking me into making a new dress."

"I live to serve. Are you seeing him again?"

"He asked me out. I want to see him." She ached with wanting to see him.

"Did you tell him about Danny?"

"I wanted to. I was going to but he told me his ex-wife won't let his daughter visit him here if he's dating me."

"That's crazy. How can she keep him from his child?"

"I don't know." Beth shook her head. "I never thought Katie would turn out so bitter. Who am I fooling? She called the cops on us."

"She has some serious control issues there."

"For real." Beth came around the back of the counter to stow her purse under it. "I want to keep seeing him, I really do. I never, ever got over him. Everything is so complicated." Beth shook her head. "Like this. We were talking about his job and he starts telling me about this super-talented kid on the Junior Sharks. Three guesses and the first two don't count as to who he was talking about."

"Oh no. Danny?"

She touched her finger to her nose. "Got it in one. Here he is gushing over Danny and I couldn't say word one. It was wicked awkward."

"Why didn't you just come out and tell him? Get it out in the open now."

"Like I told you, I was going to and then he started telling me about Katie and I chickened out."

Jenna pursed her lips. "You've got to tell him soon. Lobster Cove is so small, you can run but you can't hide."

"Both Jeff and Danny deserve the truth. I'll call him and set something up. Then we can both tell Danny together." And maybe neither of them will hate me for too long."

"No time like the present."

"He's probably teaching."

"Text him. And then get going on re-shelving the fabric bolts."

Beth nodded. "I'll text him after I finish with the fabric."

Jenna shook her head. "What am I going to do with you? Text first, girlfriend."

Beth pulled her phone out of the pocket of her denim skirt. "Yes boss."

****

Jeff stood on the sidelines of the high school football field and watched his guys running drills. Not bad, but... "Lavery, pick up your feet! Move it!"

Lavery did as he was told.

Jeff loved when that happened.

He also loved the text he got from Beth. He'd call

her back before the peewee practice and get that date set up.

He couldn't wait to see her again. Hell, he couldn't wait to hear her voice again.

He'd believed she was lost to him forever and now here she was back. No way he would let her go again.

"Hey, Coach?"

He turned to see the captain of the Sharks. "Uh, yeah, Chris?"

"Want us to start running the new plays you gave us?"

Jeff nodded. "Sounds good. How about you guys take ten and then start up with the new stuff."

"Right away!"

Jeff blew his whistle. "Sharks! Take ten!" He looked at Chris. "You, too."

"Thanks, Coach!" He jogged down the field to catch up with the others around the team bench.

Jeff knew he was in trouble when he couldn't keep his mind on practice.

****

"That's great, Tina! Can you try it again and get your wrist a little flatter?" Beth sat in a chair a little behind her piano student. "Like this." She demonstrated what she wanted from Tina.

"I'll try." Tina placed her fingers on the keys and played the scale Beth wanted.

C-sharp major. The scale with six sharps and so many black keys. Everyone struggled with that one.

"Good, keep going," Beth said as she played the exercise along with Tina. It helped both training her hands along with her ear.

The opening notes of Beethoven's Fifth Symphony

rang out of her cellphone. She pulled it off the top of the piano. "Keep going with the scale while I take this call."

"'Kay." Tina stared at her fingers and the notes she worked on.

Jeff's name popped onto the caller I.D. She smiled even though her stomach seized.. "Hello."

"Hello, Beth! I haven't been able to stop thinking of you after the other night." He chuckled. "Have you been thinking about me?"

An understatement if she'd ever heard one. "You know I have."

"Hmmmmm. So, you want to take me on a date?"

"Yes." She pressed her free hand against her heart. "What are you doing this weekend?"

"Like Saturday? Not much. Reviewing the video of Friday's game. You want to save me from that?"

"How about lunch in this place I know in Bar Harbor?" So no one she knew would witness her humiliation.

"That sounds nice. Around two?"

"Works for me." She'd convinced Anita to have Danny at her house all day.

"What time should I pick you up?"

She took a beat to think. "Let's meet there." She stopped as Tina played *Für Elise*. Making the same mistake in the same place every time. Beth closed her eyes. Nothing like practicing your mistakes.

Kill me now.

"Why don't we ride together? It doesn't make sense." Jeff sounded puzzled.

"I've got my reasons. Listen I have to go, I'm in the middle of a piano lesson. I'll text the address of the restaurant to you. I'm really glad you called. Gotta go." She ended the call before he could protest more.

Once she blew his world apart, he'd be grateful they came in two cars.

Couldn't think about it now. Tina needed her lesson.

"So, Tina, let's pick out another piece for you to play, okay?"

****

Jeff worked really hard to not be offended that Beth didn't want to share a ride with him. It felt all kinds of wrong. He wanted the emotional connection they had ten years ago. The trust.

He went into the kitchen and pulled a beer from the refrigerator. He twisted off the cap, leaned against the fridge and sulked.

He needed to cool off.

Okay, maybe she had a right to be cautious. He'd married Katie, and of course that had flattened her. He had to make it right for her. He regretted marrying Katie with every breath he took. Although if he hadn't, he wouldn't have Cookie.

He remembered the moment he'd fallen in love with her. He'd been trying to find the chorus teacher to talk to her about putting him on the ineligible list. The auditorium seemed like the best way to start. But the chorus teacher wasn't there.

Instead, he'd found Beth. She was playing the piano, totally lost in the music. Every note wrapped itself around him.

Wrapped around his heart.

He was gone, head over heels for this girl who held magic in her fingers. He'd surprised her when she finished playing. She'd thought she was alone. He asked her to hang out with him after the game on Friday night. She said yes.

When his team, the Addington Minutemen had lost, he'd been seriously pissed off and more than a little depressed. Beth had been perfectly fine with blowing off the party and just being with him.

He'd been her first kiss, her first lover, her first everything. He would have done anything for her, but he was a kid. Once her father had whisked her away he had no options. He'd had to wait until Beth contacted him.

Which she'd never done.

And Jeff had a problem of his own.

He never should have married Katie.

Damn his lonely heart. His weakness.

In his defense, he couldn't wait for a woman who'd disappeared into the ether forever. He'd had to move on with his life.

He would help her with her issues, heal all her broken places, make her trust him again.

Or die trying.

He supposed he should be happy, lucky even, that she'd called him. Beth had something going on, but so did he.

He'd bring that up on Saturday. He needed more from her. Could she meet him halfway?

Chapter Eleven

"Mom, can you take me to the Sharks' game tonight? I really want to watch the game."

Danny stood in front of her, his hands stuffed in the pockets of his jeans, looking up with hope in his eyes.

Beth crouched in front of him "I'm sorry, sweetie. I can't. I've got a lot to do." Liar, liar pants on fire.

He pulled his hands out of his pockets and fisted them on to his hips. "I need to go. All the Junior Sharks are going. I'll let everybody down if you don't take me. Plus, the team is having pizza after, at Lobster Lanes."

He took after Jeff, she thought. He had her coloring and eyes, but Jeff's spirit.

"I bet Mrs. Parks can give me a ride if you're too busy."

When had her child begun to challenge her like this?

Since Jeff Myers had become his coach and Danny had gotten a huge case of hero worship.

"I'll call Mrs. Parks."

Danny jumped up and let out a loud whoop. "Don't bother, Mom. I already asked since I knew you couldn't. She said since I'm hanging with Ben tomorrow, I can stay overnight." He lifted his eyes to her, the blue eyes big and round and manipulating.

"First, you don't tell me 'don't bother'. You should have asked me first." Her fingers tingled, but she stuck to her story. "But just this once, I guess it's okay if it's okay with Mrs. Parks. I'll call her to make double sure. Remember. This is a one-time thing. You always have to ask me first."

Danny rolled his eyes. "Why won't you come to the game?"

"I told you I have things to do."

"You never had things to do on a Friday night before I joined the Junior Sharks." He lifted his chin, an act of defiance if she'd ever seen one.

Her heart clenched. What to say? "I'm sorry, I just got some extra work. We had extra expenses this month."

"You mean my football equipment, right?" His lower lip jutted out. "It's all my fault."

"Oh no, no, no baby. There are a lot of other reasons." She ran her hand down the back of his head. "And somebody loaned us your equipment, so that's not it."

She was telling the truth this time at least.

"I'm sorry I'm so 'spensive." He leaped forward and banded his arms around her neck.

She felt the wetness on his cheeks against her. Beth had to nip his guilt about their finances in the bud. "You were and are the most precious thing in my life. I want you to do what you want to do."

"'Cept I don't want to play the piano any more." He extricated himself from her embrace.

Dear Lord. "You have so much talent, baby. You'll be sorry if you give it up." Like Beth had.

Danny stared at her. "That's what Grandfather said."

Hmmmmm. "What else did Grandfather tell you?"

"He told me sports were a waste of time, they just took time away from studying the Bible and from exploring the gift from the Holy Spirit, which was my music."

Beth's ears buzzed. She forced herself to breathe. "I wish you had told me that."

Danny shrugged.

"You are a gifted piano player, so you can't quit because you will regret it." She hated agreeing with her father, but there was no help for it.

He made a face.

"It's just one half hour a day of your life. It's not like I'm sentencing you to life in prison."

"Feels like it."

"The sooner you get to it, the sooner you'll be done, so scoot."

He dragged himself to the piano with all the enthusiasm of a death row inmate.

Too bad. He'd get over it.

****

"Who's calling now?" Jeff picked up his chirping phone. Katie's name came up on the caller I.D. "Katie."

"Jeff, I need you to come to Addington this weekend to take care of Cookie."

"Why?" Not that he didn't want to see his daughter but his ex-wife always had ulterior motives.

"A chance came to go to a spa this weekend and I'm taking it."

"Good for you. Sounds like fun." He ran a hand through his hair. "Why don't you send Cookie here to stay with me?"

"That's not going to happen, Jeff, and you know why." She sniffed. "You owe me this weekend. It's really hard being a single parent."

Here came the emotional blackmail. "Katie, I wish you'd—"

"Unless Beth's more important to you than your daughter. If that's the case, I can take Cookie to my parents for the weekend."

"No, I'll come." Beth would understand why he had to break their date. "I'll leave first thing Saturday morning."

"That's too late. I need to leave first thing on Saturday. You need to come tomorrow."

Of course. "I'll leave right after the game."

"Forget the game."

"What the hell, Katie? The game is my job! I just can't up and blow it off."

"Don't speak to me that way."

"Sorry." He did the math in his head. "The earliest I can get there is 1:30." Jeff's skin crawled at the thought of staying at his former house while Katie was there. "I'll stay at my mother's until it's time for me to be there for Cookie."

"That would be at 5:30. My ride comes at 6:00."

"No problem." A headache was brewing right behind his eyes. Katie had that effect on him. "Can I talk to Cookie?"

"Of course." Her voice held the smug note when Katie got her way.

"Hey, Daddy! Guess what!"

As usual, his daughter's voice smoothed out the rough edges caused by her mother. "What, Cookie?"

"I got a loose tooth!"

"That's awesome! I guess you're going to get a visit from the Tooth Fairy soon."

"Don't be silly, Daddy. Mommy told me there's no such thing as the Tooth Fairy and only babies believe in her." She sighed. "I'm not a baby, I'm six years old."

Who told a six-year-old that the Tooth Fairy didn't exist?

Score another one for Katie.

"Did your mom tell you that I'm coming to stay with you this weekend?"

"Yep! I'm so excited! I got everything all planned. We're gonna go to the zoo and take a boat ride and have a tea party!"

"Say good night now, Cookie," said Katie's voice in the background. "It's past your bedtime."

"Okay! Good night, Daddy!" She blew a little raspberry-like kiss through the phone.

"Good night, Cookie."

Katie came back on the line. "Five-thirty and no later. See you Saturday morning." She hung up.

He stared at the phone wondering if he should call Beth right away or wait until the morning.

The morning. He wanted to wait until he wasn't so mad at Katie.

Hey! And maybe he could talk Beth into coming with him.

He hoped she'd say yes.

Chapter Twelve

"Oh. That's disappointing." Beth pressed her lips together. Jeff was canceling their lunch date on Saturday.

"Doesn't have to be. You can come with me."

"With you. To Addington."

"Yeah, it'll be fun. And you'll get to meet Cookie."

She was totally not ready for either thing. Besides she didn't have anyone to stay with Danny while she went hauling off to meet her son's half-sister. "I don't think it's such a good idea."

"If you're worried about running into Katie, don't be. You can stay at my mom's until Katie leaves."

Beth's heart sank. "She'll find out. You can't ask Cookie to lie to her mother." And really, she thought, I don't want to be some big secret. Even though she herself had one heck of a doozy of a secret. Which made her the biggest hypocrite on the face of the earth.

He blew out a breath. "You're right," he paused, "you're right. So I guess I'll have to take a rain check. What about next weekend?"

"That'll work." She bit her lip.

"It'll have to be Sunday. The Junior Sharks have their first game on Saturday. I'd say Friday night after the game, but it's an away game."

Beth knew that. It was all Danny could talk about. She'd hoped to tell Jeff by then so she could go to the game. She'd figure something out. "Sure, Sunday sounds great. Call me when you get back from Addington."

"Will do." His voice dropped so it sounded low and intimate. "I'll be thinking of you the whole time. How about you? Are you going to think about me?"

"Yes." She wouldn't be able to think of anything else than telling him about Danny.

"Good!" Beth heard the satisfaction in his voice. "Uh, I've got to run to class. I'll talk to you on Monday."

"Sounds good. Have a safe trip and a good weekend with your little girl."

"Will do." He disconnected.

Beth sat there for a long time, trying to get her emotions under control. The longer she put this off, the worse it got.

****

"Hey, Mom!"

"Hi, sweetie." Beth cradled the phone against her ear. "Are you having a good time?"

"The best! We got pizza for dinner and the Sharks won the game! But I knew they would because Coach is the best! We got ice cream to celebrate! And the new Refractor game is mad cool!"

Of course Coach was the best. "Wow! What a night."

"Yep! I called because I want to say good night and I love you across all dimensions!"

Tears pricked her eyes. "Good night and I love you more."

"Bye!" He yawned.

"See you tomorrow!"

Beth picked up a picture of Danny and her taken last month during the Lobster Crawl Festival. She traced a finger over his chocolate ice cream smeared face and her heart beat a little harder.

She'd given up a lot to be his mother but she didn't have a single regret. He was her life, her whole world across all dimensions.

Chapter Thirteen

"Imagine that. After all these years she just turns up again." Jeff's mother Nancy had come with Cookie and him to the zoo. They sat on a bench, watching his little girl make faces at the monkeys.

"Yeah, it's pretty unbelievable. I always imagined finding her and...and boom! there she is." Jeff still had trouble believing Beth was back in his life.

"Cookie! Don't get so close to the edge!" Nancy called.

"'Kay!" She scrambled backward.

"It's hard to wrap my head around the fact that I've got another granddaughter out there and I'll never meet her."

"I know, Mom, but Beth's father gave her no choice."

"Bob Pritchard was a holier-than-thou sanctimonious pain in the butt. He tyrannized that girl and her mother. Still...once he died Beth could have gotten in touch with you."

"I told you. She decided not to because I married Katie."

She sniffed. "Marrying Katie was a huge mistake." She smiled. "At least you and Cookie are out of it."

He glanced at his daughter and felt his heart constrict. "I have to make Katie let her come to Lobster Cove. I'm calling my lawyer on it."

"Good luck. She's always been jealous of Beth. But I can't say I'm too broken up about Katie forcing you to come to Addington. That way I get to see you."

"You can come to Lobster Cove, you know."

"It's really far away. I'm too old to travel so far."

Jeff's mother had raised him by herself. He'd inherited her eye color, but that was where the similarity ended. Her hair was a little grayer, her face a little more lined, but her smile remained as bright and loving as ever. She'd worked herself nearly to death to give him the life she wanted for him. A wave of love swamped him. "You don't look old. You look beautiful." He kissed her cheek.

She laughed. "You really inherited your father's charm, that's for sure." She patted Jeff's hand. "You look so much like him." Her eyes softened.

"I wish I could remember him."

"You were so young when he died. I would have died right along with him if I didn't have you." She sniffed again, blinking back tears. "You saved my life."

Jeff cleared his throat. "You're the best mom in the entire world."

"And don't you forget it."

****

After church Beth took Danny for lunch at Maggie's Diner.

"Hey Beth, long time, no see!" Sally greeted them. "Hey, Danny!"

"Hi, Ms. Pelletier." Danny loved coming to Maggie's.

"Go ahead, grab a seat. I'll be right over." Sally picked up a coffeepot and went to do some refills.

"Thanks, Sally."

Beth steered them to an empty booth and they slid in.

"I want blueberry pancakes with blueberry syrup and whipped cream."

She grinned. "I knew you were going to say that!"

"That's 'cause I always order it." He rolled his eyes. "I even know what you're gonna order."

Beth leaned back against the blue vinyl covered booth seat. "Oh, yeah?"

"Yeah. A blueberry muffin with fruit salad."

"Oh, you're so smart."

Danny rolled his eyes again. "Mom, you always order a blueberry muffin and fruit salad."

"You're still smart."

"That's 'cause you're my mom." He winked at her.

She laughed. "That's right."

Lately he'd been so at odds with her. It lifted her heart to drift into their routine and banter.

"I'm glad we could come here after church again. I like coming here."

"Okay." Sally appeared at their booth wielding her order pad. She dropped a glass full of crayons on the table. "I bet I know what you want. You," she pointed her pen at Danny, "want blueberry pancakes with blueberry syrup and lots of whipped cream."

"And chocolate milk."

"Right. Also with whipped cream." She turned to Beth. "And you want a blueberry muffin, the fresh fruit salad. Coffee?"

"You got it in one." Beth nodded at her son. "I'm an open book."

Sally narrowed her eyes. "Are you? I think you might have a story or two to tell."

All the saints and angels! "I don't know what you're talking about."

"Right." Sally snickered. "I'll go put in your order."

Danny selected a green crayon, turned his placemat over, and started to draw.

"What are you making?"

"A football field." He grabbed his tongue with his teeth, the ultimate sign of concentration.

"A football field. Wow. I guess you really did have a good time at the game on Friday."

He didn't look up from his art project. "It was awesome. The other team didn't know what hit 'em. Coach is the best."

Of course. It all came back to Coach. "And you got pizza."

He looked up. "Are you mad?"

"Of course not, or else I wouldn't let you order breakfast with everything buried under whipped cream."

"It was really good." He traded the green crayon for a white one. "Sal makes the best pizza. Ben says so. The Sharks go there every Friday after a game, so it must be good." He added the white yard markings to the big green expanse.

Danny put down the white crayon for a brown one. "Can we get pizza sometime?"

"We'll see."

"It's so good, Mom. I love pizza." He grabbed a black crayon, one of the Sharks' school colors.

She cleared her throat and tried really hard not to be jealous. Really tried. "I guess if you like pizza so much, we'll have to get some every once in a while."

He looked up then, scrunching his brows. "Really? We can order a healthy one, with broccoli instead of pepperoni."

Oh, how she loved her son. "I don't know. Broccoli on pizza doesn't sound so good. Pepperoni sounds much more appetizing, don't you think?"

Danny's jaw dropped. "That's awesome! Thanks Mom! Can we get it after next week's Junior Sharks' game? It'll be my first game ever."

"I think I can spring for a pizza." Hopefully Anita would let Danny stay the night with Ben again, so she could go on her date with Jeff.

She wondered how things were going with him and his daughter in Addington. Beth thrust the thought out of her mind, because it led to thoughts of letting Jeff take Danny to meet Cookie.

She studied her son, her precious baby boy. Was this the last time she'd have him to herself?

A large, painful lump gathered in her throat, but she smiled in spite of it.

****

"Go long, Danny, go long!" Jeff was putting the Junior Sharks through some pass drills.

It had rained earlier that day and the field was more than a little slick. He imagined he'd have some very annoyed moms when they saw the mud covering the kids.

Danny scampered down the field, looking behind him so he could watch the ball and hopefully catch it. With ten-year-olds, it got kind of hit of miss.

As if in slow motion, Ben, as quarterback, lobbed the ball high at him, Danny leaped into the air and turned to make the catch, but lost his footing because of the mud. The ball hit him smack in the face and the kid fell like a ton of bricks. He landed hard on his ankle, crashed, and clunked his head hard on the ground.

"Danny!" Jeff ran to the kid. "Kids! Stand back." He and Kevin, one of the other dads went down on their knees.

Adrenaline spiked through his system. Usually he was Joe Cool.

Danny moaned as he tried to get up, a good sign that he hadn't lost consciousness, but it was pretty clear his nose was broken. Jeff didn't want to take any chances. "Kevin, can you stay here, practice is almost over anyway, and most of the other parents are here to pick up the kids. I'll get Danny to the emergency room."

****

"Good job today, Tina! I'll see you next week, right?" Beth stood at the door, holding it open for her student.

"Yep. Thanks, Mrs. Rawson." Tina left and Beth closed the door.

She sighed and leaned against the door. No more lessons for the day. Her shoulders and lower back ached from sitting rigid on the piano bench all afternoon. She glanced at the clock hanging over the piano. Anita should be dropping Danny back home soon, so she had to start dinner. He was always so hungry after practice.

She pushed off the door and started toward the kitchen when her phone trilled. She pulled it out of her pocket, saw Anita's name on the caller I.D. A strange tingling slithered along her spine. "Anita. What's up?"

"You need to get to the E.R. right away. There was an accident at practice and Danny got hurt."

Oh, God. She felt lightheaded. She shook her head to clear it.

"Beth, did you hear me?"

"Yes. I'll be right there." She ended the call, grabbed a jacket, purse and keys. Her worst nightmare about Danny playing football had come true.

Chapter Fourteen

Jeff sat by the gurney watching over Danny Rawson. Mercifully, the kid was asleep.

Anita Parks had called Danny's mother, the elusive Mrs. Rawson. He'd finally get to meet her.

He turned his gaze to the kid on the gurney. For some reason, Danny Rawson got to him. He was drawn to him like no other kid he'd worked with before.

"He's right in here, Mrs. Rawson."

Jeff stood when he heard the voice of the nurse. The curtain pulled back and he was face to face with Danny's mother.

Beth Pritchard.

Holy hell. He couldn't hear over the buzzing in his ears. Beth was Danny's mother. His Beth.

The one who'd told him he was the only man she'd ever been with. Obviously she'd been with someone else and lied about it. A queasy, cold feeling rose in his stomach.

What if she hadn't lied about him being her one and only and had lied about giving birth to a daughter she gave up for adoption? This amazing child in front of him may very well be his son.

A wave of love swept over him. He had a son. He didn't know how he knew it, he just did.

A son that the woman in front of him hadn't seen fit to tell him about. His jaw clenched and every muscle

79

went rigid. He forced himself to breathe. "Mrs. Rawson, I presume."

Beth, paler than he'd ever seen her, barely spared him a glance. She went straight to Danny. She gently smoothed the hair off his forehead. "Hey, baby. Mommy's here."

Danny's eyes fluttered open, like he sensed her there. "Mom," he croaked. "It hurts."

"I know, baby, I know," she crooned, her face as white as her son's.

His son.

She looked at Jeff then, her blue eyes round and lit with both panic and defiance. "How did this happen?"

"He slipped in the mud trying to make a catch and got hit in the face with the ball and got his nose broken. He sprained his ankle and wrist when he fell. He hit his head, but didn't lose consciousness, so I don't think he got a concussion. I brought him here right away."

"I was afraid of this! I knew he'd get hurt if I let him play football."

"Of course you did." He really didn't trust himself to talk to her right now. His hands fisted at his sides.

She stood. "I'm here now so you can go."

He took a deep breath. "I don't think so."

"Danny's welfare is my top priority. You can stay, but only if you don't upset him." She turned her back to him and sat once more.

He pulled up a chair to the other side of the gurney. She placed a kiss on Danny's forehead, her attention rapt. She held his hand and squeezed it. Danny squeezed back and murmured something Jeff didn't understand.

"I love you more," she said, her voice soft and

soothing.

He knew nothing about his son's life. That made him even madder.

The doctor came in and they both stood. "Mrs. Rawson." He held out his hand for her to shake. "I'm Alex McKenzie. You've got one brave little guy there."

She swallowed and gave Dr. McKenzie a wan smile. "I know. I'm very proud of him. When can I take him home?"

"As soon as I check him over one more time and go over his discharge instructions with you." He motioned to the hall outside the curtains. "Why don't you wait out there while me and my nurse get to work?"

"I don't know," Beth said.

Jeff touched her elbow. She flinched. Good. "Mrs. Rawson, let's go on out and give them room. The sooner they start, the sooner *we* can take Danny home."

"I can take Danny home without your help."

"You're delusional if you think that's going to happen," he ground out between his teeth.

She gasped, but he could see in her eyes that she knew the score. And he wanted answers. He was going to claim his son and there was nothing she could do about it.

She nodded and with one last look at Danny, she stepped out into the hall.

He followed right behind.

****

Beth's heart thumped like a caged rabbit and a chill surrounded her. Of all the scenarios she had imagined telling Jeff about Danny, this sure wasn't one of them.

Fury rolled off Jeff in waves, but Beth had faced

worse with her father lived to tell the tale. She squared her shoulders.

"Were you going to tell me, Mrs. Rawson? Or were you going to keep it a secret forever?"

She turned to face him. Those hazel eyes turned stormy and angry. "Yes. On our lunch date last Saturday."

"I see." He clenched and unclenched his hands. "And where is Mr. Rawson?"

"I won't talk about it here. We can get together tomorrow night and I'll explain everything."

"That doesn't work for me. I'm following you home and you're telling me tonight. I'm not letting another minute pass without claiming my son."

"You can't tonight! He's not ready."

"I want some answers and I will get them."

"Jeff, please, I know you're mad and you have every right to be. But remember he's just a little boy."

"My little boy." He thumped his chest with his fist. "My. Little. Boy."

Dr. McKenzie came out of the cubicle. "Looks like he's good to go." He held a sheaf of papers in his hand. "Here are the discharge instructions. Nurse Novak will go over them with you."

"Thank you."

"Danny's asking for you," the nurse said.

Beth glanced at Jeff then followed her.

But not before Dr. McKenzie said to Jeff. "Coach Myers, I've heard awesome things about you and I've been following the Sharks. They're looking good. Any chance you play softball?"

****

Beth parked in the driveway. Jeff, true to his word,

pulled in behind her.

"We're home, buddy," she told Danny. "I'll come right around to help you out of the car."

The door opened and Jeff leaned in. "I'll bring Danny in. You go get the door." He unbuckled Danny's seatbelt and lifted him as if he weighed nothing. "Put your arms around my neck, champ."

Her heart lurched seeing Danny cuddle against Jeff's broad chest. He already worshipped Coach. She couldn't imagine how euphoric he'd be finding out Coach was his real dad.

"Got that door open?"

She fumbled with her keys. "Sorry."

When she finally got the door open, he marched through carrying Danny as if he was made of spun glass. "Where's his room?"

"Please put him on the couch. He hasn't eaten dinner and I imagine he's hungry. Besides, he's filthy."

Jeff's jaw clenched even more, but he did as she said.

Beth plumped some pillows for his head and put one under his injured ankle. "The doctor said you need to keep this elevated. Are you hungry?"

"A little." He wiggled his back against the pillows.

"What do you want?"

He gave it some thought. "Pizza?"

"How about some cereal and a banana?" Beth smiled when Danny groaned, then turned her eyes to Jeff. "Do you want anything?"

"I'm good."

"Then, maybe while I'm putting his cereal together you can take him to the bathroom and help him clean up a little."

"Sure."

Beth blew out a breath. "Okay. I'll be right back." She hurried to the kitchen to get some breathing room.

Jeff was so angry. Once she explained everything she'd gone through, calmly and rationally, he might calm down enough to have a real conversation.

She put Danny's cereal on a tray and went back into the living room. Jeff had helped Danny into clean pajamas and now her baby had fallen asleep on the couch. Jeff sat on the other end watching him.

"Well, it looks like he's down for the count. Can you help me get him to his room?"

"Of course." He stood and picked up Danny. "Where?"

"Just down the hall. On the left. This way." She raised and pointed with a very shaky hand.

Jeff didn't say anything; he just took Danny to his room. He laid him on the bed.

"I need to tuck him in and get his ankle elevated." She stood in the doorway. "Go wait in the living room and I'll be right out."

Jeff looked like he wanted to argue, but he did what she said.

She kissed Danny's nose.

"I love you," he whispered before he totally went under, "across all dimensions."

She smiled and kissed him again. "I love you more."

Straightening, she turned off the lights and flicked on his Time Bomb nightlight.

She couldn't stall any more. Danny's father was in her living room, demanding answers, which he deserved. Closing the door, she went to face him.

****

Jeff prowled around Beth's house, feeling much like a lion with a thorn in his paw. It was a comfortable, homey room filled with comfortable furniture, shelves of books and games and pictures, but he felt anything but comfortable. He felt like an unwanted stranger.

Pictures predominated the room. They were mostly of Danny chronicling his growth from infant to the boy he was now.

Jeff had missed so much.

He found it odd that there were no pictures of Beth's husband, which confirmed his suspicion that Danny was the baby he'd made with her.

"He's sound asleep." Jeff turned to see her standing there. "Do you want me to make some coffee while we talk?"

Since he figured on a long night, he said, "Sure."

"Come into the kitchen with me. We'll be more comfortable and there'll be less chance we'll wake Danny."

"Why not." He selected a picture of Danny as an infant and brought it with him. Beth was already busy grinding beans, filling the coffeemaker with water.

Without turning to face him, she said in a small voice, "I think you remember that my father was a man with no kindness in him, a hard man who made rules and expected everyone to do as he said. I was sixteen and under his thumb." Now she faced him and motioned to one of the two kitchen chairs. "Sit, please."

He did, defiantly putting the framed photo of Danny on the table so only he could see it.

She sat in the other chair. "I desperately wanted to keep Danny, you have no idea how much I did, but my father would have none of it. The Gospel according to Bob Pritchard demanded I give my baby up for adoption. Do you want a cookie? I baked a batch of Danny's favorites today."

Something burned inside of him with that. He didn't even know what kind of damn cookie his son liked. "Sure."

She went to the cabinet, grabbed the jar of cookies. She arranged the cookies on a plate. "Here you go. Oatmeal with chocolate chips. No nuts. He hates nuts." She placed the plate on the table and sat back down.

"So do I."

"Good to know." She grabbed a cookie but didn't do anything with it. "Here's what you need to know." She told him the whole sad story.

Jeff shook his head. "Jesus Christ." A small part of him was relieved there was no Mr. Rawson lurking somewhere, waiting to ambush him and keep him from his son. "Your father died. Why didn't you tell me then?"

"I told you why. I looked you up and found out you married Katie. Who, by the way, called the Lobster Cove police right before she called my father." Beth's eyes flashed the fire of temper. "We'd be a family, maybe with other children. Instead you married her and had a child with her." Beth stood. "I'm sorry, but you were an idiot. A callous, clueless, idiot. She stole the life I should have had. No way I was letting her take my son away from me as well."

"What did you say?"

"You heard me. Katie called the police on us before she phoned my father. You married the woman who almost got you sent to jail. Good going."

He got a little lightheaded. "That can't be true. How do you know that?"

"My father told me."

"I can't believe it."

"Oh, believe it. He said so on his deathbed. So maybe you can see why I didn't want my son to have anything to do with the woman who called the police to keep us apart and the man who would actually marry her."

A bit of wind escaped from his sails. Katie would have used Danny against both of them. "I would have protected you both."

"You married her! How could I trust you?" She walked to the counter and filled the mugs with the fresh brewed coffee. "How do you take yours?"

The question took him slightly aback. "Black."

She poured milk and sugar into one mug then brought both to the table and set one in front of him. "We moved here because it was a way to be close to you. To have that little slice of happiness back."

He stared at her, this stranger, his first love, the mother of his child. His heart beat a little harder. "I want him to know I'm his father."

"That's so complicated. Somehow I have to tell him I've lied about his father all his life."

"Tough. I'm his father and I want the world to know it. I want him to know."

She nodded. "Yes. He should know the truth."

Finally! "Why did you name him Danny?"

Beth gave a mirthless laugh. "I didn't. My father was reading from the book of Daniel when he was born. He demanded I name him that." She grabbed a cookie. "He hated that I called him Danny. My one defiance."

She took a bite.

"Your father, the one who wanted to send me to jail for rape, named my son?" Jeff's blood pressure spiked way up.

Beth slapped her hand on the table. "I wouldn't risk losing him, especially over what to name him."

"I would have named him after my father, William. Billy."

She goggled at him. "You truly have no idea what I've been through! I've given up every dream I ever had for that boy. He is my whole life." She splayed her hand on her chest. "You come into our lives and he ends up in the hospital! Playing football for your team. And you're upset about his name?"

"Accidents happen."

"Accidents happen," she mimicked. "He's a very talented musician. What if this wrist injury means he can't play the piano with the same skill any more?"

"He doesn't want to play piano. He wants to play football."

"How do you know that?" Beth stood, chest-heaving, complexion mottled. "Get out of my home."

He also stood and used his height to intimidate her. "Not yet. I want to tell Danny he's my son as soon as possible. Tomorrow."

She didn't back down. "He won't be going to practice, not with his injuries. Come after practice and we'll tell him together." She angled that defiant chin up again. "Calmly. Civilly. And we'll present a united front. It's what's best for Danny."

He really didn't know this version of Beth, the one who called the shots and told you exactly how it was going to be.

Realizing she was right, he nodded. "Okay. I'll come by tomorrow evening." He picked up the picture of Danny he'd put on the table, took the photo from the frame and put it in his shirt pocket. He left the empty frame where it was. "I'll let myself out."

Her silence followed him.

Chapter Fifteen

Jeff's heart pounded as he finished one last lap around the track surrounding the high school football field. The early morning air held a chill and promise of autumn.

He stopped running and walked a quarter lap. His breath sawed in and out of his lungs, his eyes watered, and sweat poured off his forehead. He hadn't slept at all last night. His eyes were gritty, his mood foul. He grabbed his water bottle and slugged down the contents.

He had a son. He and Beth had created a son, an amazing boy.

A son Beth had kept away from him for ten years.

He actually shook with anger. He needed to get it under control .

Never mind Katie's part in the whole mess. He'd deal with her later.

He planned to contact an attorney to find out what his rights were and how to change Danny's last name to Myers. He also had to tell his mother and Katie. He didn't look forward to either call, especially the one to Katie. She would totally go off the deep end and use visitation with Cookie as a weapon.

That not only punished him, it punished his daughter.

He was in a real awkward situation and Beth was the person who put him there. One thing he knew for sure, he was not letting her come in between Danny and him.

****

"How are you feeling today, baby?" Beth sat on Danny's bed.

"Not so good." Danny rolled his eyes. "And I'm not a baby any more."

"You'll always be my baby." She drank in the sight of him. "I think you can take the day off of school today."

"Really?"

Beth nodded. "Really. But I'll call to let the school know and get today's assignments for you."

"Can I watch The Refractor movie again?"

"Sure. Now let's get you settled on the couch. Want some breakfast?"

"I can eat."

"Good." She looked at Danny with his hurt ankle and bloody, bruised nose and wanted to cry. "I'll go fix you some pancakes. How's that?"

"Yummy! I love you Mom, in every dimension!"

She hoped that was still the case after this evening. "I love you more."

****

Jeff hesitated before he got out of his car and started up the walk to Beth's front door. Once this secret came out, their lives would change forever.

What the hell. He'd missed ten years of Danny's life. He wasn't waiting a minute longer. He pressed the button for the bell.

Beth appeared. "Hi." She stood back. "Come on in."

"Thanks." He stepped into Beth's front hall for the

91

most important conversation he'd had in his life. "Where's Danny?"

"In the living room. Give me your jacket. Can I get you something to drink?" She folded his jacket over her arm. "Have you eaten dinner? I made a ton of mac and cheese and we can't possibly eat it all."

Jeff studied the woman. Her eyes looked haunted and it was clear she'd gotten about as much sleep as he did. She wore sweat pants and a T-shirt with a picture of that damned Lionel Lobster cartoon. "No, thanks. I'm good."

"Come on, then. But remember. Calmly. Civilly. No accusations, no recriminations. Just the simple truth. You got that?"

"Yeah, I do. No worries."

She plastered a toothy fake smile on her face and led the way into the living room. "Hey, Danny! Look who's here to see you."

"Coach!" Danny's face lit up and Jeff's heart skipped a beat. His son!

"Hey, champ! Mind if I sit on the couch with you?"

"'Course! How was today?"

"We all missed you and the other kids are happy you're okay."

Pulling a chair to be near Danny, Beth sat. "Danny, Coach and I have something to tell you."

Danny looked from one to the other. "You look sad, Mom. Is it bad news?"

She brushed his hair back, the gesture lingering. "No, sweetie, it's good news." She sighed, pressed her lips together, and took Danny's hand. "Coach, I mean Jeff and I have known each other a long time. We loved each other a lot, enough to try and get married."

"Cool! Do you want to get married again and Coach be my new dad?"

Jeff heard choirs of angels when he saw Danny's excitement. Beth looked at him and nodded. "Here's the thing, champ. I already am your dad."

Danny's head swiveled to face Beth. "Is that true, Mom?"

"Yes, sweetheart. It's true. Sometimes when people love each other so much they make a baby. That's what Coach," She nodded at Jeff, "and I did. We made you."

Danny started to blink a lot and looked back and forth from Beth to him. "Why didn't you be my dad right away?"

Beth brought his attention back to her. "He wanted to. Remember your grandfather? How he made all kinds of rules and was real strict about them? Like we talked about the other night?"

"Yeah." His eyes narrowed.

"He didn't like Jeff, didn't want him to be your father and took us away where he couldn't find us."

His fingers started to pull at the blanket covering him. "Did you try?" He turned his attention back to Jeff.

"Yes. I tried but your grandfather hid you guys good."

Danny sat still and silent, barely even breathing.

Beth squeezed his hand. "What are you feeling, baby?"

"What about my other father? The one you told me about?"

Beth's lips thinned and took a deep breath. "Your grandfather made me make him up because he didn't want anyone to know that I wasn't married when you were born." She grabbed his other hand. "I'm not proud of it and I'm sorry I lied to you. I had a good reason at the time. Your grandfather would have made me give you away to another family and I loved you so much I couldn't give you up."

"You told me there was never a good reason to lie," he whispered.

Jeff's eyes stung. Something shifted between them right before his eyes, a tragic loss of the absolute trust Danny had in Beth.

Jeff had done his own damage so he might as well 'fess up. "When I couldn't find you and your mom, I got married to someone else."

"You didn't love my mom any more?" Danny's nose started to run.

"I did love your mom and I wondered every day about how she was and what she was doing. But since I couldn't find her, I gave up and married someone else."

"Are you still married to her and that's why you can't be my dad?"

"I'll always be your dad, champ. And no, I'm not still married to her. We got a divorce. You know what that is, right?"

"Yeah. A couple kids in my class got divorces."

"So you understand." Jeff smiled. "Here's the good news. You have a sister."

"Where's she live?"

"Back in Massachusetts in the town your mom and I grew up in. Her name is Cookie. I know she'll be so happy to have a big brother."

Danny scowled as he digested that little factoid. "I don't want a sister. Girls are stupid. And Cookie's a stupid name."

"Danny! That's not a very nice thing to say. Give her a chance," Beth said. "I think it's great that you have a little sister and I can't wait to meet her. You'll have so much fun."

"I don't want to meet her. She can stay in Massachusetts."

Jeff had never seen Danny's inner brat. He should have expected it. "You've got a grandmother who can't wait to meet you. She's really nice and she makes the best cookies."

Danny's eyes narrowed. "What kind? I only eat oatmeal and chocolate chip cookies."

"That's not true, baby. I know you eat all kinds of cookies."

"If you can lie, I can too."

Beth sucked in a harsh breath and closed her eyes.

Jeff knew he had to step in. "No, you can't. You also can't talk to your mother like that. Tell her you're sorry."

Danny, to his credit, looked ashamed. "Sorry."

Beth stood. "Do you have any questions right now?"

Danny shook his head as he gave a jaw-cracking yawn.

"Then I think we've talked enough tonight," she said, her voice even and cool. "Danny, it's time for your bath. I'll get it ready." She left the room.

He watched this boy, this miracle, his son, and felt a rush of love so strong and pure, the same as he felt when Cookie was born.

Anger over the lost years bubbled up in him again at that thought, but he tamped it down. It didn't do anybody any good for him to go around being mad.

Especially when the man who deserved all his anger was dead.

"Danny, your bath is ready."

Jeff looked up to see Beth watching them both. He couldn't get a bead on her.

"I haven't finished reading my new comic yet." The kid made the tortoise look like Jeff Gordon.

"C'm'on, champ. Finish up. Bath time is calling your name."

"Are you gonna be here tomorrow when I wake up?"

"No. Sorry. I live in my house and you live in yours with your mom."

"What if I don't wanna live with my mom? What if I wanna live with you?"

Tread lightly, he warned himself. "Well, your sister lives with her mother, and you live with yours. But I'm going to be around. A lot. You'll probably get sick of me."

"Did you ever live with her?"

It didn't take much to figure out that her equaled Cookie. "Yes, when I was still married to her mom, we all lived in the same house. I moved out when Cookie's mom and I got divorced."

"If you lived with her, why can't you live with me and Mom?"

Man. He hadn't counted on sibling rivalry so soon. "We're not married. I promise you'll get to spend lots of time at my house."

Beth's eyebrows shot to the top of her forehead and her eyes widened.

"For tonight, it's enough that you know I'm your dad."

"Danny, you need to take your bath." She came fully into the room. "Let me help you up."

Danny pulled away when she touched him. "I want my dad to help me."

Beth put her palms up and took a couple of steps back.

"I'm right here, son." Jeff lifted Danny. The kid winced a little, but didn't make a sound. "Where's the bathroom?" Jeff asked.

"Down the hall on the right. Across from his room."

"Got it."

Beth brushed past them as she did that rabbit thing into the living room. "I'll just clean up. I've left clean underwear and pajamas on the counter."

Man, she looked rough. He almost felt sorry for her.

Operative word being almost.

He nodded and hauled his kid down the hall to the bathroom.

****

I will not cry, I will not cry, I will not cry, Beth repeated in her head as a mantra, a plea, a prayer.

She knew it'd be tough, but the reality turned out to be worse.

If you can lie, I can too.

By the end of his life, Beth had lost all love for her father. Actually, she lost the love when he made her make that terrible, terrible agreement. She was ashamed that she was relieved when he'd died. She shouldn't have been so jealous of Katie. But she couldn't stand to watch Jeff love Katie and not her. To prefer Katie's child and not Danny.

She talked a good game about being all about Danny, but in the end her jealousy had kept Jeff and Danny apart. Playing God. Just like her father. She guessed the leaf didn't fall far from the tree. A sob clogged her throat at the thought.

"Hey, Beth?" Jeff stood in the entrance to the living room. "Danny's done with his bath and is changed and ready for lights out."

"I'll be right there." So weary, she passed him and made her way to Danny's bedroom. He was already in bed and looked away from the door, giving her the cold shoulder. By rote, she turned on his Time Bomb nightlight. "Hey, baby."

"I'm not a baby. Don't call me that ever again."

"Okay." She swallowed as she sat on his bed. "Did you say your prayers?"

"Didn't have to. God gave me my real dad tonight."

She could barely breathe. "I love you, Danny. Across all dimensions."

Danny turned his back to her and pulled the covers over his head.

"Good night," she choked out. Flicking off the light, she closed the door and made it to the wall. Since she couldn't stand up any more, she slid down the wall and dropped her head onto her knees.

Her son, her very reason for being, hated her. She choked back tears and took some deep breaths to compose herself. She would not let Jeff Myers see her cry.

He came out of the bathroom and crouched beside her. "I cleaned the bathroom."

"Thank you." What else could she say?

He held out a hand to help her up. "Let's go to the kitchen."

Why not? She let him help her up. "That's probably best."

As they passed through the living room, he said, "Let me pick up the dirty dishes."

"Leave them. It'll give me something to do when I can't sleep tonight."

"I know the feeling." He brought her into the kitchen and let her drop into one of those two chairs. He sat across from her. "This is what's going to happen next."

"What?" He'd been so supportive all evening. She hadn't expected it and was grateful for it. Apparently he had another agenda.

He heaved a sigh. "I am making an appointment with Nate Cavanaugh to find out what my rights are here. I'll be honest. I want to adopt him. Put my name on him."

"Put your name on him, like he's some kind of shiny new toy you don't want anyone else to have?" Her stomach twisted like Nancy Kerrigan flying through the air, doing triple axels. She bolted out of her chair and threw up into the sink. He'd been right there to pull her hair out of the way and rub her back.

It brought back all her memories of their mad dash to get married. She'd been puking her guts up the entire trip. He'd been that solicitous then. She pushed him away. "I'm okay."

"You sure?"

"Don't worry about it." She rinsed out the sink, got a glass of water. "I'm used to taking care of myself."

"I'm prepared to pay child support."

"Oh, God." So many new wrinkles.

"Calm down." He touched her arm, his manner totally businesslike. "I do need it on record that I'm Danny's father," he pointed to himself, "not some figment of your imagination."

She heard the derision in his tone. She'd taken enough hits tonight. She wasn't taking any more. "I did what I had to do. Would you have preferred I let my father give my baby away?"

"No, of course not." His gaze darkened. "What a mess."

"Why didn't you ever try to find us?" The question came flying out of her mouth before she could stop it.

"I was afraid of some crackpot sending me to jail."

"Believe me, you don't have to be behind bars to be stuck in a prison." She pulled up some pride. "If anyone was responsible for you going to jail, it would have been your wife. You're right, it's a mess."

He turned his eyes to the floor. "I'm not trying to hassle you in any way. I'm just trying to get back as much of the time that you stole from me."

She'd had enough. "I didn't steal anything from you and I'm sick and tired of that tune right now. I won't try to keep you from building a relationship with Danny, but I won't stand here and...and," She choked. "Please. If you ever loved me, just go. I can't take any more tonight."

She watched him turn on his heel and leave. While she expected him to slam the door, he left without a sound.

When her father died, she'd vowed that no man would ever control her life again.

Jeff Myers walked back into her life and thought he

could call the shots. Why did the men who professed to love her only want to control her?

Well, she wasn't taking it any more, that was for sure.

Chapter Sixteen

"I don't feel good enough to go to school today. I need to stay home."

Beth knew this was coming. Whatever she suggested, Danny immediately resisted. Protested. Refused.

Jittery, every nerve she had rubbed raw, she lost her patience. "You're going to school. Your wrist is strong enough to handle the crutches. There will be teachers to help you."

"I don't want teachers to help me. I want my dad."

Lord, give her patience. "He works in the high school. Your teachers will help you." Light bulb. "Besides, you don't want everyone to think you're a baby, do you?"

"No."

"Well, if you expect your father to step in every time you get hurt, the kids won't think very much of you, especially if you brag. Don't you want to earn respect on your own? No one respects someone who hides behind his father."

He arched a brow and looked so much like Jeff. "Whatever."

She wanted to shake her precious boy. If she'd learned anything the previous night, Jeff would at least make Danny mind his manners.

"You may be mad at me right now but I'm still the

boss of you. The doctor cleared you to go to school on crutches." Danny's wrist sprain had ended up no big deal. "If you want Jeff to cancel all his classes and devote his time to you, I've got to tell you, bab—"

"Don't call me baby ever again."

She picked her battle and ignored that dig. "I guarantee you won't win any friends by bragging that the coach is your dad."

"What do you know?"

"More than you. You didn't like it when other kids bragged about who their dads are."

"I used to, but it's okay now, I've got a real dad."

Lord, give me strength. "You don't want me to call you baby, but you want everyone to watch your dad, the coach, treat you like a baby? Think about it."

"He knows I'm a big kid."

Time to take a new tack. "You can see Coach—"

"Dad."

"Okay, Dad." She gave that word the gravity it deserved, because it was important to him and it was the truth. "If you want to be respected for your talent, do you really want to have the kids like you just because you're the coach's son?"

"They'll be afraid of me, because they won't want me to talk smack about them to Dad."

Who was this creature and what had he done with her son? "I don't think this is your best plan."

"I'll ask Dad about it and tell you what we figure out." He crossed his arms against his chest.

She gave up. "Grab your crutches and go out to the car. I'll be right there with your books and your lunch."

Before she dropped him at school and got him settled in his classroom she texted Jeff about Danny's delusions of grandeur.

He'd have to talk some sense into the boy. Lord knew Danny wasn't listening to her.

****

"Hi, Julia, do you have a minute?" Jeff caught up with the high school principal in the outer office.

"Sure, come on in. Alex told me he talked to you about the softball team the other night when one of your Junior Sharks got hurt." She sat behind her desk and he sat in one of the chairs in front of it. "What's up?"

"I've had a change in my personal life and I want to tell you before you hear it from someone else."

"You've got my attention." She leaned forward, elbows on her desk.

"I just found out that I have a ten-year-old son, that Junior Shark Alex told you about."

"Just found out?"

"It's a long story. I was kept in the dark for ten years. Now that I know I have a kid, he's not going to be a secret any more."

"Who is he?"

"Danny Rawson. Beth Pritch—uh, Rawson is his mom."

Her eyebrows slammed up her forehead. "Danny? Of course I know Danny. Beth is the organist at St. Joseph's. She's a lovely person." She stood. "I'm shocked. How did you find out?"

"The other night at the hospital. I knew Beth by her real name, Pritchard, but my son had a different last name. I never would have known if Danny hadn't gotten hurt and I'd taken him to the emergency room." The hurt was still fresh. "I just wanted to let you know about my changed circumstances."

"Wow. That's a lot to take in. I never would have guessed—" She shook her head. "Never mind. You're going to be very busy between having a son here and a daughter down in Massachusetts."

He frowned. "Nothing I can't handle."

"Okay. Thanks for letting me know." She gathered some files from her desktop. "I've got a meeting. Good luck!"

He followed her out the door. He would need every bit of that luck Julia wished him.

****

Beth had gotten Danny to school early so she could let his teacher know what was going on.

Of course, the minute they got to the classroom Danny announced as loudly as he could that Coach Myers was his real dad and how awesome that was.

She'd never forget the shocked look on Mrs. Bailey's face. Or the judgmental one that followed. She might as well get used to it.

Jeff hadn't answered her text yet.

Beth's next mission? To tell Anita. They were meeting at Maggie's Diner for lunch.

Anita was already seated when Beth got there.

"Hi," Beth said. "Thanks for coming to meet me."

"It sounded important."

"It is."

Sally brought over the coffeepot and turned over the heavy white mugs already on the table. "The soup today is fish chowder. Do you need menus?"

Anita shrugged. "I don't. I want the lobster burger."

Beth decided on the chowder and a blueberry muffin.

"Coming right up!" Sally went back to the kitchen.

"There's something you need to know. I've been keeping a big secret." She clasped her hands on the table. Might as well pull off the Band-Aid fast. "Long story short, Jeff Myers is Danny's biological father."

Anita's jaw dropped. "What," she squeaked. "Jeff Myers? As in Coach Jeff Myers, Hunk Extraordinaire?"

"Yes."

"Why didn't you tell me?"

Beth felt her face flush. "It's complicated. Jeff didn't know and I needed to tell him and Danny first." Well, except she'd had to tell Jenna, but Anita did have to know that. "He found out at the E.R. the other night when Danny got hurt."

"Why didn't you tell him?" Anita shot Beth an accusing glance.

"It's a very long, complicated story."

"That's why you needed my help getting him to and from practice."

"Yeah, well, I can help out with that now that Jeff and Danny know."

"Why didn't you tell me? I wouldn't have told anybody."

"Like I said, I couldn't tell anybody before I told Jeff and Danny. I made plans to tell him last Saturday, but he had to go back to Massachusetts to see his daughter."

Anita's eyes widened. "He has a daughter?"

"Yes. With my ex-best friend from high school, now known as Skankarella."

Anita laughed.

"They got married but they're divorced now." Thank the Lord for small things. "Then I was going to tell him tonight after the Sharks game, but it's an away game at Stockton Springs. With the boys' first game on Saturday afternoon, I had to wait for Sunday." She added two creamers and a sugar packet into her coffee and stirred. "Danny's accident took care of that."

"He must have been so mad."

"An understatement. They both were. He is working with me when it comes to helping Danny get used to it."

"What'll happen next?"

"I have no idea. Danny turned overnight into a kid I don't recognize. He worshipped Jeff before he knew he was his dad. Now?" Beth sighed. "Dad walks on water and I'm a big fat liar who kept him from his father."

Someone gasped. They both looked up to see Sally standing next to their table with their food.

Great. Just great.

"Are you saying that the new football coach, who is amazingly hot by the way and gives Tom Brady a run for his money, is Danny's biological father?"

Nope, nothing wrong with Sally's hearing. "Yes."

Sally put down their food on the table. "If that don't beat all."

"Thanks, Sally, everything looks good." Anita picked up her lobster burger.

Sally took the hint. "Just holler if you need anything else." She walked away, her steps reluctant.

"It's going to be all over town by tomorrow."

Beth picked up her spoon and dipped it into her soup. "I know. It would be anyway. I told Mrs. Bailey this morning so she could deal with Danny's new attitude. By now, every kid and teacher at Lobster Cove

Elementary knows." She put the spoon of soup in her mouth. It looked good and smelled heavenly, but it tasted like ashes.

Thank God for Anita. She might be Beth's only friend after this shook down.

****

"Hey, champ." Jeff sat on a bench on the sidelines next to Danny.

"Hey, Dad." His face shone with adulation and joy. "Wish I could practice with everyone else today."

"Stay off that ankle and you'll be back out there in no time." He ruffled the kid's hair. "I need to talk to you about something."

"'Kay."

"Your mom texted me this morning that you thought you'd get special treatment over the other kids because I'm your dad."

Danny's face turned beet red. "She's a tattletale."

"No Danny, she's your mother and she shared information with me that I needed. That's what parents do. So here's the deal. I'm going to treat you like any other kid on the team. If I hear you trying to push other kids around, I'm going to have to kick you off the team."

Danny's lip trembled. "You wouldn't do that!"

"I would. That's just really poor sportsmanship and would ruin the morale of the team."

Danny swiped at his eyes with the back of a grimy hand. "Okay. I probably wouldn't have done anything. I said it 'cause Mom was making me mad."

"I'm glad to hear you didn't mean it, but I don't like you saying stuff like that because you're mad at your mother." He stood. "I've got to get back to watching the practice. We okay?"

"'Course, Dad."

Jeff jogged back to his post. That had gone well, but he and Beth better brace themselves for more trouble with Danny.

Chapter Seventeen

"Two visits in two weeks! To what do I owe the pleasure?" Jeff's mother stood on tiptoe to kiss his cheek.

"I've got some news, Ma." He grabbed a Sam Adams—that she kept only for him—out of the fridge, sat at the kitchen table, and popped the top.

She put a bowl of tortilla chips in front of him along with some salsa. "It must be important."

"It is." He took a swig of his beer and enjoyed the cold bitter fizz in his mouth before he swallowed it. "Remember I told you that Beth was living in Lobster Cove."

"I remember thinking it was a real coincidence."

He dove right in. "She didn't give our baby daughter up for adoption. Instead she had a baby boy who she kept. His name is Danny and he's on the kid's football team I coach on the side."

"What?" His mother slapped her hand over her heart. "How did you find out?"

"He got hurt last Wednesday and I stayed with him in the Emergency Room until his mother got there. She couldn't keep him a secret any more."

"How could she lie to you about having a son?"

He told her the whole sad story. "So that's it." He took another pull on his beer.

"You're kidding! I want to kill her."

"Which one?"

"Your ex-wife. She was the one who got you busted? Didn't she know that lunatic wanted to send you to jail?"

"Stand in line. That's why Beth didn't want Danny anywhere near her."

She sniffed. "Knowing Katie, that was probably a good plan."

He grimaced. "I've got to tell her. Katie, I mean. She won't take it well."

Nancy sniffed. "Do you have any pictures of this surprise grandson of mine?"

Jeff grinned. "I do." He pulled out his phone and brought up the pictures he'd taken of Danny. "I took some of him at practice on Friday. I got this one from Beth." He drew his wallet out of his pocket and showed her the photo he'd stolen from the frame the night he'd learned the truth.

She smiled and tears came to her eyes. "He looks just like you did at that age. Except for the blue eyes and freckles."

I don't know. I think he looks a lot like Beth. You know. With that whole blue eyes and freckles thing." His mother handed him back the photo and he traced the outline of Danny's tiny, infant, scrunched-up face.

"How will you handle things with Beth?"

"I've got an appointment with a lawyer tomorrow to talk about adopting him and changing his last name to Myers. I don't want any kid running around out there without my name on him."

"Do you think Beth will fight you?"

"She'll do whatever she has to do to for Danny's good. She's not like Katie." He hoped.

Oh, how he hoped.

"When are you telling her?"

"'Bout an hour from now. I'm dreading it. She's already miffed that I showed up out of the blue and she had to change her afternoon plans." He finished off his beer.

She stood and put a maternal hand on his shoulder and squeezed. "Do you want me to go with you so I can make sure Cookie doesn't hear? I can take her out for ice cream or something."

"Thanks, but I've got to do this alone. And I've got to tell Cookie anyway." No need to have his mother around when her mother goes berserk.

****

An hour later, Jeff knocked on the door of what used to be his home. He heard excited screams and grinned.

Cookie threw open the door and launched herself into his arms. "Daddy!" She wrapped her arms around his neck so tightly he thought he'd choke.

"Hey, Cookie!" He laid his cheek on top of her head and inhaled that little girl scent. "Let me see what you're wearing."

She let him put her down and did a couple of twirls. The ensemble consisted of a purple sparkly top over a ruffled pink skirt that flared out when she circled. A plastic tiara studded with big square "jewels" completed the look. He squatted so he was at eye level with her. "Well, don't you look beautiful."

She giggled. "You always say that, Daddy."

Katie entered the room on a cloud of White Diamonds. "Okay, Cookie. You run to the playroom so your father can tell me what's so important that we had to change our plans."

"Okay." She put a hand on each cheek. "Scratchy! You need to shave." She kissed him on his nose. "Don't leave without saying good bye."

"You know I won't." He stood as she scampered out of the room.

Katie turned her back and walked into their family room. He sighed and followed. She perched on one of the sofa's arms. He sat in what was once his favorite chair. He'd wanted to take it with him when he moved out, but Katie hadn't allowed it.

It was just a freakin' chair. He didn't get it, but what else was new?

"So, what's this big news you have for me? Though I imagine I know what it is."

"Uh, no you can't. I have a son with Beth, a boy named Danny."

"What?" Katie's jaw dropped. "You told me she had a girl and gave her away for adoption."

"Apparently she didn't. But now I know about him and I'm going to be a big part of his life, which means he's going to be part of his sister's life."

She jumped up. "Cookie is not that boy's sister. I'm not letting him anywhere near her. She won't understand."

"She absolutely is his sister, whether you like it or not, and she will accept him if we tell her the right way. I bet she'll love having a big brother."

Katie started to pace. "I won't allow it."

"You will, and you know why? Because Beth told me what you did. You were the one to call the Lobster Cove police." He hung onto his control by a very thin thread.

"What are you talking about? Beth is telling more lies."

Give me strength. "Her father told her, Katie…on his deathbed so I have no reason not to believe him. You do know you could have gotten me thrown in jail."

Katie sniffed. "I know no such thing. How can you take the word of a maniac over mine?"

He couldn't believe her but he knew she'd stick to her story with her dying breath. "Cookie will meet Danny and have a relationship with him."

"Over my dead body."

He resisted the obvious threat that usually followed that statement. "You'll have no choice. Make no mistake, if you get in the way of this I'll take you to court so fast it'll make your head spin."

She stopped and glared at him with narrowed eyes. "You get out of my house right now." She pointed to the door.

"Excuse me? Who still pays the mortgage on this place?" What a piece of work. A strong sense of regret descended on him that he had ever touched, kissed or married this woman. "And not before I tell Cookie."

"I'll call the police and have them throw you out."

"Yeah, 'cause you're so good at that. Katie, it's my house. I have a right to be here. Like I said, I still pay the mortgage on it. Now, I'm going to the playroom and tell my daughter about her brother. You can come if you like, but you can't stop me."

"I hate you."

Jeff laughed right in her face. "Ditto." He remembered Danny and Beth's little phrase. "In every dimension." He turned on his heel and left.

She scrambled after him.

Cookie had wrapped a silver boa around her neck and was having a tea party with her American Girl doll, the one they'd had made to look just like her, all fluffy blonde curls and big brown eyes, the bear they'd made the last time they went to Build-A-Bear and what looked to be a brand new Barbie. "Hi, Daddy. Do you want to have some tea?" She lifted the toy teapot to show him.

"Not right now, Cookie girl. I've got some good news for you." He took off his jacket and sat cross-legged on the floor next to her. "Guess what!"

"What?"

"You have a big brother."

"I do?" Her little brows furrowed under the tiara. "How come I don't know him?"

"That's because I didn't know about him. I just found out on Wednesday."

"What's his name?" She put down the teapot.

"His name is Danny and he's ten-years-old." Jeff brushed a blonde curl out of her eyes. "And he can't wait to meet you." Well, not right now, but Jeff was going to fix that.

"Where is he now? Did he come with you?"

"He stayed with his mom back in Lobster Cove."

"Does he live with you?" A little bit of jealousy tinged her voice, but after Danny's reaction to Cookie, he'd expected the same from her.

"He lives with his mom in her house."

"Are you going to marry his mommy and be a family there?" And, yes indeed, the world famous Cookie pout blossomed on her face.

"I don't know. Things are all mixed up but I'm going to bring him down so he can meet your grandmother and you."

"Do I have to share Grandma with him?" Cookie adored Jeff's mother.

"Yes, but she'll still see you all the time and love you all the same."

Cookie took that in. She looked up at Katie, who was standing in the doorway. "You don't have to meet him if you don't want to, sugarplum, not if it upsets you."

"It's not going to upset you. It'll be fun to have someone else to play with. He's nice. You'll see."

"Do you want to play tea party with me now?" She was obviously done talking about Danny. He shouldn't push the issue.

"I would love to! What kind of tea are we having today?"

Cookie giggled. "The pretend kind! You're so funny, Daddy." She poured and handed him the tiniest cup he'd ever seen.

He lifted it to his lips. "Delicious!"

****

"I warn you, Jeff. I'm not letting you force Cookie to have a relationship with Beth's son. He is not her brother."

Exhausted, Jeff rolled his shoulders to get rid of the pain in his neck. Time with Katie did that to him. "Biology says otherwise."

"And I will not tolerate Cookie spending any time with Beth."

"After what you pulled ten years ago, Beth understandably doesn't want Danny anywhere near you, so it looks like you're both on the same page."

Katie sucked in a breath and glared at him.

Bulls-eye!

"I've never lied to you. I did not call the Lobster Cove police. Beth's crazy father did."

"Whatever, sweetheart. You keep saying that." He looked at the elegant woman who'd betrayed her friend and almost sent him to jail.

"If you don't have anything new to say, I've got to head back to Lobster Cove." He threw on his jacket and started down the porch stairs.

"To her."

He knew *her* meant Beth. "Yes."

For once Katie kept her mouth shut.

****

"Hey, let's give this man a cigar!" Sally shouted as Jeff walked into Maggie's Diner. "Congratulations! It's a boy!"

Jeff stopped in his tracks. How had word gotten around so soon? "Thank you."

"What can we get for you today?" Maggie beamed at him. "It's on the house."

"Uh, wow. No need for that." Seriously. Jeff walked up to the counter. "I just need a Moxie to go and a fish sandwich with fries."

"Haddock or flounder?" Maggie asked.

"Flounder, I think."

"You got it." Maggie scurried off to make his order.

"So, how does it feel to find out you've got a ten-year-old son?" Sally perched on a stool behind the cash register.

Jeff's chest puffed up at the mere thought of his son. "It feels great! Danny's a good kid." And while he had huge issues with Beth, he wouldn't let anyone bad mouth her. "Beth's done a good job with him."

Sally nodded. "She has. She's had to work so hard since her husband died. It's terrible how we treat our veterans and their families. Now that you're in the picture you can help her out."

Jeff saw red at the mention of Beth's war hero husband.

Beth's pretend war hero husband. All of that was totally made of wrong.

But not that he'd let on in public, because who dissed a veteran? Not Nancy Myers' baby boy. "I'm going to do everything I can for my son."

Sally sighed. "Your son. I think you like the sound of that."

He smiled. "I do."

"Too bad the Sharks lost last Friday night at Stockton Springs. People got used to them winning."

"You shouldn't count on winning every time, especially with a high school team." The team hadn't lost. Jeff didn't have his head in the game. He'd let his players down.

No more. Now that everything was out in the open, he had a plan, he wouldn't be distracted again.

"Here's your food!" Maggie brought a takeout bag. "Sally, get Coach's Moxie."

Sally sighed, reached into the cooler and clinked out a bottle. "Here you go."

"Thanks, Sally." He liberated his wallet from of his back pocket. "What do I owe you, Maggie?"

"I told you it's on the house. You just make sure the Sharks win the next game."

"I'll do my best."

Sally laughed as she brought his Moxie to him.

"Give 'em hell, Coach!"

"Thank you, ladies." He had to get out of there. "And thanks for supporting the team."

As he left, he realized just how fast gossip got around in a small town.

Chapter Eighteen

"Thanks for seeing me, Father Zack."

"Of course, Beth. I'm always here for you." He leaned back in his chair. "What can I do you for?"

Beth folded her hands in her lap, but didn't look down. She looked him right in the eyes.

"Danny knows Jeff is his father. He's overjoyed, of course. But Father," she said, "Danny knows I lied to him and it's a problem."

"As in 'if you can lie, I can, too' kind of a problem?"

She closed her eyes, grateful for his gentle acceptance. "Yes."

"He's mad at you."

Beth smiled. "Got it in one. He's furious, really furious." That smile melted off her face. "I'm a liar and Jeff walks on water."

"Jeff Myers does not walk on water. I lost fifty bucks on last Friday's game. He needs to pull himself together A.S.A.P. before I lose more."

"You bet on children?" Her jaw dropped.

"No." Father Zack gave a rueful shake of his head. "I bet on a football game. There's a difference."

"You're terrible," she teased. "Talk about splitting hairs."

He waved his hand as if to brush Beth's opinion away. "No split hairs at all. It's the same thing as

Bingo, which, as we know, makes a lot of money for St. Joe's. Which goes toward your salary."

His eyes twinkled. "And I lost to Ralph Sykes, of all people." Ralph Sykes was a math teacher at Lobster Cove High who had stood in the way of setting up a daycare in another church for the children of teen mothers so they could stay in school.

As a single parent and teen mother, Beth didn't have much respect for Ralph Sykes.

Truth to tell, she wasn't quite a single parent any more. She had a real live, breathing, in the flesh, baby daddy who wanted to be totally hands-on.

"Is he offering to pay child support?"

"I'm not sure he can afford it. He says he can, but he's obviously paying child support for Cookie. He can't afford to support Danny, too, not on a teacher's salary," Beth murmured. Confusion and guilt swelled up again to drown her. "I don't want his money, I don't want his anything. I've always taken care of Danny by myself. I don't need his money."

"You do work really hard but I know money is an issue for you. You should let him help financially."

"I just want him to love Danny and make sure everything he does protects Danny from harm."

Father Zack's face remained a mask, interested, but void of opinion. "Is that your only issue?"

Here came the crux of the matter. "No. I don't want my son anywhere near Jeff's ex-wife."

"Is she a bad mother?"

She thought about the question, knowing that totally her jealousy and anger at Katie colored her vision of Katie's being a good mother or not. She was angry with Jeff for not seeing through Katie's bull. She was mad at herself for letting Katie stand in the way of her telling Jeff about Danny. Her anger had caused her to make some really bad decisions.

Back to the question at hand. "I have no idea whether she's a good mother or not. She blocks Jeff having his daughter visit him up here, according to him, because she can."

"Does she have a reason?"

"Who knows? I don't think so. Jeff is a good dad, I think. He makes sure Danny minds his manners. It's all about Jeff's gullibility where Katie's concerned." Beth shrugged. "I don't trust my son's welfare with her and Katie refuses to let Cookie visit here because of me." She blew out a huge, cleansing breath. "But she is the mother of Danny's half-sister. I just have this bad feeling about it." She continued to look Father Zack in the eyes. "It's most likely jealousy and worry."

"I'd be afraid if you weren't worried and confused. Considering what she did, I think you're right to keep Danny away from her until the situation settles down." He shrugged. "But what do I know?"

"I thought priests were supposed to have all the answers, all the time. Like 24/7, 365 days out of the year."

"We don't. The best we can do is pray and trust God to lead the way."

Her shoulders slumped under what felt like the weight of a truckload of bricks. "I've got to make things right with Jeff and Danny."

"You already told the truth. The ball is in his court and he does have some issues to own up to and make right."

"I can't even begin to make it straight with Danny.

I tell him to be honest in every situation and now he finds out he has a real live father I never told him about, and a legendary father, who was just that. A legend."

She sniffed and looked for the box of tissues that usually sat on Father Z's desk. She grabbed several of them, riffling them out one at a time. "He will never, ever trust me again."

"That is a problem."

"It's the biggest problem. But I'm happy this is all out in the open. I just can't figure out how to repair my relationship with Danny."

"Are you his mother?"

What? "Of course I'm Danny's mother.

"Have you protected him and loved him all the days of his life?"

"Of course. I made a deal with the devil just so I could keep him. I even let my father name him. Jeff got so angry about that. He says I shouldn't have."

"Why do women always feel at fault when things happen beyond their control? I think Jeff needs to get over it."

Wow. "I don't know. I just feel I did everything wrong."

"No you didn't," Father Zack said. "Everyone can see what good a job you're doing to raise your son."

"From your mouth to God's ears."

"That's usually the way it works, with this priest thing I've got going on. But here's the thing. You were abused."

"My father never raised a hand to me."

"Abuse takes place in many forms. Your father emotionally abused you. He took away your mother, who was also abused, by the way, and he took away your choices. Your power. He shut you down every step of the way and pressed you at every turn." He leaned back in his chair and rested his hands on his considerable belly. "That's abuse, Beth. It's amazing that you are the woman you are instead of being a victim."

Beth hadn't thought about being abused. She'd just called it her life, but Father Zack had brought up things she had to think about. However, "I still shouldn't have lied to Jeff once I found out he'd married Katie."

"I can understand why you did. Does it make it right? No. But God forgives you." He gave her the gentlest smile she had ever seen. "You have to forgive yourself and that's the hardest part of all."

"I'm feeling guilty about deceiving Jeff, but Danny?" She shook her head. "That's my worst sin."

"Would it have been better for him to know he had a father out there who didn't want him?"

"I believe Jeff did want him, but Katie certainly wouldn't have."

"Didn't you trust Jeff to keep Katie in check?"

"No. He married the person who blew us up and I didn't think that showed very good judgment." Beth knew this better than she knew her own name. She sighed. "I'm stuck. I have no idea what to do any more."

Father Zack gave her an understanding smile. "Lots of lies going on here. Seems like forgiveness is the order of the day." He leaned forward. "My money's on you, but I'll still pray for you and Danny and Jeff."

She laughed for the first time since her whole deception blew up in her face. "Can you put in a good word for me, then?"

"You don't even have to ask. I've got it covered." He stood and came around the desk. "God forgives you without reservation or hesitation. Accept it and don't give away any more of your power, because little sister…you are nobody's victim."

Warmth grew in her at his words of comfort and his good advice. She'd already lost too much control of the situation. She couldn't let any more slide out of her grasp.

****

"So, Dad, do you want to stay for dinner tonight?"

Jeff had decided he would drive Danny home from practice every evening. "I don't know, champ. Your mother might not appreciate a last minute dinner guest."

"It'll be okay. She always makes a lot of food."

He chuckled. "Famous last words, son."

"Really! It'll be okay." Danny paused. "Can you talk to Mom about letting me stop my piano lessons?"

"Why do you want to quit?" He really didn't believe in forcing a kid to do something he hated. He remembered the horror of finding out he had to sing in a freaking chorus way back in high school.

"The piano is stupid. I wanna play football now. I don't want to play the piano any more and she'll never let me quit."

"Are you any good?"

"I dunno. She says I am."

"Maybe you can play for me when I get you home."

Danny chuffed out a breath. "I guess. Will you talk to Mom? She'll listen to you."

He snorted. He doubted that very much. "I'll see

what I can do."

Jeff remembered the moment he'd fallen in love with Beth. His heart had been hers from the minute he opened those auditorium doors at Addington High School and heard the music circling through the room.

He'd managed to get himself on the ineligible list by being a real jerk in chorus. The teacher, Andi Nelson, now Mrs. Coach, failed him and his buddy and put them on the ineligible list, meaning they couldn't play football until she changed the grade. The only way to get off the list was to jump through the hoops Andi Nelson put in front of them. Desperate to play ball, he'd gone to the auditorium to ask her for some extra credit stuff to do.

Mrs. Coach wasn't there, but Beth sat at the piano, lost in her music. He'd never seen nor heard anything so beautiful.

He shook his head. He was lost in the past while his son wanted answers.

"So please, Dad?"

"I'm sorry, champ. What were you saying?"

"Can you also talk her into buying me The Refractor video game? She won't get me one because it takes time away from the piano and schoolwork, especially now that I'm on the team. If I can quit the piano, I'll have time to play the game."

He used the eternal parental dodge. "We'll see."

****

"Mo-om! I'm home!"

Just the sound of Danny's voice made Beth smile. She washed her hands and left the kitchen. Oh, and lookee here. Jeff came with him. She'd hoped he would just drop Danny off and then vamoose.

Danny flung his backpack onto the couch. "I invited Dad to have dinner with us. He can stay, right, Mom?"

Her gaze met Jeff's. "Of course. But maybe he has other plans." Please have other plans!

"I don't."

She whooshed out a breath. "Okay then. Danny"— she pointed down the hall—"you need to wash up before you come to the table. Face and hands."

Danny looked at Jeff. "I'll be right back." He ran to the bathroom.

"Danny!" Beth called. "You walk, not run in the house."

"Okay!"

Beth's instruction didn't change his speed. He ignored her.

Again.

"I know this isn't how you thought the evening would go."

She took a deep breath and turned to face Jeff. "Really? What was your first clue?"

He crossed his arms over his chest. "I want to spend as much time with him as I can. I deserve to spend this time with him."

"You keep saying that and I'm not trying to keep you away from him. I'd just like a little warning."

"Danny sprang it on me in the car and I couldn't say no."

"You could say no. But you're here now so stay for dinner. Danny will be disappointed if you don't."

"I appreciate it." He glanced toward the kitchen. "Do you need any help?"

"I've got it." She'd been working and cooking

dinner for Danny all on her own for a long time. She did not need his help. "Why don't you sit and relax. I'm sure Danny will be done washing up"—she looked at her watch—"about now."

Like clockwork the water in the bathroom turned off.

Jeff's mouth thinned into two tight lines. "I guess you know him right down to his toes."

"I'm his mother. He's been the reason I got out of bed and put my shoes on every day and trudged on no matter what life threw at me for the last ten years, so of course I do." She motioned to the couch and the copy of the *Lobster Cove Anchor* on the coffee table. "Why don't you sit and read the paper while I put the finishing touches on dinner. I hope you like spaghetti and meatballs."

"Sounds good." He took a big sniff. "It smells even better."

Whatever. She needed to get a little distance from him. "You relax. Danny will be flying down the hall any second."

"Dad!"

"Here he comes." She turned on her heel and went to the kitchen.

She closed her eyes. What didn't kill you made you stronger.

Chapter Nineteen

"Dad? Can you tell her now?" Danny's version of a whisper could not be defined as soft and secret. What the kid knew, the world knew.

Beth picked up her water and took a slow, deliberate sip. "Tell me what?"

"Dad says I don't have to take piano lessons any more."

Beth turned horrified eyes toward Jeff. Who wanted to sink into the floor. He cleared his throat. "That's not exactly what I said."

"Yes it is," Danny said. "You said you'd tell Mom about the piano lessons."

Jeff saw virtual lightning flash from Beth's eyes and fingertips. Way past time for some damage control. "You promised me you'd play something for me." He concentrated all his focus on Danny. "Go play the piano for me."

"Do I have to?" Jeff might as well have said, "Go eat some raw liver."

"'Fraid so. You promised me."

Danny started to get out of his chair. Beth cleared her throat. "Aren't you forgetting something?"

Danny stood next to his chair. He rolled his eyes like the champ Jeff called him. He rolled his eyes all the time these days, like it was his job. "May I be excused?"

"Thank you. Go and play." Danny whooped. "I meant the piano." Danny stopped mid-whoop. "I love to hear you. Play the Bach *Two Part Invention* you've been working on." Beth smiled.

Danny glanced at Jeff. The kid clearly expected him to step in.

"Go ahead, champ. Let me hear what you got."

Danny trudged off with all the enthusiasm of a convict going to the electric chair.

****

Beth skewered Jeff with a glare. "Once you hear him play, you'll know why I won't let him quit." No matter what, she wasn't letting Danny squander his musical talent. "He's got a rare gift."

How dare Jeff come in at the last minute and try to order her around? He'd find out she wasn't the powerless little girl she'd been ten years ago. Her son was meant to play the piano.

Danny began to play. Badly. Loudly. Wrong notes and wrong rhythms on purpose. Beth sighed.

"He's making mistakes on purpose," she said.

"Yeah, even I get that. But, Beth, if he hates the piano lessons so much, talent or no talent, why make him suffer?"

Beth felt her jaw drop. "You're kidding, right?"

"No, I'm not kidding. You shouldn't make him waste time on something he hates."

Beth wanted to take her dinner fork, reach across the table and stab him. "You have no idea what Danny wants or needs. You don't have the first clue about him."

"And that's my fault, how?" His eyes glittered with rancor.

Beth had had enough. "I think it's time for you to leave," she said, fronting more calmness than she thought was possible. "Go say good night to Danny."

"Beth," he said, his voice laden with exhaustion. "I don't want to fight with you all the time."

"Then don't."

"I want him to have my name. I need him to be Danny Myers. I want to change his middle name to William. What is his middle name anyway?"

"Paul. After the apostle." She forced herself to keep it together. "We need time to work things out. I don't want to keep you from Danny. I haven't denied you any time with him. As for last names, he probably will want that too and be thrilled to have his middle name changed to your father's."

"Good." He stood and took his plate over to the sink. "Here's the thing. The fall break is next weekend. I want to take Danny to Addington to meet my mother and Cookie."

"You're crazy, right? Your mother must have dropped you on your head all twenty-eight years ago." Beth couldn't believe he was serious. "There is no way I'm letting you take Danny to spend quality time with Katie." Even though she'd known it was coming.

His eyes went flinty and cold. "Danny will meet the rest of my family. And Cookie is his sister, whether you like it or not."

"You can't take him without me."

"I don't want you to come. It'll be easier without you." He shook his head. "You've got to work with me on this."

Danny ran back into the kitchen. "So can I stop my piano lessons?"

"That's between you and your mom, but I don't see why you can't take a break from the piano for a while."

Danny wrapped his arms around Jeff's waist, hugging him tight. "Thanks, Dad!"

What? How dare he? "Danny, it's time for your homework."

"Can I wait until Dad goes?"

The air started to snap, crackle, and pop around her. "I need to talk to your dad before he leaves. Say good night then hit the books."

Both Danny and Jeff seemed to know she had had enough. About time.

Jeff knelt in front of Danny and ruffled his hair. "Good night, champ. Now go and do as your mom tells you. I'll see you tomorrow at practice."

"'Kay!" Danny hugged him again. "G'night!"

"Go get your books and bring them in here. You can work on the table while I clean up the kitchen." Beth looked at Jeff. "I'll walk you out."

Danny ran to get his books, mercifully out of earshot.

"I really wish you'd work with me on this," he said as she handed him his jacket.

"I really wish you wouldn't undermine my authority with him." She folded her arms under her breasts. "I appreciate the back-up you've done already, but don't start to cross me. Danny's keeping up with the piano."

His brow furrowed. "I don't see why he has to."

The urge to slap his face had her palms tingling again. "He's got talent, real talent. If he keeps up, he can have the career I gave up to keep him. You have to respect that."

"That career was your dream. Don't impose it on him. Let him find his own."

She closed her eyes. "Just go, Jeff. Please."

"I'll be in touch."

Oh, goody. Something to look forward to. Dandy. Just dandy.

Chapter Twenty

Danny had begged and pleaded with Beth to take him to the Sharks' game on Friday night. She gave in, knowing how much it would mean to him to see Jeff in action. Dressed in jeans and his oversized black and silver Lobster Cove Sharks hoodie, Danny could not sit still. He wiggled and fidgeted like someone dropped fire ants down his pants.

He'd wanted Beth to wear the same thing, but she didn't have anything like that, so Danny made her dress in the school colors.

Clad in black jeans, a gray Irish fisherman's sweater, and a purple ball cap she'd pulled her ponytail through the back of, Beth remembered that last year in Addington when she went to every game Jeff played.

He was her first kiss, her only boyfriend, her only lover.

She'd adored him.

Now, sitting in the stands, all those feeling rushed back, the love, the adoration, the obsession. She trembled with the force of those emotions.

She did not welcome them.

Not one little bit.

Danny nudged her shoulder then pointed down to the sidelines. "Look, Mom! There's Dad!"

Beth followed Danny's gesture down to the field. Yep. Jeff was down there looking at a clipboard. He'd dressed in a pair of black dress pants, a lavender button down shirt with a silver tie, covered by a black blazer.

He'd always looked scrumptious to her. She'd thought him the most handsome boy in the world.

He'd only improved with age.

The opposing team, the Ellsworth Eagles, ran onto the field, spurred on by their cheerleaders, kicking it into high gear in their maroon and gray uniforms.

A hush came over the crowd as the Sharks cheerleaders moved into place carrying a huge paper covered wooden frame. The paper was painted with picture of a shark on the hunt, toothy mouth open wide, and the words Fight! Score! Win! Go Sharks!

The pep band launched into Queen's 'We Are the Champions,' and the hometown boys ran through the frame, tearing the paper as the Sharks burst on to the field.

The crowd leapt to its feet, screaming and clapping. Teenage girls in black, silver, and purple uniforms cartwheeled back to their places on the sidelines.

They faced the crowd and whipped the Sharks' fans into a frenzy. Danny was one of those fans. He whistled and cheered with the loudest of them. Pride radiated out of him, pride that he was the coach's son. Beth's heart jumped up and lodged in her throat. She'd never seen her son so intense, so captivated.

Her son had fallen in love with his father.

She tried not to feel jealous, since Danny had finally gotten his dearest wish, a father.

That Jeff was back in her life didn't make a difference as long as her son was happy.

Boy, she really was a liar.

It had been just the two of them, she and Danny, for so long. She mourned the loss of that closeness. Danny watched the game with a focus Beth hadn't seen in him before. Ever. Danny was all about the game.

And against her will, Beth was all about the coach. She couldn't take her eyes off him. She wanted to hate him. It would make her life so much easier. Instead she was drawn to him more than ever; damn her hormones.

Half time came and went. She let Danny get food from the concession stand, something she'd never let him have before. He just wore her down. And, in the current situation, she didn't want to be the parent who always said no.

Since Jeff had become the fun parent.

She'd stretched her rules, but it felt a lot like bribing Danny. Actually, truth to tell, it was exactly like bribing Danny. She glanced at her son and was again struck with how much Danny already admired Jeff. Emulated Jeff.

Loved Jeff.

The future shrouded in uncertainty, Beth wanted her perfectly controlled life back. Didn't look like that would happen anytime soon.

"Mom, can we go with the team to the victory party at Lobster Lanes?

"You're not part of the team, Danny. Besides, it's past your bedtime and the Junior Sharks have a game tomorrow."

"I can so go. Dad will let me."

"Dad's not got the last say here, I do. Dad or no dad, it's a party for high school kids, and in case you hadn't noticed, you're not one."

"But Mom!" His blue eyes were filled with

rebellion.

"No. We're going home."

****

The Sharks won by the skin of their teeth. Way from satisfied, Jeff fumed.

He'd been painfully aware of Beth and Danny in the bleachers. Too distracted by their presence, he could barely keep his attention on the game. Thankfully, Ellsworth blew it in the last quarter. He had to get his head back on straight. To not concentrate on his son in the stands.

Not to mention his son's mother. He knew she'd been watching him and it really wrecked his focus.

"Hey Coach!" Jeff looked to his left to see Ethan, his best running back. "You coming to the Lanes for a victory celebration?"

"You know I am. The pizzas are on me!"

"Schweet!" Ethan pasted a shit-eating grin on his face. "We almost blew it tonight but you got us through. Thanks for believing in us."

"You guys did all the work. I only cracked the whip a time or two." His team had a lot of heart that was for sure.

It only took a couple of minutes to get to Lobster Lanes and Sal's Pizzeria. Sal already had ten huge pies hot and ready for them, extra cheese, pepperoni, veggie and a Sal's special, one loaded with everything, all smelling gloriously of garlicky tomato sauce, melted mozzarella, and spicy sausage.

Food worthy of the gods.

Soon their tables were piled high with sodas, plates and pizza and the guys were letting off steam while celebrating their win. It brought him back to his high school days quarterbacking for the Addington Minutemen, hoping Beth could stay a little longer after sneaking out of her father's house to go to the game. She and Katie would come together. Sometimes he and Beth left the after party early, just wanting to be alone.

Katie. He'd told Beth the truth, that he didn't know Katie had turned them in. He'd been such a sap. And sap that he was, he gave in to nostalgia. So he'd looked up and saw Beth and Danny in the stands. He wished they were both here with him now.

He wanted the whole father and son experience with Danny that he hadn't gotten with his own dad, since he'd died when Jeff was so young.

The door to the bowling alley opened. Jeff glanced to see the newcomer, and son of a bitch. All his blood rushed to his head in a huge *whoosh*.

Danny. What the hell? He strode over to his son. "Hey, Danny. Didn't expect to see you here." He looked past Danny's shoulder. "Where's your mom?"

Danny's chin jutted out. "She's at home. I came by myself on my bike."

"What? She let you ride your bike, at night, all by yourself, to come here?" Disbelief mixed with temper snapped at him.

The boy looked at his feet. "She doesn't know," he mumbled. "I snuck out."

"You what?" Jeff roared and Danny flinched. "You wait right here and don't move a muscle."

Danny started to say something but Jeff cut him off at the pass. "Not one word, not one muscle." Jeff wanted to throttle the kid. He went to the counter and had Sal run his credit card to pay for the team's food, then marched back to deal with Danny. "Come with me. I'm taking you home."

"I don't want to go home. I want to be here with the team."

"Quiet, kid. Not another word."

He got Danny settled in his truck, loaded his bike in the back, and pulled out of the parking lot. When he could trust himself to talk, he said, "This will never happen again. You will not sneak out of your mother's house, especially at this time of night to ride your bike God knows where. You got that?"

Danny stared straight out the front window and didn't answer.

"I asked if you understand what I'm saying."

"Yeah," Danny whispered, his head bent low. The kid looked miserable. Good.

He pulled up in Beth's driveway and parked behind her car. He was still angry with Danny, but he was also pissed beyond all belief that the kid could sneak out and his mother didn't even notice he was missing. His hands shook with it.

Jeff didn't bother to knock he just opened the door and dragged Danny in behind him. "Beth!" he yelled. "Guess who I've got here with me!"

"Jeff?" Beth appeared in her hallway, wrapped in a long pink terry cloth robe. Wet tendrils of her hair framed an angelic face covered in confusion. "Why are you here?" Her eyes widened when she saw Danny. "Danny?" She looked at Jeff. "What's going on?"

"Our son snuck out of the house and rode his bike all the way to Lobster Lanes so he could party with the team. At ten o'clock at night." And in case she didn't notice it… "In the dark."

All the color left her face. "Danny—you did this?"

"Unless he has an evil twin," Jeff said, "he did this."

"Beth stared slack-jawed at her son. "Why?" She walked to him. "How?"

Danny did the best imitation of a mute Jeff had ever seen, and he was having none of it. "Tell your mother what you did."

No one disobeyed Jeff Myers when he used that voice.

"I pretended to go to bed and waited until you were taking a bath to sneak out," he mumbled to the floor before glancing at Jeff for some back-up.

Wasn't happening. "Do you know what could have happened to you?" Jeff worked hard to keep from yelling at the kid.

Beth covered her mouth with her hand. She gripped the couch with her other one. "Danny, you could have gotten hurt."

Danny wouldn't look at her.

Oh, no. "Danny, answer your mother."

She kneeled in front of Danny and took a deep breath as she put her hands on his bony little shoulders. "Why did you do this?"

The kid tossed his head and wrenched out of Beth's grasp. "I wanted to go to the party and you wouldn't let me."

"That doesn't mean you can do dangerous things to get what you want. What if someone ran you over?"

"I wore my helmet. I have reflectors on my bike."

"Not enough, Danny." Jeff inserted himself into the scene. "You were wrong." He rubbed his chin. "I don't know about tomorrow's game. If I can't trust you on something like this, how can I know you're going to follow the rules during the game?"

"I can, Dad! I can follow the rules!"

"Then you have to prove it by following your mom's rules."

Danny looked from Jeff to Beth. Then he focused all his attention on Jeff. "Okay."

Beth stood. "Go on now and get into your pajamas. I'll be back to tuck you in when I'm done talking to your dad."

"I don't want you to tuck me in," Danny muttered as he left.

Jeff waited until Danny was out of sight. "How could you not know he was missing? What kind of mother loses a kid? You have one job, know where your kid is. It's not rocket science."

"I put him to bed and like I usually do on a Friday night, I brewed a cup of tea, ran a bubble bath and spent a little me time relaxing. I'm not accountable to you."

The thought of a naked Beth inside a hot tub filled with bubbles, wearing only a welcoming smile, flitted across his mind. He pushed it to the way back.

"Is he getting too much for you?" Jeff steeled himself to deal with the temper that would surely come from her. "What happened tonight is unacceptable."

"What? Of course it's unacceptable. I'll deal with it." Her blue eyes sparked with fury.

"I wonder if you can handle him any more. He clearly doesn't respect you."

"You stupid jerk," she ground out. "I never had any problems with him until you showed up." She pointed to the door. "You barely know him. You can take your judgmental butt and leave my house. And don't you ever talk to me like that again."

"You're not getting rid of me that easily. The boy needs a strong hand. I've got two of them. I won't let you cut me out."

"Then don't be a judgmental ass. I fought my father, I brought up my son, and I'm damned"—she jabbed her finger into his chest—"if I'm going to let you take over now. He never defied me before you came along. Chew on that." She showed him the door.

He gathered up his righteous indignation and took it along with him.

Chapter Twenty-One

"We need to figure out a way to deal with Danny after last night's stunt." Beth's voice crackled as Jeff listened to her on the phone.

"We do." Jeff put a Pop-Tart into his toaster and glared at the coffeemaker trying to make it brew faster.

"He has to face the consequences of what he did."

"What do you suggest?" The toaster started to smoke, telling him the pastry was done just the way he liked it. Incinerated. Well, he really didn't like his Pop-Tart charcoaled. He just couldn't figure out how to get the toaster to work right.

"My first impulse is to pull him off the team, but that would get in the way of his relationship with you." She sighed. "As if I'm trying to keep you and him apart, and that's not the case."

Finally coffee filled the pot. He poured a cup and inhaled the brisk, nutty scent. And moaned in ecstasy. What mortal man could resist? Not him.

"Are you okay?"

Oops. "Yeah," he grunted, took a sip, and winced at the heat. "How about we take him someplace after the game and talk to him about it." And do something he and Katie never did for Cookie. "Present a united front."

"That could work. Maybe just go grab some ice cream or something."

"Agreed."

"I guess we'll decide where to take him after the game, so I'll let you go now. Jeff?"

"Yeah?"

"Thank you for being willing to work with me."

"He's my son, too."

"See you later." Beth clicked off.

He'd been really rough and way out of line with her and he needed to apologize. He could do that when they talked to Danny. Jeff put down his phone and picked up a piece of black Pop-Tart. Beth would forgive him and they could move into a better relationship from there. He felt his chest expand, his heart open.

Hope jumped right into that big ol' space.

Even though they were at odds, he still loved her. Things needed to be settled, for sure, but God help him, he still loved her.

He probably always would.

Chapter Twenty-Two

Beth sat with Anita on the bleachers watching their sons play football. A lovely fall day, a slight breeze, fluffy white clouds floated in a perfect blue sky.

"They are so cute," Anita laughed as the boys ran up and down the field. "Better than I thought they'd be."

Beth smiled and nodded. "Especially considering all that equipment they're wearing."

"Ben sleeps well after all—" Anita jumped up. "Look! Is that Ben running down the field?" She shielded her eyes with her hand. "And that's Danny falling back to throw to Ben!"

Beth also leaped up. "Oh my God! It is!"

She bounced from foot to foot as Danny threw a perfect pass to Ben, who caught it and took off toward the goal post. She cupped her hands around her mouth and yelled for all she was worth. "Way to go, Danny!"

Anita joined in with a hearty whistle and shouted, "Run, Benny! Go, go go!"

Score! The Junior Shark moms and dads screamed in jubilation as the boys jumped all over each other then ran to the sidelines to Jeff.

The memories of another football game hit Beth, memories of Jeff making a pass like that to his buddy Tim, scoring a touchdown. The guys piling on each other and Coach Mike running onto the field.

She remembered sneaking out of the house to meet Katie and go to the game together, how nervous and excited she'd been. She and Jeff had skipped the party after, to go somewhere alone and talk. How young they'd been. Her skin prickled and she felt a soft pull of warmth. Jeff was grinning at her from across the field. Pride rolled off him, pride in their son.

She grinned and waved back. He turned to the boys and she felt a pang of longing for what could have been.

She ached with wanting all that. How foolish, especially after he'd been such a butthead last night. Maybe this little outing with Danny after the game would be a step in the right direction, because she would make it very clear that he was not rolling over her.

****

Danny danced around in front of Jeff and Beth as they walked to the docks. They'd stopped at Julie's Coffee and Sweet Shop after the game for treats and now were headed toward the shore to talk to Danny and maybe feed a seagull or two.

He glanced at Beth from the corner of his eye. She wore her hair in a ponytail she'd pulled through the back of her silver and black Sharks ball cap. Dressed in a simple blue T-shirt that matched the color of her eyes, topped with a brand spankin' new Sharks' hoodie and a pair of well-worn faded jeans, she looked like the high school girl he'd fallen in love with.

She turned and caught him staring. "What—do I have ice cream on my face?"

He shook his head. "Just thinking that you don't look old enough to have a ten-year-old son."

She snorted. "There are days I feel old enough to

146

have a one-hundred-year-old son." Her tongue snaked out to lick her pistachio ice cream. "While Danny's floating on Cloud 9, we need to talk about what we're going to tell him."

"First things first. I need to apologize for last night. I was really out of line and I'm sorry. My only excuse is that I was so panicked I didn't think before I spoke."

"I'm glad you said that because you can't talk to me like that again, especially in front of Danny. I'm serious. I won't let you disrespect me in front of my son. She took a deep breath. "So about Danny."

"I figure he's got a right to be mad, but he's got no right to be fresh with you and just make his own rules up because he's mad."

"He wants to live with you because he hates me."

Something lit inside of him. "Would that be so bad? Katie and I shared Cookie when I still lived in Addington."

"This is totally different. You and Katie have a legal agreement, with joint custody. Danny wants to live with you because he's trying to punish me." She pursed her lips. "He's trying to play us against each other."

Jeff stayed silent as he digested that. "True. But what would it hurt if he stayed with me some of the time? I really want to get to know him."

"I know you do and I want that too, but we have to keep that part out of the mix for a little bit so he doesn't think he's getting rewarded by being a little snot."

He laughed, the sound coming from deep within him. "I never thought I'd hear you call your precious son a little snot."

"Let me clue you in on something. He's not always

so precious."

"Was it hard raising him on your own?"

"When my father was alive, it was very hard. All those rules." Beth took advantage of a trashcan and dumped her melting ice cream cone into it. To Jeff it looked like she'd lost her appetite.

"Danny was—is—a very active little boy. Father demanded a quiet well-mannered child who never gave anyone a moment's trouble." As she spoke, Danny ran ahead of them, kicking rocks like they were tiny little footballs. "I walked a tightrope for the first six years of his life, keeping my father in check while letting Danny have as much of a normal life as possible. Although sometimes things fell through the cracks." She sighed. "Danny had learned to make collages in pre-school and wanted to make one for my father for Father's Day. I got him all the supplies he needed and magazines galore and let him have at it."

"You let him play with scissors?"

"No, I gave him a machete and told him to have at it." She saw Jeff make a face that could only mean *you dufus*. "He wanted it to be a surprise and didn't want me to see it, so I didn't. Father's Day came and my father opened Danny's collage and I thought he would have a heart attack."

"What? Did Danny find some porn magazines on his own?"

"That might have been better. Oh, no. Danny had cut the storybook version of *The Bible* to shreds." Her eyes shone. "He wanted to give his grandfather pictures of all the people he admired and talked about."

"Your father didn't like it?" Jeff couldn't imagine his mother hating something Cookie made for her.

Beth sighed. "The book had been blessed by a priest. So, to my father's way of thinking, Danny had disfigured a holy book. He called the collage an abomination. Thankfully Danny didn't know the meaning of the word." She shuddered. "I had to take Danny out of the room—out of the house, and try to explain why his grandfather didn't like the gift."

"Jesus." Jeff didn't know what else to say.

"You have to understand, Jeff. That's what our life was like. It got worse after my mother died. If I'm protective, that's why."

Jeff's body heated with each word. He wished Bob Pritchard wasn't already dead so he could kill him again. "I wish you had found me, told me.

"And married to the person who let everyone know we were eloping." She shook her head. "It's old ground. On to the task at hand." She gestured toward Danny.

"Maybe he's just rebelling—"

"This is not rebellion. This is temper."

Jeff saw that. The kid couldn't feel free to take off whenever he wanted because he didn't like the rules. "Got it. So what do we do?"

Beth chuffed out a breath. "I want to lay out the facts, objectively, and make him realize how wrong he was and how he should make it right."

Jeff grunted. That sounded a little too 'New Age' to him, which in his not so humble opinion, would not work. "There has to be a consequence, Beth."

"Of course there does. What do you suggest?"

"Military school?"

That made her laugh, as he hoped it would. Then she got real serious. "The worst thing he could experience right now is being kicked off the team."

No, Jeff thought. Just no. "I can bench him, not let him play, but not kick him off the team. Have another idea?"

"Yeah, but it won't have the same impact as benching him. The only thing he loves more than football right now is The Refractor, this superhero he's totally into. I let him buy the comics, but I don't let him play the computer games."

"I remember from when I was in his room." He didn't know The Refractor from Donald Duck. "So?"

"We can cut him off cold turkey, like Time Bomb exploded and made everything go away."

"Time Bomb?" This felt a little bit more like his territory than any Barbie Cookie had ever made him play with.

Beth studied him, like she was trying to get a bead on him. "Time Bomb is The Refractor's arch enemy. He can explode at will and then re-form back into his physical shape when he wants to. He works together with Mega Mole." She blew out a breath. "Please don't make me explain Mega Mole."

"Okay, I won't. But someday you'll have to school me on Barbie shoes."

She stopped walking, clasped her hands in front of her, like a nun, and turned the saddest eyes he had ever seen to look at him.

"I wasn't allowed to have Barbies. I only got to play with them when I went to Katie's house."

And there she was, the elephant in the room, also known as Katie.

And if Katie knew that he thought of her as an elephant in any way shape or form, she'd totally explode.

Much like The Refractor's arch enemy Time Bomb.

Beth's shoulders drooped. "I can't believe you married her."

His chest ached. "Now that I know the whole story, I can't believe I married her either."

Beth's eyes caught fire. "You must have loved her."

"I told you. I thought I did love her. She pulled out all the stops and I was lonely. Now I realize that she was the closest thing to you that I could have."

He prayed that she'd get it. He'd told her before, he knew, but he really needed her to understand that.

That he'd really never loved Katie.

Which, of course, made him the biggest asshole in the whole universe, but it was in the past and he couldn't fix it. He could only live in the now.

And the now was all about fixing Danny.

"I will make it clear that he can't play me against you," he said. "You have rules and he has to follow them."

"Thank you," she said, simple as pie.

"He lives with you and by your rules, but he can stay with me regularly."

"I can do that."

"There's one more thing. I want to take him to Addington to meet my mom and his sister over Columbus Day weekend.

Beth didn't flinch, didn't blink. "That's what you said and I've thought about it. So, it's fine. But only if I go with you." Her clear blue eyes held no sign of doubt or giving in.

Oddly, the moment held more intimacy than he'd

felt in a while. Well, since the date she'd gone on with him.

Then he saw her looking at him expectantly. "What?"

"I'm going, end of story. I'll find some place to stay, but I will go."

"I'm not sold on the idea. Katie will only make things more difficult between Danny and Cookie. I think it's better if I go alone."

Beth sighed. "We're at an impasse, I guess."

Yeah they were and she held all the cards.

For now.

They reached a row of benches. He stuck his hands into his pockets. The wind had picked up now that they were on the waterfront and a hint of salt tinged the air. Looking out over the wharves, he could see a storm rolling in, chasing away the blue skies and fluffy clouds from earlier in the day.

Danny ran over to them. Jeff crouched in front of him, so they were eye level. "We gotta talk about what happened last night, champ."

"I don't want to."

Beth sat on one of the benches. "I'm sorry, but you don't have a choice."

"I know you're having a hard time with your mom since we found out I'm your dad. But here's the thing." Jeff made sure Danny was looking right at him. "You've got to follow her rules and treat her with respect."

Danny glanced at Beth. "But if you're my dad, I can live with you."

"No you can't. You can stay with me sometimes, but you still live with your mom and she calls the shots."

"Her rules are dumb. She treats me like a baby." Danny kicked the sand and rocks at the edge of the bench.

"Her rules aren't dumb. They're to keep you safe. And they would be the same at my house." He looked at Beth to assure her of the same thing.

"You could have really gotten hurt last night," Beth interjected. "You just can't go off whenever you want without telling me."

"I wanted to go to the Lanes and you wouldn't let me."

"That party was for teens, Danny. Not for kids still in elementary school. You didn't belong at a party for teens."

"Dad was there."

"And I had to leave my team to bring you home, which wasn't fair to the guys." Jeff put his hands on Danny's shoulders. "What you did was wrong and next time you do anything to break your mother's or my rules, I'm benching you."

He cocked his head to one side. "What's that mean?"

"You can still be on the team but you can't play in the games."

Danny swung his head from Jeff to Beth then back to Jeff, the movement more than a little frantic. "You can't do that!"

"We can and we will." Jeff stood. "The choice is yours. Follow your mom's rules and start to treat her with respect again, or no football."

Danny stared at the ground, his lips pressed into a thin line.

"You need to tell us you understand the deal here," Jeff said.

He hesitated. "I understand," Danny said finally, but he didn't sound happy about it.

"Good. Now apologize to your mother for what you did last night."

Another hesitation. "I'm sorry, Mom." He didn't sound happy about that, either.

Too bad. Beth stood. "It's getting cold and I think it's starting to rain. We should get home." She pulled the hood of her sweatshirt over her head. "Would you like to come for dinner? It won't be fancy, just some crockpot chicken thing, but you're welcome to join us."

And what was this about? Maybe she thought she could change his mind about the trip to Addington if she was nice?

"Please, Dad?" Danny pleaded. "I can show you my new *Adventures of The Refractor* comic book."

He had a slew of things to do at home: lesson plans, watching last night's game video, working out some details for the football clinic with the Nelson twins.

It all paled against the opportunity to spend more time with his son.

Well, much as he hated to admit it, after today's truce, he wanted to spend time with Danny's mother too. "Thanks. I think I'd like that."

Chapter Twenty-Three

"So, see The Refractor can control light and stuff. His hair changes color when he uses his powers. Like this." Danny held up his favorite Refractor action figure, pressed a button and the hair went from black to blond.

He'd dragged out all his action figures to show Jeff. Beth listened as she got dinner on the table.

Hey, Dad, she thought. Welcome to the wild, adventurous world of The Refractor.

"Cool," Jeff said.

"And this one is Dr. Pierce Powers and he can control other people's powers, like make them stronger or weaker whenever he wants."

"He's a good guy?" Jeff's voice rumbled in her ears.

"Yep!" Danny said. "The Refractor, Pierce Powers and this one, Princess Arabella, are all on the same team. She comes from the planet Moreese from a far off galaxy in another dimension. That's where the whole 'across all dimensions' line comes from."

"A girl superhero, huh? That's cool."

Beth could almost hear Danny wince. "She's okay for a girl, I guess. She does a lot of spooky stuff," Danny said.

"Who's this one?" Jeff asked. "He's pretty scary looking."

155

"That's Mega Mole. He got hit with some radiation that turned him into a huge, power hungry mole. "He can't see very well, but he can really dig."

"Hmmmmm. I guess being able to dig is a real important skill to have."

Beth smiled and peeked into the pan of rice she had cooking on the stove.

"This one is Syr Duke and he's from Moreese like the Princess. He wants to destroy her."

"Why is that?" Jeff asked.

"He wants to steal her powers and go back to Moreese and take it over."

"He's pretty evil, then."

"Yes!" Danny's voice raised a couple hundred decibels.

Beth got the food into serving bowls. Time to leave Moreese behind and come to the dinner table.

She wiped her hands on a dishtowel and moved into the living room. "Danny, go wash your hands, dinner's ready."

Danny dropped Syr Duke and ran to wash his hands. Jeff stood. "I should do the same thing, to set a good example."

"Great idea." Beth went back to the kitchen and waited for the boys.

She still didn't know why she'd invited Jeff over. She didn't want to examine it very closely.

Danny clattered into the kitchen with Jeff right behind him.

"Smells good," Jeff walked around the table to hold out Beth's chair for her.

She warmed at the gentlemanly act. "Thank you," she said as she sat.

"You're welcome." Jeff went to his own place at the table.

Silverware clanged against Beth's best dishes as they dug in. Danny shoved food in his mouth as fast as he could. "Slow down there, Danny. You're going to choke," Beth warned him.

"This is really good, Beth." Jeff smiled at her.

Pleased, she said, "You're welcome."

As they sat there eating a meal together, the three of them, it felt dangerously like everything she'd dreamed of all those lonely years ago. She thought that maybe she'd stopped wanting them to be a family.

Looked like she was wrong. Because it looked like she did want that very much.

Even though Danny's father was a big-time butthead.

****

Jeff stood at Beth's door, ready to leave. "Thanks again for dinner. It was really good."

He was working very hard to not give in to the impulse to kiss her.

"You're welcome." Her pink lips parted, practically inviting him to lean in for a smooch.

Or two.

Or three.

"I really want to kiss you right now." He kept his voice low, so the kid wouldn't hear. "Would that be okay?"

Beth licked her lips then cast a glance behind her. "Maybe one little one."

His heart thumped as he lowered his head to touch his lips to hers. He felt her pulse skitter and beat against his body.

Lifting his mouth from hers he whispered, "We can make this work, Bethy. I want to make it work."

Her body trembled all over. "Let's take it one day at a time. I don't know if I'm ready yet."

Not the answer he was looking for, but it'd have to do.

Exit stage right. "Good night. Thanks again for dinner." He stepped out of her warm living room and onto her chilly porch.

"Don't mention it." She closed the door and shut him out of hers and Danny's world.

Not for long, though. Not for long.

****

"I loved the pictures you sent me." Jeff's mother sighed. "I can't get over how much he looks like you when you were that age."

"I don't see it." Jeff pressed pause on the TV remote.

"Of course you don't." She chuckled. "I bet he can't sit still for five minutes at a time."

Jeff shook his head and laughed. "You're right. The kid's always moving. So I'm bringing him to Addington to meet you and Cookie on Columbus Day weekend."

She sighed. "I can't wait! I still can't believe I have a ten year old grandson."

"Yeah. The thing is, he's having a really hard time with all of this."

"With you?" Indignation rushed across the satellite connections.

He sighed. "Not so much. But he's been acting out a lot with Beth."

"I think that's understandable. Um, I hate to bring

158

this up, but how does Katie feel about this little visit? Is she cooperating?"

"Haven't talked to her yet. It's my next phone call."

"Good luck."

"Thanks. I'm going to need it."

"Just remember to breathe and focus on Cookie."

"Mom." Jeff just felt his mouth fly open. "Do you think it would be okay if Beth stayed with us during this visit?"

Heavy sigh. "I should have realized. Just like Katie, Beth's not letting you take your child on a vacation."

"It's not quite the same, Mom. Right now I don't have any rights to Danny." That would be fixed up real soon. "She's only going to let him come if she comes along with him."

He listened to his mother breathe. Then, "That is probably a good thing. Even if he's mad at her, she's been his anchor all his life. Since things will probably be real confusing for him, I think it's a good idea. Of course she can stay here with us."

Jeff let out a breath he hadn't known he was holding. "Thanks, Mom."

"I'll put it on your tab."

An old inside joke. Just like Beth and Danny's "I love you across all dimensions."

The strongest love he'd ever felt drenched him. He took a second so he wouldn't embarrass himself by sobbing into the phone. "I've never deserved you."

"True. But I took pity on you once I saw your ugly face and those sticky out ears of yours." She paused. "You got those from your father of course."

"So you've told me." The devil sat on his left shoulder. "But you may be lying."

"Say what?" She sounded just enough outraged to really make him relax.

"You say I got my big ears from my father, but I sometimes look at you, and, well, Mom?" He couldn't hold back a snort. "Your ears are kinda big."

"Kinda?" she asked, in a tone of voice that if they were in the same room, she'd box *his* ears. "What does that mean?"

Jeff sat back in his chair and felt his muscles unkink for the first time in a couple of weeks. He grinned at his phone. "I've heard tell that things like big ears skip a generation. Since Danny is channeling Dumbo, I've got to just follow the evidence, you know."

She sputtered. "I don't have big ears. I don't have big anything if I don't want to."

Something more inside him loosened. He adored her. It had been only the two of them from what he could remember. Ever.

Danny had the same relationship with Beth that he'd had with his own mom. The realization hit him smack in the face.

He tried to swallow, but it took a couple of attempts. "We were a team. I always knew that."

"Your father would have loved the man you've become." She paused. "He would have never let you marry Katie."

Another huge pause. Jeff waited.

"One of my biggest regrets is that I was too busy working to put food on the table to give you the supervision I should have."

"Mom, I turned out all right."

"Except for getting the most over protected girl on the planet pregnant."

"You were so mad."

"Think how you'd feel if some jock got Cookie pregnant."

"I'd kill him." Just the thought made him all twitchy and ragey. "She's not going to date until she's thirty."

"Unless she lies to you about staying at her friend's house and sneaks out to date behind your back."

His stomach rolled. "Damn."

"Don't swear," she scolded. "I'm going to tell you something."

"I'm sure I can't stop you."

"Don't be fresh! I always felt sorry for that girl. Beth, I mean. That father of hers was a sick, mean person." She looked at a wall, clearly back into a memory. "He confronted me once." She made a noise that was a combination of disgust and amusement. "I was a single mother, the worst thing in the world according to Bob Pritchard."

His mother continued. "I would have done anything to keep him from having you arrested. I'll always be grateful to Mike Kelly for making sure that didn't happen."

An explosive noise sounded in his ear as she moved the phone from one ear to the other. "He put that girl and her mother through hell. I can't imagine what happened to them when he took them on the run."

"Beth's only told me a little about it and it wasn't good." He frowned. "She said that Danny was the only thing that kept her going."

"So that's the reason I can forgive her for keeping his existence a secret."

Jeff grunted. "I'm still working on that."

His mother gave a gentle sigh. "I don't blame you. But think about this. With that father of hers, I don't think there was a lot of forgiveness in her life."

"Yeah, I guess you're right." He'd never really thought of that. Love for the woman who raised him drenched him. "I'm really lucky to have you for a mom."

"And don't you forget it."

****

"So my advice to you, Mrs. Rawson, is to let the adoption happen."

Beth sat ramrod straight in a green padded leather chair in Brody Collins', her lawyer's office. "What do you mean?"

"He's got some things going on in his favor, like the fact that the father listed on Danny's birth certificate never existed." Brody leaned forward and rested his elbows on his desk. "He's got a steady job, a good income, although we can use that to make a case for him paying child support."

"I don't want his money."

"Yes you do." Brody smiled. "Trust me."

"He already pays child support to his ex-wife in Massachusetts."

"That doesn't make a difference in the eyes of the court. I'll check and see if there are any differences between support standards in Massachusetts and in Maine, but I don't think there are. He has to provide the means for Danny to have the same quality of life that he does for his other child."

She pressed her hand to her stomach. "So you want me to let him adopt Danny and change his name."

"Yes."

Adoption. Such a big step. Beth shivered as icy fingers chased up and down her spine. On one hand, she owed Jeff this. On the other hand, she ached at the thought of sharing her boy.

But she could see that it was the right thing to do for Danny. She was already the town's favorite topic of gossip. She'd noticed that people stopped talking when she entered a room.

Jeff adopting Danny would just give them something more to talk about.

Danny would be happy. So happy.

And that made all the difference. "Okay. Let's go ahead with this. I won't fight Jeff adopting Danny and changing his last name."

"Good." Brody smiled. "This is the best thing for everyone. It short circuits whatever Nate Cavanaugh can put together, and once Jeff adopts Danny, it will be easier to get child support from him."

Somehow, Beth didn't feel comforted by that. It felt like selling her child. But if it stopped Jeff from taking Danny away from her, her very worst fear, so-be-it.

****

"So," Jeff said to Danny as he gave him a ride home after practice, "we're taking a trip to Massachusetts next weekend so you can meet your grandmother and your sister."

"I don't want a sister."

"Too bad, champ. You've got one."

Silence.

163

"Will my grandmother like me?"

Jeff's brows knit across his forehead. "Of course she does. She loves you. Why do you ask?"

More silence.

"My grandfather didn't like me very much. He was mean to me and Mom."

Jeff remembered his conversation with his mother about Bob Pritchard and the hands wrapped around the steering wheel tightened and shook. "Your grandmother is nothing like your grandfather. She loves you even without seeing you, because that's the way she is. You know what? She talked to me when I told her about you and she knew your grandfather."

"Yeah?"

"Yeah." He glanced in the rear view mirror. "She told me about how bad he treated your mom. How hard he was on her and how he made her do stuff she didn't want to do."

He sniffled. "Like tell the lie about you?"

"Like tell the lie about me. My mom told me to try to forgive your mom and I'm going to do it. Here's the thing, champ. I think you should forgive your mom too."

"But she lied to us, even after Grandfather died."

"Yes, she did. But haven't you ever done something you weren't proud of? Something you had to apologize for?"

"Yeah," Danny said grudgingly.

"Didn't you feel really bad until the other person forgave you?"

"I guess so."

"Here's what I think, champ. Your mom has been there for you every second of your life, loving you no matter what, taking care of you, even though that meant changing your poopy diapers." Jeff smiled. "I bet your diapers were really gross and nasty."

"I bet mine were the grossest ever!" The kid sounded positively gleeful over the thought.

That's my boy! "I wouldn't be surprised. And for sure I wouldn't have wanted to change them. If I'd been around, I'd have made your mom change all of them and you know what?"

"What?"

God forgive him for this lie. "She would have changed them without one single complaint. She loves you that much. Across all dimensions, like Professor Pierce and Princess Arabella."

"Yeah," he said slowly. "I guess."

"You've been really mean to her since you found out about me and I think you need to remember how good she's always been to you. She's your mom, the only one you're ever going to get. Think about how you'd feel if she was gone and you could never see her again. There'd be a big sized hole in the shape of your mom in your soul if that happened and you'd never ever be able to fill it. Not even with me around."

Did he hear a sniff or two from the peanut gallery? "Think very carefully about it."

Danny was silent for quite a while.

"Can Mom come with us when we go to Massachusetts?" Danny's voice was barely a whisper.

If he hadn't already made the decision to bring Beth along, that question would have cinched it. "Yes. Your mom can come along."

"Okay."

Danny definitely sounded relieved.

He wanted to talk to Beth and have them both of them explain to Danny about the whole adoption thing. Grateful that Beth had agreed to it, amazed that Beth had agreed to it, just humbled him in general.

With this agreement to the adoption and the name changes, Beth was giving him everything he wanted, all tied up in a shiny red bow on a shiny silver platter. It really made holding onto hard feelings look pretty petty and mean.

"You've got family you haven't met and they love you already." Jeff flicked the blinker on to signal a left.

Danny went silent, something totally outside of Jeff's experience with his son. He stayed that way until Jeff dropped him off at Beth's.

He followed Danny in, since he needed to talk to Beth.

Danny threw the door open and flew through it while he yelled, "Mo-om! I'm home!"

Jeff caught it before it slammed behind him. Beth stepped out of her kitchen, wiping her hands on a dishtowel.

"Jeff," she said, her eyes clouded and unreadable. "Thanks for bringing Danny home."

"I'm happy to. We need to talk."

"I guess we do. I assume you've heard from my lawyer."

"Yes." But he didn't want to talk about lawyers. "I still want to take Danny to Addington next weekend and I want you to come along."

Beth blinked. "Wow. What changed your mind?"

He shifted his weight from one foot to the other, happy that she didn't remind him that he couldn't take Danny anywhere without her. "And thank you for not fighting the adoption. I've figured out that Danny doesn't know yet."

"He doesn't."

"I'd like to tell him together tonight."

She looked back to where Danny had disappeared. "It's as good a time as any."

"There's more." Jeff wanted to hug her, but knew a hug from him might not be welcome. "My mother is okay with you staying at her house when I take Danny down to meet her."

"That's generous of your mother. I'll make arrangements to get a sub to play at mass on Sunday and hope Jenna can do without me at the shop. Might be tough since it's a holiday weekend." Beth would not meet his gaze. "What about Katie?"

"What about her?" He did not want to talk to Beth about Katie.

Beth gave him a sour look. "She's not going to be happy about this."

"What she wants doesn't matter."

"I believe you think that but I think the reality is very different."

The next thing he knew, Danny clattered down the hall, twirling around like Mega Mole tunneling through the Earth. "Dad! Are you staying for dinner?"

His son wrapped his arms around his waist. Jeff peeled the arms away and crouched. "No, not tonight." He smoothed Danny's hair down. The hair didn't cooperate and sprang back up. "But we've got something to tell you."

"What did I do?" Danny frowned.

"Nothing, sweetie," Beth said. "This is a good thing."

Jeff barely spared her a glance while he hoisted Danny up underneath his armpits and deposited him on the couch. "What do you think about changing your last name from Rawson to Myers?"

Danny's face went blank. "What do you mean?"

He looked over to Beth and she smiled. "Your father wants to adopt you and give you his name."

Danny's eyes showed confusion. "Then my name will be different from yours."

She soothed a comforting hand across his cheek. "It's the name you should have had all along."

"Will it hurt your feelings, Mom?"

Well, this was a change for the better, Jeff thought. Their talk in the car about Beth's father had made a difference.

"It's not going to hurt my feelings one little bit. How do you feel about changing your middle name from Paul to William?"

"Why?"

"Because William was your dad's father's name."

Danny shrugged. "Okay."

Beth lifted her gaze from Danny to stare directly into Jeff's eyes.

Not for long. She resumed giving all her attention to Danny. "You're going to meet your grandmother and your sister and have a lot of fun."

"Will she be there?" Danny whispered.

Beth glanced at Jeff again then focused on Danny again. "She, who?"

"The other lady who Dad married and had a baby with." Danny looked at Jeff. "Why did you marry her mom and not marry mine?"

Jeff didn't know how to answer, but Beth saved

him. "I know you remember your grandfather."

Danny nodded.

"And I know you remember how strict he was."

Danny nodded again.

"And you remember when we told you that your grandfather wouldn't let me and your Dad get married." She nodded at Jeff.

"If he loved you so much, why did he marry someone else and have a kid with her?"

Jeff itched to say that Cookie wasn't some random kid, but this was the Beth and Danny show.

Danny stared at his mother, like he was trying to pull the truth from her brain. "I don't know why your father married Cookie's mother," Beth said, her voice reassuring. "We don't need to know." Beth smiled. "Let's focus on meeting your grandmother who loves you without knowing what a stinker you are."

Danny laughed and flung his arms around her neck. Jeff really, finally got the bond between them.

"I'm glad you're coming, Mom," Danny said.

"I wouldn't let you go anywhere without me, whether you like it or not."

Danny sniffled and wiped his nose with his sleeve.

Jeff winced. Beth didn't skip a beat.

She grabbed her son and held him so tight, Jeff worried that Danny couldn't breathe. "It's all going to be good, Danny. You'll see."

Danny wiggled free. "All right. I'm hungry."

"Dinner's coming right up." She met Jeff's gaze. "Are you sure you don't want to stay?"

Jeff did want to stay more than just about anything else right at that moment, but he had things he had to do. "No, thanks, I can't. But can I get a rain check for another time?"

"You got it."

They stood there staring at each other for a moment. Beth looked away first. "I'll walk you to the door."

"No," Jeff said. "You go on and feed our son. I'll show myself out. Thanks again for not fighting the adoption."

She shrugged. "You're welcome."

"Mo-om! I'm hungry!" Danny bellowed from the kitchen.

"I need to go take care of that."

"Right." Jeff stepped away and went to the door. "Good night."

After he let himself out, Jeff felt lighter than he had in weeks. This could all work out.

He remembered how much he had loved Beth then, how much he wanted to be with her when he first found her here in Lobster Cove.

He tried those feelings on again and they felt pretty good.

Chapter Twenty-Four

Danny's sense of co-operation lasted until Beth told him to practice piano. Again he rebelled by playing poorly on purpose. So badly, in fact, that Beth gave serious consideration to getting some earplugs. She pinched the bridge of her nose in between the thumb and forefinger of her right hand.

Thinking Danny was turning back into her happy, eager to please little boy, Beth thought she could finally breathe a little. Apparently, that was not to be. She guessed for every step forward they made, they'd get two steps back.

She had to have patience with him, had to remember how much his world had shifted. At least he didn't overtly hate her any more. And just when she thought they were back to playing Princess Arabella against Syr Duke fighting for control of MoReese, he ran up to hug her tight and said, "I love you across all dimensions. I'm sorry my diapers were so disgusting," and ran off to take his bath.

What?

She just prayed that he'd behave when he met Nancy Myers and Cookie. Only time would tell. For that one brief moment she and Jeff had stood in front of her door, when Danny had run to the kitchen, she'd thought he might kiss her.

She'd wanted him to kiss her. For just that little

space of time to kiss her and let the years melt away and feel as totally in love as she felt about him then.

What the hell was she going to do about that?

****

"So, I'll be there early Saturday evening to get Cookie. Please have her ready." Jeff worked to keep his voice calm and level.

"She's really nervous about meeting Beth's son."

"He's my son, too, and Cookie's brother. So please get her so I can talk to her?"

"She's already had her bath and gone to bed."

"Really. It's just 7:30."

Katie sniffed. "She had a busy day. I can wake her up if you insist."

"Please do." Cookie wasn't asleep.

He didn't have to wait long for his daughter to come to the phone.

"Hi, Daddy."

"Hi, princess. Guess what?"

"What?"

"I'm coming to visit you this weekend and I'm bringing your brother with me so you can meet him."

Silence.

"He's a really nice boy and I know you're going to have a lot of fun."

Katie came back on the line. "Cookie wants me to say good night for her."

Right. "Whatever. Give her a kiss for me. I'll see you this weekend and Katie?"

"What now?"

"No games, okay. Don't make this harder than it has to be."

He clicked off the phone and hoped like hell that

Katie wouldn't sabotage this visit.

He just wouldn't let her.

End of story.

****

Saturday brought blue skies, lots of sunshine, and a little of the heat leftover from summer. Beth and Anita sat together in the bleachers, cheering their boys on.

The kids played hard, but lost by one touchdown. Danny and Ben scuffled their way off the field to the sidelines.

"Good game, buddy!" Beth touched his shoulder. "You tried really hard and did a great job."

Danny shook his head. "We lost."

"Doesn't matter," Anita said. "You still played your best."

"Except that our best wasn't enough." Ben was just as bummed as Danny.

"What did Coach say?" Anita asked.

"He said what you said, that what was really important was that we did our best." Ben and Danny both shook their heads and stared at their feet.

"Well, I'm proud of you anyway." Beth put her hand on Danny's shoulder. "Let's get you home and cleaned up so we're ready to leave when Dad gets there to pick us up."

Danny didn't say anything; he just followed Beth to the car. He moped for the entire ride home. Well, Beth thought, he had to learn how to lose gracefully. One more life lesson learned. Maybe this football thing wasn't so bad.

Danny was barely out of the shower when Jeff showed up. "You all set, champ?"

"Guess so."

"Where're your bags?"

"In my room."

"Go on back and get them and we'll be on our way."

Danny trudged to his room. "Where are *your* bags?" He turned to Beth.

"Right there by the door." She wrinkled her nose. "I didn't know what to bring, so I may have overpacked."

Jeff raised his eyebrows when he saw the three bags. "You know we're only going to be there tonight, all day tomorrow and Monday morning."

She felt her face heat up. "I want to look appropriate for whatever comes up."

"Okay, sunshine. You're lucky you've got a big strong man to take them to the truck for you."

She chuckled. "My hero."

He laughed.

Danny came back dragging his bag and his backpack. "Here," he said.

"Here? You're carrying those out by yourself, champ."

Danny looked at Beth. "Mom?"

She always dealt with his bags, but Jeff was right. He could take responsibility for that task now. "You heard your dad."

He grimaced but kept dragging his stuff out the door. Jeff hoisted Beth's suitcases. "Oof! What do you have packed in there—cinder blocks?"

"Ha, ha, very funny. I can carry it if it's too much for you to handle, hot stuff."

"Hot stuff?" Jeff laughed, the sound coming deep from inside him.

"What? Afraid you're not going to be able to live up to the hype?" Nerves jumped up and down all under Beth's skin as she started flirting with him.

She'd never really flirted before. It was about time she did.

****

"He's out like a light," Jeff said to Beth as they headed down Route 1.

"He didn't sleep at all last night and he always gets wiped out after games. After practices, too."

"He works hard." Jeff put on his blinker to move into the left lane to pass a mini-van. "Has he said anything more to you about this visit?"

Jeff himself had hardly slept due to worrying about how this weekend would go. He was glad he'd relented and included Beth because he now knew he needed her support.

"No," said Beth. "Not a word. It's worrisome, but he's a happy, friendly boy. He should do fine once he gets the lay of the land."

"Huh. Cookie's a real girly girl, I think I've told you." Jeff moved back into the right lane. "I'm really hoping they can find some common ground."

"Take them to the playground. That might be a good place to start. What kid doesn't love a swing set?"

"That's a good idea. My mother probably has some ideas on how to make some bonding happen."

"How is she?" Beth asked. "Your mother I mean."

"She's good. Still working hard, but she'll never stop working."

Beth looked out the passenger side window. "She probably hates me."

"She was mad at first, but has come around to see

your side. She remembers how unforgiving a man your father was and decided you needed a little forgiveness. She's really excited to meet Danny. She and Katie do not get along."

He saw Beth knuckle tears out of her eyes. "I'm sorry, I shouldn't cry. What an amazing woman. I can't believe how generous she is." Her nose made a snarfly sound and she rummaged in her purse and pulled out a tissue. "I'm sorry she doesn't get along with Katie. That must make things difficult for you."

He snorted. "Katie makes things difficult all on her own."

Beth didn't say anything about that, just pushed a long brown curl of her hair behind one ear.

She looked impossibly pretty, impossibly young dressed in jeans, a blue turtleneck and an aging black pea coat. The only jewelry she wore was her watch and a pair of earrings made with some kind of blue stones. He was pretty sure she hadn't put on any makeup.

He felt himself falling in love with her all over again. He might as well face facts.

He'd never stopped loving Beth in the first place.

****

Beth had never expected to see the "Welcome to Addington, Massachusetts. Home of the Minutemen!" sign ever again, especially crossing the town line with Jeff Myers.

The acrobatic part of a flea circus had taken over her stomach. She hadn't realized how difficult it would be to go back to Addington. She kept her hands clasped in her lap so Jeff wouldn't see them tremble.

She had to take care of her own nerves so she could take care of Danny's. She should probably wake him up. She turned around in her seat, reached over and jostled his knee. "Danny."

Her son's eyelids fluttered open, shut, then lifted again. His hair stuck out every which way and his face squished up so it resembled a bug's and exuded *eau de grumpy*.

"Wake up, sleepyhead. We're almost there."

He yawned. "Where?"

"Almost to your grandmother's house."

"'Bout five minutes left to go, champ," Jeff added.

Danny looked out the window and kicked his feet against the backseat. "Where did you live, Mom?"

"Not far from where your grandmother lives."

"Do you want to drive past it?" Jeff glanced at her out of the sides of his eyes.

She shivered. "No, thank you." She never wanted to see that house ever again. Her heart pounded a little faster when Jeff turned right on to Gosnold Street, past a white house, a yellow house, and came to a stop in the driveway of a little green house, with a big red 8 on the mailbox.

Jeff's childhood home.

He'd barely cut the motor and gotten out of the car when a gray haired woman appeared in the front doorway. Nancy Myers.

Jeff's mother.

She ran down her front stairs. "Oh, you're here!" She wrapped her arms around Jeff.

He kissed her on the top of her head. "Hey, Mom."

Beth helped Danny out of the car and put her arm around his shoulders while he gained his sea legs.

"Beth, I'm so happy to see you!" Nancy beamed at them even as tears welled in her eyes. She obviously knew enough to keep a little distance from them. "And who is this handsome young man?"

Danny leaned into Beth. Jeff came up to his mother and put his arm around her shoulders, just like Beth had done with Danny. "Mom, this is my son, Danny."

Her hands flew to her cheeks. "He looks just like you when you were that age. Cowlicks and all."

Danny looked up at Beth. "What's a cowlick?"

"The things that make your hair stick out all over the place." She braced herself. Time to let him go. "Danny, why don't you go over to your grandmother and say hello?" She took her arm from around his shoulders.

In spite of how he'd recently been acting, he had been brought up with manners and to show respect for adults. Taking a couple of hesitating steps toward Nancy, he held his hand. "Hello. I'm Danny."

Nancy didn't hesitate, she took the hand he offered and shook it. "Hello, Danny. I'm your grandmother, but you can call me whatever you want. If Grandma doesn't work, Nancy will do."

"Why don't we try out Granny Nancy?"

The newly christened Granny Nancy elbowed her son hard in the ribs. "You think you're so funny."

"I am."

"I bet you're hungry, Danny, so let's go in and get a snack to tide us over until dinner?" Nancy kept hold of Danny's hand and led him into the house.

Beth's stomach unkinked a little bit. Nancy clearly already loved Danny.

Jeff slung a heavy muscled arm around Beth's shoulders. "Come on in, sunshine. Let's get this party started."

Chapter Twenty-Five

While his mother fussed over Danny and Beth, Jeff took a minute to give Katie a call to make sure Cookie was ready when he got there to pick her up.

No answer. Typical Katie. He'd just get there at the arranged time.

And so it started. He had no doubt that this next couple days would not go easy. Far from it. Thank you, Katie.

But consistent love, understanding and boundaries would make a good start. He went into the kitchen where his mother had Danny sitting at a table with a glass of milk and a plate of cookies. "Mom?" What was Beth going to say about this? She watched Danny's diet like a hawk. "You're going to spoil his dinner."

She waved him away. "A grandmother's prerogative. Go fetch Cookie."

Danny stiffened at the mentioned of his sister's name and picked up his glass of chocolate milk to take a drink.

On second thought, champ, Jeff thought, have another cookie or three. I might be a while picking up Cookie. The poor kid might slip into a sugar coma before he could grab his daughter and get back.

"See you in a bit, buddy," Jeff said as he brushed his knuckles across his son's head. "You too, Mom." He walked to her and gave her a slight hug and a distracted kiss on her cheek.

She pulled back. "Just remember. This too shall pass."

"Sooner rather than later, I hope," Jeff told his mother.

It didn't take long to get to his former home with Katie and Cookie, even if he hadn't set the roads on fire trying to get there. He parked his car in his old driveway and took a deep breath.

Tap-dance time. Good thing that when it came to Katie he kept his dancing shoes on all the time.

He bounded up the stairs to the porch and remembered at the last moment he had to knock or ring the bell.

Ah, the world according to Katie. He leaned on the button. Finally she pulled the door open. "You shouldn't have made so much noise. Cookie's sick and it disturbs her."

He stepped into the house. "Cookie's sick?"

Yes, and the Kardashians were shy.

"She's gotten so upset about meeting Beth's son that she's throwing up. I don't think she should go."

Oh, Katie, you never disappoint. "I'll go talk to her."

Katie stood there, tapping the toe of one beige patent leather pump, which was the exact same color of her pants, top and jacket. "Don't badger her. She's sick. I won't have you harassing her."

"Katie." He rubbed the back of his hand across his forehead. "Back off. I'm her father. I love her. I won't hurt her, and if you think I would, you're living in another universe." He closed his eyes. He just couldn't believe her. "I'm going to see my daughter and I'm going to take her to my mother's. My mother has a toilet or two she can puke in."

"Your mother only has one toilet, one bathroom. With her company, there might be a problem."

Jeff nearly turned into Time Bomb. He thought the top of his head would launch off his shoulders. "Don't you dare criticize my mother! She worked hard to buy that house." He shook his head and uncurled his fingers. "Forget it. I'm not going to do this with you. You said Cookie's in her room?"

"Yes. But you have to be quiet."

Sweet Baby Jesus on a cracker, please help him. "Fine. I hope you have her bags packed, because she's leaving with me within the next ten minutes."

"I won't let you take her if she doesn't want to go."

"I've got joint custody and I'm not taking her out of state. We arranged this visit a week ago. And you had no problem with me taking Cookie to my mother's a couple of weekends ago when you needed to go to the spa." He turned from his mission to check on Cookie. "Go run and call your lawyer. He can call Nathaniel Cavanaugh at the law firm of at Jordan and Jordan in Lobster Cove. Oh, and FYI? Nate takes no prisoners."

"So dramatic." She checked out her manicure. "You must get that from hanging around with Beth."

What? Seriously? There wasn't enough zen in the universe to help him deal with this. "You and I both know Beth doesn't do dramatics."

"I don't know any such thing. Ten years is a long time. People change."

"I'm going to go get Cookie." He ignored Katie's sputtering and took the stairs up to his daughter's room. The door was closed so he knocked then opened it.

"Hey, Princess. Are you ready to go?"

Cookie laid on her bed, surrounded by some Barbies, her look-alike American Girl doll and some clothes piled by an empty Hello Kitty backpack. "I have a tummy ache."

He crossed the room and perched on the edge of her toy box. "I'm sorry to hear that. Do you think it's a nervous tummy?"

She turned those big brown eyes of hers at him. "I'm afraid of the boy," she whispered.

"The boy has a name and it's Danny. And I'm pretty sure Danny's a little afraid of you too."

"Really?"

"I'm pretty sure. So, why don't you pack some of these clothes," he gestured to the glitter encrusted, pastel colored pile on the floor, "and get ready to go. Your grandma's made your favorite cookies and she's waiting for you to get there so we can have dinner."

He felt rather than heard Katie come into the room. Standing, he turned to face her. "Can you help her get ready? We really have to get going."

Katie pasted a totally fake smile on her face. "Come on, sweetie. Let's find your prettiest outfits."

"Make sure you pack some play clothes. I see a trip to the park in our future."

"'Kay, Daddy." Cookie slid off the bed and dived into the job of choosing the clothes she wanted to wear.

He leaned against the doorframe.

Katie picked up a pair of shoes covered in lavender glitter and big hot pink hearts. "You don't have to supervise. We'll be down in a minute."

Oh, look. Katie wanted to get rid of him, most likely so she could feed Cookie more things to worry about. "No, it's okay. I'm staying right here."

Katie lifted a shoulder. "Whatever."

He smiled at her. He could nearly see smoke come out of her ears.

Sometimes it was good to be him.

****

"Thank you for letting me stay here this weekend." Beth chopped tomatoes for the salad she was assembling.

Jeff's mother stirred the spaghetti sauce she had simmering on the stove. The scents of garlic, basil, oregano, and thyme spread through the room. "It's no problem. I think it's best for Danny to have you here. I've got a relationship with Cookie, she feels at home here. It's all new for Danny."

"Everything's new for Danny." Beth sighed. "He's been having a hard time with it."

"I'd be surprised if he didn't. But you and Jeff both love him and will guide him through this." She put down the wooden spoon she held onto a ceramic spoon rest next to the stove. "My son is good man. He's strong and fair, but mostly he's a great dad and loves his kids."

Beth reached for a carrot she had on the cutting board and started peeling it. "I'm letting him adopt Danny. It's the right thing to do for both of them. I'm even letting him change Danny's middle name to William."

"After my husband—Jeff's father?" She stopped stirring her sauce. "Thank you. You have no idea how much that means to me! To Jeff." Tears sprang to Nancy's eyes. She wiped them away with her apron. "My husband died when Jeff was so young. I regret that he didn't have enough time with him."

"The name Paul means nothing to him or me, but William is important to Jeff. It's not a big deal."

"It's a very big deal to us." She gave Beth a brief hug. "It's very brave of you."

"Brave?"

"Yes. You've had him to yourself for his whole life. You've been everything to him and I can tell he's everything to you. You're dealing with some big changes very graciously. That's brave."

"I haven't always. It's only right."

"What's right isn't always easy."

Beth felt her eyes watering up and changed the subject. "What's Cookie like?"

"I imagine Jeff told you that she's a delightful little girl who loves her daddy. He dotes on her." Nancy chuckled. "She had him tied around her little finger from the moment he first laid eyes on her."

"They have a really strong bond."

"As strong as yours and Danny's. Jeff wants the same relationship with Danny that he's got with Cookie." Nancy put a warm hand on Beth's arm. "Don't worry. It'll all work out." She gave her a pointed look. "Love makes all the difference."

They both looked up as the front door flew open. A scurry of tiny footsteps raced into the kitchen. "Grandma! I'm here!"

While Nancy laughed and hugged Cookie, Beth studied Danny's stepsister. A tiny girl, with fluffy blonde curls framing her impish face and big brown eyes underneath insanely thick eyelashes and a button for a nose, she looked exactly like a fairy princess.

Nancy and Cookie stepped apart and Cookie

peeked up at Beth from under those ridiculous lashes. Nancy said, "This is Beth, Danny's mom, and she's staying with us, too. Can you say hello?"

Cookie wrapped her arms around Nancy's right leg with enough vigor to cut off her circulation. For a minute it looked like the girl was going to stick her thumb in her mouth, but that moment passed.

"Cookie, say hello to Beth." Jeff's low voice brooked no disobedience.

"Hello," she whispered.

Beth crouched in front of her and marveled at this tiny, beautiful miracle, all rancor toward Katie forgotten. "Hello. I'm very happy to meet you."

Cookie hid her face behind Nancy's back.

"I'll go see what Danny's up to," Beth said, knowing Cookie needed some space.

And what do you know? Beth needed a little space herself. She should have been better prepared for outright rejection. "I'll be right back."She'd pounded it into Danny's head that he had to be exceptionally polite if he met his half-sister's mom.

She made a hasty retreat. When she got to the room she'd be sharing with Danny, she took a second to appreciate her son. She was still puzzled about the poopy diaper comment. Where had that come from?

He sat in the middle of the room making juicy explosion noises as his Refractor action figures rained death and destruction upon each other.

"Danny," she interrupted, "put the battle for the universe on hold for a bit. Cookie's here and it's almost time for dinner. Come down and meet her."

He stopped mid-cataclysm and turned wary eyes up to her. "I'm not hungry."

"That may be, but you are expected to be polite, remember? Your grandmother has made a yummy meal and Cookie is also her guest. She's only a little girl while you're a big boy. So man up, buddy."

She could tell Danny wanted to protest but in the end he did as he was told. Pride filled her. "Let's go. Your grandmother is counting on you."

Danny moved with an uncharacteristic lack of enthusiasm. Where was the boy who threw himself headlong into life? He'd finally gotten the father he'd always wanted. Okay. She got it. Now he had to face a little girl who had a prior claim. No wonder he wasn't enthusiastic. "Don't worry, buddy. Everybody loves you already. Especially me and your dad."

He sent her a hopeful, yet reluctant look. The situation took a toll on him. Hopefully she and Jeff could guide him through it.

Cookie sat on the living room floor with an army of Barbies accompanied by hundreds of pastel tiny shoes, little sequin, satiny dresses and one small hairbrush. She stopped attacking the hair of one doll with the brush and looked up when Beth and Danny came into the room.

"Danny, this is Cookie," Beth said, her tone of voice as gentle as she could make it. "Cookie, this is my son Danny."

"Hello," Danny mumbled.

Cookie blinked then returned her attention to her dolls.

Ooooo-kay. "Let's go into the kitchen and see if Granny Nancy needs any help. I bet it's almost time to set the table."

"'Kay."

"Hey, Nancy, Danny's here and he wants to help."

Nancy turned and grinned. "I'm sure we can set him up with a job. Dad, show Danny where the silverware is so he can set the table."

"You got it, Ma." Jeff moved smoothly to where his mother kept the cutlery and pulled open the drawer. "Let's get what you need, champ."

Danny got right down to it. Beth shared a smile with Jeff over Danny's head.

It didn't take much longer to get the meal on the table, spaghetti and meatballs, garlic bread and a big mixed salad, all served family style.

"I'll go get Cookie. Be right back." Jeff wiped his hands on a dishtowel and went to fetch his daughter.

Danny watched his father leave the room. Something was going on in his head, but you had to be an expert in Danny-o-logy to see it. Her son was fronting big-time. His gaze got really stormy when Jeff carried the little girl into the room but he kept a smile on his face.

"Let's get going! I'm starved." Jeff sounded a little too cheerful." He plopped Cookie on to a chair with a booster seat. "There you go, princess."

The rest of them sat. The bowls piled high with food were passed around, though Jeff put together a plate for Cookie, cutting everything into bite sized pieces for her. He pulled out the mushrooms and the green pepper slivers from her salad.

Beth's father had no tolerance for picky eaters so Danny had never been coddled or indulged. He ate what was on the plate or he didn't eat at all. Originally Beth had hated that as she watched Danny choke down bite after bite of food he didn't like. When her father died she had relaxed that rule, but the early training had never left Danny. He ate everything and enjoyed it.

Beth also knew that making kids eat according to really strict rules didn't, in general, work. Danny was a happy exception.

"Grandma?" Cookie looked up from pushing around the food on her plate. "Can I have a peanut butter and jelly sandwich?"

"I thought you liked spaghetti?" Jeff frowned down at the little girl.

"It's too spicy tonight." She turned doe eyes up to Jeff. "It burns in my mouth."

"It's the same as I always make it. You've always loved it," Nancy said.

Tears threatened to burst out of Cookie's eyes. "I want a peanut butter sandwich."

"You should always be grateful that there's food on the table and eat what's put in front of you." Danny sounded very much like Beth's father.

Yikes! "Danny," Beth started, "please. Eat your own food and don't worry about Cookie. Please say you're sorry."

"Sorry," Danny grumbled.

Beth felt a flush of pride in her son.

Danny glared at Cookie as he forked a huge chunk of tomato sauce covered meatball and stuffed it into his mouth.

"Daddy, he's chewing with his mouth open. It's gross."

Beth glanced at Danny and, yes, he was chewing with his mouth open. Gleefully and on purpose. That flush of pride dissipated faster than it had come.

So much for those superior manners he was

supposed to have. "Danny, please chew with your mouth closed."

He hesitated, but he did as he was told. The minute he stopped, Cookie opened her mouth and showed off the mostly chewed food in her own mouth.

Jeff and Nancy might've thought this would go well, but Beth knew better. Neither kid felt like making this easy.

Jeff seemed totally involved with the spaghetti. Nancy, however, watched the whole thing between Danny and Cookie. "Cookie, baby girl, please close your mouth when you chew."

She just slowly spit out the food from her mouth. "This doesn't taste good."

"This is your favorite thing for Grandma to make." Jeff frowned.

"I want a peanut butter sandwich." Cookie thrust out her lower lip, apparently possessing a killer boo-boo-lip.

Jeff looked torn and confused. "Okay," he said, obviously trying to ward off a brewing temper tantrum. "I'll have it ready in a minute." He left the table.

True to his word, he had the sandwich made in a jiffy and put it in front of Cookie. "Here you go, just the way you like it." White bread, crusts removed, cut into four triangles.

Cookie just stared at the plate.

Beth bit back a sigh. Nope. Not going to be even the least bit easy.

Chapter Twenty-Six

"So, what movie are we going to watch?" Jeff posed the question to the two sullen children sitting on the couch.

"I want the Barbie one, Daddy! The *Barbie on Sparkle Island* one!"

Danny gave Cookie a look of pure disgust. "I want *The Adventures of The Refractor*." Beth cleared her throat. "Please," he added.

"I don't like The Refreckatator."

"The Refractor. Re-frac-tor," Danny repeated slowly. "Do you even know who he is?"

Cookie pulled out her killer pout again. "I know he's a stupid boy."

"He's not a stupid boy! He's only the greatest super hero ever!"

A band of tympani drums had set up shop right behind Jeff's eyes. "How about I find one you'll both like?"

Cookie and Danny stuck their tongues out at each other. Jeff pretended not to notice and went through the DVDs his mother had.

And what did you know? Absolutely nothing a kid like Danny would like. Maybe something about animals. What kid didn't like animals? "How about *Max the Monkey*?"

Both kids shook their heads. Finally. Something

they agreed on, *Max the Monkey* hate. "Or we could play a game."

"What kind of game?" Danny crossed his arms across his chest.

"We could play *Candy Land*" Cookie perked up. "I like that game."

"*Candy Land*? Only stupid babies play *Candy Land*."

"Danny, apologize right now. We don't call each other stupid.

Danny grunted and looked at Cookie. "I'm sorry you're stupid."

"I think you need to change that, son."

Danny sighed. "Okay. I'm sorry I called you stupid." He flung himself back against the couch. "Don't you have any big kid games?"

"Like what?" Jeff closed his eyes.

"Like *Totally Gross*."

"We don't have *Totally Gross*." He didn't even know what *Totally Gross* was.

"It's only the best game ever! If you get the right card you have to check the other players for boogers and toe jam or describe the last time you puked! The best game ever!"

"Daddy! I hate that game!"

Cookie had never encountered the game, but Jeff actually kind of agreed with her.

Although his inner ten-year-old yelled "Yeah!"

"We don't have *Totally* Gross and even if we did, your sister wouldn't like it."

"So what do you have that's fun and got nothing to do with Barbies or ponies?" Danny lifted his chin, like a challenge.

"We've got *Candy Land, Memory, Sorry* and *Mystery Date*." Cookie ticked the games off on one hand.

"You like to play *Sorry*, right Danny?" Beth came in the room wiping her hands on a dishtowel.

Jeff had never been so glad to see someone in his whole life.

Danny shrugged. "I guess."

"And it sounds like Cookie likes *Sorry*, too." She smiled at his daughter, who wouldn't look at her. "Sounds like a plan."

Jeff wanted to grab Beth and kiss her. However —

"I'll go get the game." Jeff wasn't giving either kid a chance to disagree.

He dropped onto his knees and threw open the game cabinet. He rummaged a bit until he found the battered game box. As he dragged it out, he prayed all the pieces were in there. All he needed was for some to be missing and each kid didn't get enough soldiers.

"I'll just set it up here on the coffee table."

Beth had perched herself on the arm of the sofa next to Danny. "Do you need any help?" She directed her question to Jeff. Danny didn't need any assistance playing *Sorry*.

Jeff glanced up at her. "I think I got this. I am a professional, after all."

She laughed. "Then I'll leave everything in your more than capable hands. Just give me a holler if you need me." She left for the kitchen.

He watched her leave, watching the sway of her denim clad ass.

"Dad, do you need a hand getting the board set up?" Danny's voice brought his attention back to the kids and off his mother's ass.

Damn.

"Sure, Danny, I'd like that."

****

"How's it going out there?" Nancy finished pouring some boiling water into a teapot.

Beth wrinkled her nose. "The two of them are not giving him an inch. They're determined to not have a good time. I can work on Danny, but Cookie?" Beth shrugged. "I don't dare."

"Sounds like a job for Granny Nancy." She stood and put a hand on Beth's shoulder. "You're a good mom, Beth. Danny'll come around because you'll help him. Bring me a cup of tea in about ten minutes, okay?"

"You got it."

"I knew I could count on you."

Beth watched Nancy leave the kitchen. She wondered how different her life would have been like if she had had a mother like Nancy Myers.

****

"I'm hungry." Cookie's whining had reached the volume of death threat.

"Maybe you should have eaten some of the p.b.&j you asked for." He said it before he thought and paid the price. Cookie crumpled.

Bashing his head against a wall would be more productive than mediating between these two kids. Dammit! He was good with kids. He led kids. He said jump and they said how high.

Why were a ten-year-old boy and a six-year-old girl so difficult to keep in line?

"I'm hungry," his princess daughter repeated.

Damn. "How does ice cream sound?"

"Vanilla with rainbow jimmies?" He knew what Cookie wanted. It never changed.

She nodded.

"How about you, Danny? Do you want some ice cream?"

"Yes, please!"

His son had a hollow leg. He ate constantly and wasn't fussy about it. "I'll be right back." He unfolded himself from pretzel position he'd been suffering through for the past half hour.

Relieved for the break, he took several deep breaths while he scooped out vanilla ice cream into bowls and loaded rainbow jimmies over the top of it.

Ice cream fixed everything.

He carried the bowls into the living room and put one, with a spoon, in front of each child.

Cookie dug in with gusto.

Danny stared at it like it was rat poison.

Oh, shit. "Something wrong, champ?"

Danny wouldn't meet his gaze.

"C'mon kid. What's up?"

Danny still wouldn't look at him. "I don't like vanilla ice cream."

So much for the kid being a food Hoover who would eat whatever you put in front of him.

Never mind him being the kid who preached that you should be grateful and eat everything that was put in front of you was refusing to eat vanilla ice cream.

"I think there might be some chocolate in the freezer," Nancy said. "Let me go check." She turned her attention to Danny. "Are rainbow jimmies still okay?"

Danny nodded. "Yes, please."

"I got it." She shook her head at Jeff. "You stay here and finish the game."

Please don't make me. Please, please don't leave me alone with them. "Thanks, Ma."

She skewered him with a look. "No problem, Dad."

Somehow he thought his doting mother was messing with his head. After looking at her face, he knew she was.

Why couldn't everyone just cooperate and get along?

Chapter Twenty-Seven

Beth stood in front of the doors to The End Zone and watched Jeff's truck's taillights get smaller and smaller as they drove away. She hoped the afternoon at the playground would turn out well and make a good solid step forward with regard to the children's bonding process.

It felt like Cookie and Danny were playing good cop/bad cop, trying to keep the ground shifting underneath the grownups. If that was so, they rocked it hard. She just wished Danny would try.

She ran her hands down the denim skirt and straightened her loden green sweater. She'd worried all week about what to wear when she came to confront her past. In the end, what did it matter? She was no glamour girl and felt totally ridiculous fretting over with pair of sensible flat shoes she should wear to go meet people she hadn't seen in ten years.

Uh-oh! She hadn't been their equal when she knew them. Andi Nelson Kelly had been her mentor and Beth loved her, but she'd never been her equal. She refused to speculate about Jeff's mentor Mike Kelly, who she knew hated her.

With a tiny sigh, Beth studied the door keeping her out of The End Zone. One push and she could step inside and see people she'd loved so many years ago.

More people she'd let down. She took a deep

inhale and held it for a time to calm her fraying nerves. It didn't help.

Oh, well. She'd just have to open the door and face them. Aaaannnddd … no time like the present.

One push and she entered the restaurant. The place jumped and hummed with loud voices, laughter and the sound of about ten TVs showing ten different sports and games. The aroma of grilled burgers and French fries hung like a delicious cloud over the room.

Beth never ate fried food, but smelling the delicious aromas in The End Zone, she truly regretted her decision. Tables filled the majority of the space between the door and the bar. Off to her right a row of booths lined the wall. She craned her neck around to find Andi Kelly.

As she searched, a blonde woman flew out of one of the booths and launched herself at Beth and gave her a big hug.

Andi.

The epitome of elegance, she still styled her hair in an elegant French twist. Even for a Sunday afternoon having lunch in a sports bar she dressed in light gray wool slacks and a periwinkle blue cashmere twin set, the neckline set off just perfectly by the strand of pearls around her neck. A pair of sapphire studs blinked in her ears. She still smelled reassuringly of Chanel No. 5.

Andi released her and moved an arm's length away. "Let me look at you."

This woman had been her rock, her mentor, her confidante, her savior. When Beth learned she was pregnant, Andi had stepped in and taken her to Boston to see a doctor and bought her first prescription of pre-natal vitamins.

Thanks to Beth's father, she'd almost lost her job because of it.

"You're so beautiful," Andi said, a tremor present in her voice. "Come on and join us." Andi steered her to the booth where she'd been sitting. Beth held her breath.

Several other people sat tucked in there. Mike Kelly, Andi's husband, Jeff's coach and mentor. Mr. Mason, the vice-principal of Addington High School back then, and a very pretty dark haired woman Beth didn't know, but who seemed to belong to Mr. Mason.

"Beth." Mr. Mason slid out of the booth to give her a hug, "It's so great to see you. We all hoped you were doing well."

Beth couldn't breathe, couldn't move if she'd wanted to. Frozen in place, again a teen living with an oppressive father, always the good girl, always terrified to do something wrong.

Oh, God.

Mr. Mason pulled back, giving her space to breathe. "Here, slide in. Ainslie," he told the dark haired woman, "this is Beth Pritchard, the brilliant pianist who went to AHS. Beth, this is my wife Ainslie. Her son Ruark is training for a career in opera."

"I'm so pleased to meet you," Ainslie said, her voice dripping with the slow music of the south. "Andi's been telling us all about you and how talented you are. Maybe we can talk you into accompanying my son so we can hear my baby sing."

Beth slid into the spot Andi made for her. "I don't really play any more. I have a decent sized studio in Maine and play at the local church, but no," Beth shook her head, which suddenly felt like it weighed one hundred pounds. "I don't play any more. I had to give it up when Danny was born."

And there it was. She knew beyond the shadow of a doubt that these people loved Jeff and had to be so angry with her for lying to him about her son. Jeff's son.

"Jeff says your boy is quite a ball player. Throws like he was born a Manning brother. Or maybe even as good as a Nelson brother." Mike Kelly, the legendary Coach Mike, looked at her with something that might be kindness in his eyes. "When the twins go up to do that football camp next summer, make sure Danny gets some time to work with Brock. He'll be one hell of a mentor."

They all swiveled their heads to look at Mike.

"What?"

"Language?" Andi prompted.

Beth laughed. "I'm a grownup now. I think I can handle hearing the word hell. I may have even used it a time or two myself, and not in the context my father meant it."

Silence.

She immediately pulled back. After all, he'd tried to get Andi fired. "I'm sorry. I shouldn't have mentioned him."

"Was it very hard?" Andi reached across the table for her hand.

"It was." Beth sat up straight and squared her shoulders. "Worse after my mother died. But please, it's done and I don't want to talk about it." For real. Seriously. "I hear the food is really good and I'm hungry."

"Let's get you a menu." Andi got out of the booth

like a woman with a life and death mission.

"Bobby's really charged up the menu for this Addington's Tables competition. If you thought the food was good before, now just turn it up to eleven." Mr. Mason chuckled.

Beth licked her lips. "Mr. Mason, this is the first time I've been here. I don't think sixteen year olds were allowed in back then."

Mr. Mason didn't miss a beat. "I didn't even think of that. You look so grown-up now and you were always so studious back then." He leaned back against the booth back. "And please call me Dave. You're not a student any more."

No she wasn't a student any more. "Dave it is."

Andi came back with a menu and handed it to Beth. Everything's good here. You can't go wrong."

"A Bobby burger with onion rings is as close to heaven as you'll get here on earth," Mike offered.

Andi rolled her eyes. "If you have more refined," she aimed that word at Mike, "tastes, take a look at the specials. Bobby is really going all out to upgrade the menu."

Beth cracked open the menu and tried to read it, but tears prickled her eyes but she'd be damned if she'd let them fall. How could these people treat her so nicely when she'd lied to them all?

"I don't know much about your situation." A southern accent caught her attention.

Beth snapped up her head to look at Mrs. Mason.

Mr. Mason said, "Uh, Ainslie?"

She ignored him. "But I do know about mine. When I moved here from Charleston with three children and no skills except how to dress pretty and plan a party, I felt like I'd hit rock bottom. Do you know why I had to move away from Charleston?"

Of course she didn't, Beth thought. Where was this going? "No."

"Ever heard of Bobby Lee Logan? Venture capitalist extraordinaire?"

The name pricked a memory, but for the life of her, Beth couldn't retrieve it. "Maybe."

Dave brought his and Ainslie's entwined hands to rest on the table. Ainslie gave him a look of pure adoration.

"Bobby Lee Logan was the Darth Vader of crooks. He made Bernie Madoff look like Elmo, the most adorable Muppet of all." Ainslie reached for her glass and took a big glug of water. "I trusted him with all my heart and soul, but he robbed and cheated and stole from every single one of our friends. By the time the whole thing was over, I had no friends and no money. Since being a former Miss Carolina isn't really a career, I had no job skills." She paused as Dave lifted their entwined hands to kiss her knuckles. "I moved here so the stigma wouldn't haunt my children every day. It was hard, trust me, it was hard, but we did it."

Great story, but, "Why are you telling me this?"

Ainslie looked at Dave then at Mike, who nodded to her. "I know what it's like to do whatever you have to for the sake of your precious babies."

Beth took a deep breath and pressed her lips together.

"Ainslie told the truth, even if it is a bit, abrupt, but this is now, and no one at this table holds anything against you, okay?" Mike told Beth. "Let's not dwell in the past and let's go from here." He stopped himself.

"Actually, why don't we just drop all the bullshit from—"

"Mike, little pitchers." Andi shook her head at him.

Beth had to laugh again. "Andi, along with the word hell, I think I might have said bullshit before. Who's all grown up?" She pointed her thumbs to herself. "This girl."

"I'm sorry. I still feel so protective of you. It's going to take a while to get used to the new you."

Mike turned his gaze to Andi and his whole demeanor softened. As far as Beth saw and sensed, Mike adored his wife. "Spud. Everything's okay. Relax and let's have a meal."

A very blonde, perky waitress showed up and took their order. Beth hadn't had time to even look at the menu, much less understand it, so she went with Mike's suggestion of a Bobby burger and some onion rings instead of fries.

Once they stopped talking about her, she breathed easily. They spoke of normal things, everyday things having to do with all things Addington. Dave and Mike talked about stuff at the high school. Ainslie gossiped about the upcoming cooking competition and how Ainslie's boss, Hope Monahan, the woman who owned the restaurant Ainslie coordinated events for, had started dating her main competitor. It looked like it was getting hot and heavy.

Andi took Beth's hand. "I'm sorry about the loss of your music."

"I didn't lose it. I just put it somewhere else." Beth pulled her hand free. "A lovely dream that a young girl once held close to her heart. I had a choice, Danny versus a career as a concert pianist. In the end there was no choice. Danny has always come first. And he's way more talented than I ever was. Seriously."

Andi's lips thinned as she pressed them together. After an interminable second or two, she smiled. "I so admire the woman you've become."

"Y'know, spud? You should challenge Beth to a game of foosball."

Andi turned to look at him with the same WTF look in her eyes that Beth knew was in hers.

Mike only grinned broader. "I know you've been practicing," he told his wife. "Go out there and kick some skinny foosball butt."

"But our food..." Andi looked at her husband as if he'd grown two more heads.

"I'll let you know when it gets here. Go," Mike said, his voice now full of meaning. "Take a little time to get to know your girl."

Andi traded a significant look with her husband, their bond so thick and undeniable. Beth wanted the same thing with Jeff. They'd made a good start last night, but could she trust it?

"We don't have to play foosball if you don't want to. Mike was just trying to tease me. He does it a lot, but I love him anyway." Andi threaded her arm through Beth's.

"That's good, since I don't know how to play." Where would she have ever gotten the experience? Had her father even known what foosball was?

She didn't think so.

"Hey, Andi, what do you need?" A tall brown haired waitress stopped next to them.

"Hi Sandy. I'm just looking for a quiet corner so I can catch up with my friend here."

Sandy looked around. "There." She pointed to a tiny table in the corner next to the bar. "It's the staff break table and we're busy enough that no one is going on break any time soon."

Andi smiled. "Thanks."

Beth followed her to the table and they both sat. "I expected Coach Mike to hate me for what I did to Jeff."

Andi shook her head. "He understands that you weren't in control of any of it. He also knows what Katie did to you both—calling your father, telling him you two'd run away. Tim and Katie both came to me and Mike, but I just can't understand her going to your father, knowing what he intended to do to Jeff."

"My father didn't call the Lobster Cove police. Katie did."

"Katie?" Andi goggled at Beth. "She called the Lobster Cove police? I don't get that girl."

"Join the club."

Andi was off and running. "Granted, running away wasn't the right answer. Mike and I took a really painful road trip, in whiteout conditions, may I remind you, to catch the two of you and bring you back home before anyone knew you were missing."

"I'm sorry!" Beth slumped back in her chair. "We were so scared of what my father would do to Jeff and so crazy in love and wanted to be together. We were stupid."

"You had people here to deal with your father and his plans for Jeff. There was no way Mike would've let anything bad happen to him. And he had the nuclear option named Deke Nelson." Andi sighed. "My father loved Jeff and would have used all his considerable clout to do what had to be done. You're the one we couldn't save."

Beth swallowed around a great big lump in her throat. "That's not true. Danny saved me. I did what I had to do for his sake. I would go through all of it again to make sure he was safe with me."

"Well, that's all in the past. What's going on now?"

"Pretty much my life revolves around Danny, which is the reason I don't have a full time job." Beth shrugged. "I give piano lessons, I play organ at the Catholic church and I work at Happy Thoughts, a sewing, knitting, quilting, whatever you need store." She chuckled. "If you need it, Jenna, my boss, makes sure she has it."

Andi looked very sad. Beth didn't get it. Oh, well.

"So it's a good place, Lobster Cove?"

"It's a great place to bring up a child." It was a great place to live in general.

Andi sighed. "What a coincidence both you and Jeff ended up in the very same town you ran away to."

"Who knows?" Beth confessed to the one person she could always turn to for unconditional love. "I just felt, uh, drawn there. I really can't explain it."

"Well, I for one think it's fate bringing you two together and giving you a second chance." Andi twisted the gold band of her wedding ring.

Did Beth dare to dream about a second chance. Her heart leaped at the sound of a second chance with Jeff. Something she wanted more than anything else in the world right now. "I don't know about that. We need to be careful and go slow so we don't give Danny false hope. He adores Jeff. And then there's Cookie to consider."

"Jeff's a good man, Beth. I know I didn't think so at first, but we bonded because we both missed you so much."

"You missed me?" Beth couldn't believe it.

"Oh, I did, I really did. Jeff got a job here bussing tables and we talked about you all the time. He really loved you."

"Ladies," Sandy said as she came up to their table, "Mike sent me to tell you that Chelsea has just arrived with your food."

"Thanks Sandy. You're a doll."

"I know! I tell Bobby that all the time." She grinned. "You'd think he'd do something nice like give me a raise or throw me a parade. He's such an ingrate."

Andi laughed. "I'll tell him when I see him."

"Mrs. Coach, you are a goddess." Sandy looked up as someone signaled her for attention. "Ah well. Duty calls. Enjoy your lunch!"

"Thanks," Beth murmured. She followed Andi back to their table.

And ran smack dab into Katie.

As in her former best friend and Jeff's ex-wife. Yee hah!

"What are you doing here?" Katie's voice could have turned water into ice cubes on the edge of Mount Doom looking over the river of fire.

Beth couldn't think of a word to say.

This woman bore no resemblance to the girl Beth had known in school. Her blonde hair was clearly the work of an expensive stylist. Of course she hadn't been a blonde back then. She wore designer everything, from gorgeous tan calfskin boots and Ascada jeans to a raw silk T-shirt the color of platinum.

Beth fought the urge to fuss with her clothes and hair. She won but just barely.

"I thought I told Jeff I didn't want you anywhere near Cookie," Katie spat through clenched teeth.

She would not apologize about being there for Danny. "I thought it best if I came to help Danny in case he got overwhelmed."

Her neatly plucked and penciled eyebrows shot up to the top of her head. "You thought? Since when do you get a say in any of this?"

Okay. Now Katie was just making her mad. She straightened her shoulders. "Since the minute I gave birth to Jeff's son."

Katie threw back her head, tossing those expensively foiled blonde curls over her shoulders. "Stay away from my daughter. Jeff you can have. He's a poor excuse for a husband, but I will not stand for you playing mommy to Cookie. You got that? I will make sure Jeff never sees my daughter again in his lifetime."

"How could you do that to him? He loves her."

"The exact same way you kept his son hidden for ten years. Go away, Beth. Nobody missed you and nobody wants you here now."

"Beth, come on. Your food's getting cold." Mike appeared and put a gentle hand on Beth's elbow. He nodded in obvious dismissal. "Katie."

"This isn't over and if you think you can trump me, you're delusional." Katie gave them each a hard look then turned on her three-inch heels and stalked away.

"You okay?"

Beth blew out the breath she'd been holding. "Yeah. Just surprised is all."

"She's a real peach, that one." He slanted a glance

at her. "She was supposed to be your best friend. Bad choice, I think."

Beth shrugged. "What can I say? My life is all about bad choices, except for doing whatever I could to keep Danny."

"I get that." He nodded. "I tried to stop Jeff from marrying her. I sensed right from the get-go that she had an agenda and that she didn't really love Jeff. He deserved—deserves better. I still really can't understand why he got with her."

That made two of them.

****

Jeff and his mother watched both children on the swings. The leaves twirled to the ground and the air light, the perfect Indian summer day.

For Jeff, it brought back all those fall afternoons when he and his buddy Tim would pile up leaves they'd jump in over and over again. Nothing brought back the memories of his childhood like fall weather.

Laughter rolled over the park as groups of children romped and played games with each other. He smiled at Nancy. "I think they're getting along. What do you think?"

"Looks like," she said.

Tires screeched as a slick sports car barreled into the parking lot, stopping short of running them over.

Jeff pulled his mother behind him. "What the hell? You could have killed someone!"

Katie leaped out of the car. "How dare you lie to me!"

"Jesus, Katie! What are you doing here?"

"I'll go check on the children." Nancy walked off.

"I told you I didn't want Beth around Cookie!"

Spittle spewed from the twisted grimace of her lips.

"Katie, get a grip. I told you she was going to meet her half-brother and that's what she's doing." He reached for her, hoping the contact would calm her down.

She yanked away from him. "Don't you dare touch me. I'm here to get my daughter and take her home."

A hair-raising Cookie-sounding scream came from the swings. "Mommy! I want my mommy."

"If that boy has done anything to hurt my little girl, there'll be hell to pay!" Katie ran/limped in her heels across the playground."

Cookie met her halfway. "Mommy! The boy's being mean to me!" Tears streaked down Cookie's face.

Jeff figured it had taken two to tango. "I want you kids to apologize to each other."

Danny sighed. "I'm sorry."

"Cookie girl? What do you say?"

She only sobbed harder.

Katie scooped the wailing child up. "Come on, sugar plum. I'm taking you home." Sparing one last poisonous glance at Jeff, she picked her way over the field.

"Wanna tell me what happened?" Jeff sat on the swing next to Danny's.

"Am I in trouble?"

"No." Jeff couldn't believe Danny would pick on Cookie.

He smudged his sneaker in the trough under the swing. "She started saying that her mom was prettier and better than my mom and other stuff." He hiked up a shoulder. "She said you love her better because she has the same last name as you." He lifted up his eyes, full of misery. "Then her mom came and she started screaming like I hurt her. I promise, Dad. I didn't do anything to her."

Jeff touched Danny's arm across the space of the swing.

"That's pretty much the gist of what I heard when I came over here," Nancy offered.

"'Kay, champ. Let's blow this popsicle stand."

The sooner the better, as far as Jeff was concerned.

Chapter Twenty-Eight

"It was that bad?" Jeff heard Beth's soothing voice behind him.

He put down the beer he'd been nursing, slid over sideways on the back porch stair, and patted the space next to him. "Yeah."

She took the seat. "I'm sorry. I guess it was dumb luck to run into Katie at The End Zone."

"What the hell was she doing there? She hates the place."

Beth wrapped her hands around her mug of hot chocolate. "Maybe waiting there to see if I'd show up? Although," she paused slightly, "she looked pretty stunned to see me."

He grunted before taking another swig of beer.

"What did they fight about?"

Jeff put a hand behind his neck and squeezed, trying to alleviate the cramped muscles. "They were getting along great, or so I thought. Katie pulls up and reads me the riot act about how could I let you near her precious baby girl, she wasn't going to let us play house and pretend to be a happy family, blah, blah, blah. Next thing I know Katie is howling like a cracked out banshee." He made a conscious effort to unclench his teeth. "Ma had gone over where the kids were playing to, I don't know, to distract them I guess from Katie and me arguing."

211

"That's so wrong. Doesn't Katie see that fighting you on this also really hurts Cookie?"

"You'd think." He snorted. "Ma said they were having a tit for tat about which mom was the prettiest." A smile crept across his face. "Danny defended you quite adamantly."

"He did? I'm no way near as pretty as Katie." Surprise tinged her voice.

"You're prettier than her in more ways than you know. Did Danny defend you? He sure did. Ma said he was a regular Sir Galahad. So here's where it all went wrong. Danny is saying you don't need fancy clothes, jewelry and makeup to be beautiful."

Pride radiated out of Beth, pride and pure love. "Oh, my."

"Yeah, I'm proud of him. Then Cookie tells him that her mom told her that if she didn't wear jewelry and makeup that the boys wouldn't like her."

"Poor thing!" She took a sip of her hot chocolate. "I don't know where that came from. Katie was never like that in high school."

He grimaced. "Well, I didn't really know her in school. Anyway, after Cookie gives Danny the whole spiel about makeup and such, Danny told her that no boys were ever going to like her, even with all the fancy stuff, because she was a stupid baby."

"What am I going to do about that? I can't have him trashing his sister to her face." Her posture slumped a bit. "He apologized, I hope."

Jeff nodded. "Right after I told him to. Cookie, however, only cried like it was her job." He played with the moisture-beaded label of his beer bottle. "Katie took Cookie home. End of story."

"I'm so sorry. That must have been so hard for you."

He expelled a huge sigh. "You know, I went into this weekend thinking I could make it work, that the kids would get along and Katie wouldn't have a thing to complain about. Then it turned into one of those going-to-hell-in-a-hand-basket events and blew up in my face."

Beth put her hand on his arm and rubbed it up and down. "I guess Hallmark doesn't have a card covering those occasions."

"'Fraid not, sunshine." He bowed his head, the weight of it totally unbearable. "What am I going to do?"

"Nothing right now. Sometimes you have to wait until the time is right. I ought to know. I knew I'd get control of my life back from my father sooner or later. I just had to put one foot in front of the other and keep breathing."

"You were great with her this morning." The picture of Beth helping Cookie stop the helpless little girl act hung up front in his mind. "She's usually not so manipulating. Katie could, however, teach master classes in manipulation, that's how much of an expert she is."

Beth laughed. "I don't care. Making sure Danny can make a bowl of cereal on his own is no biggie. Believe me, making sure kids can do some things for themselves is a crucial skill when you're a single mom. With Danny it was easy. Mr. Independent from the get-go."

"You've done a great job with him." His skin tingled where she rubbed it. It would be so easy just to lean over and kiss her.

His soul was desperate for him to kiss her, so he turned to face her. "I really need to do this." He lowered his head and coaxed her with a finger under her chin to lift her face high enough for him to taste her soft, pretty mouth.

Beth trembled as her mouth opened for his kiss.

Opening up just for him.

He was Beth's first. Her only.

Try as hard as he did to deny it, Beth was his woman. If that was old fashioned, then so-be-it.

He broke the kiss, that light, gentle meeting of their lips, took the mug out of her hands and set it on the porch next to his beer. She faced him, her rosy lips slightly parted, her breath coming in hesitant, erratic hitches.

He pushed her hair back then framed her face with his hands. Her skin felt as fragile as rose petals, as smooth and supple as silk. He went in for a deeper taste of that tempting mouth.

"Mmmmmm." She didn't hold back, didn't hesitate, just opened to him as the kiss spun and blossomed with the promise of more to come.

She tasted of the chocolate she'd been drinking, all warm and seductive. He wanted using his tongue to coax hers to come out and play. She opened up and welcomed him in. Her arms wrapped around him. He took his hands away from her face and hauled her onto his lap.

When he'd been a horny kid and was into instant gratification, he'd ignored the beauty of her body in favor of getting off.

That was a thing of the past. His hands and mouth

longed to explore this woman.

Thank the Lord the time was right. This was their moment. He knew it deep down in his soul.

He cupped her breasts underneath her sweater, and she gasped. As he raked his thumbs over the hard points of her nipples, she trembled.

She tore her mouth away from his. "We can't do this out here. What if your mother..." Beth moaned as his thumbs traced around the peaks of her soft breasts, "or Danny" another moan, "come out?"

She was right, but, "Just a little bit longer, sunshine. It feels so good to have my hands on you again."

Her head fell backward and he pressed tiny little kisses on her neck, where her pulse beat like a conga drum underneath his lips.

"Jeff, please," she murmured, her voice breathy and low.

"Please what?"

"Oh, God. Take a guess." She pressed her breasts firmly into his hands. He kissed a path back up her neck and took her mouth again.

"Mom?" Danny called from back in the house. "Where are you?"

Beth pulled away, her eyes wide and a little frantic. "What do you need, buddy?" She clambered up the stairs.

And left him pretty much high and dry and with a pounding erection. He carefully rearranged himself and pulled his shirt out of his pants to hide his hard-on. Limping only a little bit, he picked up his beer and Beth's mug and made his way to the kitchen.

Damn. They'd always had to hide their love,

except for that one time they'd gone to dinner in Lobster Cove.

No more hiding. He was bringing their relationship out of the dark and into the light.

It was damn well time.

****

"I don't feel good."

Danny didn't look too good either. Beth pressed the back of her hand to his forehead. "You don't have a fever."

Face pale, every freckle on his cheeks standing out in relief, Danny shook his head. "I think I'm gonna—"

Puke, Beth finished in her head as her son hurled all over himself and Nancy's clean kitchen floor. He burst into tears.

"Oh my gosh, baby. Let me get you cleaned up!"

Jeff came in at that point and, being a rocket scientist and all, figured out what had happened. "You take care of him. I'll clean the floor."

"Thanks." Beth picked up her sobbing child and took him to the bathroom where she removed his soiled pajamas and washed him with a warm facecloth.

Jeff showed up with a glass of ginger ale. "I'll leave this here in case he's thirsty."

She glanced up at him and relief flooded her. Someone to help her, someone who knew what to do. Heaven. "Thank you. Could you do me a favor and get a clean set of pjs and underwear from his back pack?"

"Sure. Hang in there, champ. You'll feel better in no time."

"Are you thirsty? Your dad brought you some ginger ale. Maybe that will help your poor tummy."

Danny sniffled. "'Kay."

"Just little sips. We don't want to give your stomach any surprises."

Jeff came back with the things for Danny. "Here you go."

Beth felt him watch her as she got Danny ready to go back to bed. She reached to pick him up but Jeff was right there. "Let me grab him. He's probably pretty heavy."

"I never feel it," she murmured as Jeff hoisted their son into his arms and took him to his bed.

He sat on the edge of the mattress and watched her tuck in Danny. Poor thing was almost asleep again. Beth rubbed his back as she hummed a little tune.

"Do you think he's got a stomach bug?"

Beth shook her head. "He doesn't have a fever. I should have remembered this." She didn't take her eyes off of her boy. "When he's had a really heavy, emotional day, he gets sick to his stomach. I'm surprised he didn't toss his cookies the night we told him the truth about you."

"I guess today could count as a heavy on the emotional side kind of day."

Beth took a deep breath. "I should have been here with him instead of—"

"Making out on the back steps with his daddy?"

She bit her lip and gave him one nod. "Yes."

"That's bull, Beth. You sitting in here and watching him sleep wouldn't have prevented him from getting sick."

"I know, I know, but he couldn't find me. His whole life he's known exactly where I'd be when he didn't feel so hot and tonight, he didn't."

Jeff put his hands on her shoulders and started to

squeeze them. "Your muscles here are pretty tight. Let me touch you. Help you relax."

"Oh." His warm fingers found every knot and kink in her neck and back.

"You're not alone any more, sunshine. You've got help now. A partner in crime, so to speak."

Her own mother hadn't even helped her with Danny. Her father had prohibited it. "You're going to have to be patient with me until I get that into my thick head." Into my fragile heart.

"You know," he whispered in her from his perch behind her, "I can't count all the times I lay on this bed, dreaming of you being in it with me. Now I can promise this wasn't exactly how I pictured it, but I like it."

"You like watching over a kid who might barf on you any second?"

"No. But I love sitting with you like this, taking care of our son together."

Lord help her, Beth liked it too.

It felt like a family. A real family, one that didn't judge and tear each other down, one that worked together to lift each member up.

Oh, her heart ached. She craved that family more than anything in the entire world.

Chapter Twenty-Nine

"So, tell me! How was your weekend?" Jenna sat across the table from her at Maggie's Diner. She'd even closed the shop for an hour so they could do lunch sitting down.

"Interesting. It didn't really happen the way Jeff planned."

Jenna squeezed some lemon into her water. "No?"

Beth sighed. "It turned into a total disaster. The kids didn't get along and it didn't help matters when I ran into his ex-wife while having lunch with some old friends."

"Ouch. I gather it was unpleasant."

"Katie went full on nuclear meltdown. Jeff hadn't told her I would be there. So, yeah, Katie was pretty shocked to see me." She felt bad about that. She'd had a clue even though she didn't think she'd run into Katie at The End Zone.

Sally came and brought their lunch orders. "Lobster burger for you. It's such a shame your handsome hunk of a husband is allergic to shellfish." She put that plate in front of Jenna. "Smoked Salmon Reuben for you." As she dropped Beth's plate, she asked, "Do you need anything else right now?"

"No, we're good. Thank you, Sally." Jenna smiled.

"Yes, thank you."

"Give me a yell if you need anything."

Jenna took her fork and stabbed some sweet potato fries with it. "What happened?"

Beth sprinkled salt over her potato salad. "She ripped me a new one. After that, she took off and went to the park where Jeff was with the kids."

Jenna raised her eyebrows. "And—"

"She ripped Jeff a new one to match mine, grabbed her daughter and took off."

"Poor guy." Jenna shook her head.

"Jeff was pretty upset." Beth picked up half of her sandwich. "Danny, too. He got himself so wound up, he got sick."

Jenna pouted. "Poor kid." She took a bite of her lobster burger.

Beth watched as Jenna moaned in lobster-induced ecstasy.

Jenna swallowed. "God that's good. Why do I think there's more to the story?" She took a sip of her water.

Beth had to tell someone. "We, uh, before Danny got sick and all, had a kind of, uh, romantic moment on the back steps of his mother's house." Beth's face heated up.

"Romantic, eh?" Jenna grinned. "How romantic was it?"

"Amazing. Terrifying." She leaned in and looked around to see if anyone was listening. "We were going at it like we were kids again in the back of his mother's car. Then Danny came looking for me with a case of *vomitus eruptus*."

Jenna eyebrows took a trip north on her forehead. "Did he see anything?"

Beth sat back. "No. Thank God I heard him before

he could get to the back door."

"Holy petunia! Do you think it was just a one-time thing or is there more coming up?" Jenna took a wistful look at her burger. "And I don't mean Danny tossing his cookies and ruining the," she fluttered her eyelashes, "moooooodddd."

Beth had always thought Jenna to be a savvy woman. Right now she had her doubts.

"I want there to be more." She wanted it so much her heart pounded and her body ached. "He pretty much said he wants more."

"The awesomest of awesome, my girl!"

Beth rubbed a hand over her stomach. "Maybe. What if it doesn't work out? What if we can't make what we had ten years ago?"

"You'll never know unless you try. But do you want to go back ten years? You know a whole lot more now."

Beth hadn't thought of that, but she really should have. "You're right. I'm not the same person I was then. I'm free now. No," Beth said as Jenna opened her mouth. "I will never go back there. Not ever again."

"I don't blame you." Jenna took another bite of her burger and her eyes crossed. "Damn this is good."

"I don't want to tease Danny with the possibility of being a family if Jeff and I can't make it work. That would just break his heart."

Jenna swallowed. "There is that. Either way he's going to be a fixture in Danny's life. You can't change that so why not go for it?"

"It might be too much, too soon. I don't know." She frowned. "I just don't know."

****

Jeff stood looking at the clipboard with his plans for today's practice. White clouds dotted a brilliant blue sky and the green leaves of the trees had turned yellow, red, and orange. The wind was up, though. Should make for interesting conditions to work on throwing the ball around.

"Dad?"

"Yeah, Danny?" Jeff looked at his very penitent posture. "What's up?"

Danny kicked his feet against the chair leg. "Cookie told me that it doesn't matter that I'm a boy and I'm older. She says she counts more because you married her mom."

Jeff mentally counted to ten. "I love both you and her the same, no matter who your moms are. I don't know where Cookie got the idea that I love her more, but it's not true." Actually, he knew exactly where she learned that little tidbit. "It's not a contest and it never will be. Can you forgive her? She's only six, so I hope you can."

He changed his position so he could look Danny straight in the eyes. "You're my boy, champ. My son. I loved you from the minute I heard you were coming."

"Really?"

"Really." He remembered the day Beth told him she was pregnant. He'd cried then, right along with Beth. He'd been scared shitless, but ready to man up and do the right thing.

"I wish you had married my mom."

Jeff's heart jumped. "What would you think if I started to date your mom?"

"For real? Like real dates, like buying her flowers and taking her out to fancy places for dinner?"

"Of course real dates. Are you okay with that?"

Danny looked away and went to his thinking place. After a couple of minutes, he turned his gaze to Jeff's. "My mom hasn't ever dated anybody ever." He scrunched his nose as he thought about it. "You gotta be romantic."

Jeff wanted to hug this truth teller, his amazing son. "I can do romantic."

"I mean not just flowers. I mean all that gross stuff girls like."

"What does that mean?" He loved the way this kid looked out for his mother.

Danny scrunched his face again. "Go someplace special, where she has to get dressed up and all, give her some flowers to wear. Like taking her to a ball, like in Cinderella." Then Danny got down to business and grimaced in clear disgust. "You might have to kiss her."

Jeff laughed out loud. The joy just burst out of him. "Kissing her doesn't sound like a punishment. Gotta tell you..." He leaned in close to Danny. "I really like kissing your mom. A lot."

Danny shut up for a second or two, again a rare occurrence. "Maybe she likes to kiss you. She's never kissed anybody else for as long as I've been around."

Jeff's chest expanded with pride. Beth had never even kissed anyone other than him. He'd known that in his head, but now he had confirmation.

Beth was his. No one else's.

"I'm gonna grow up someday and leave her, but I don't wanna leave her alone." Danny met Jeff's gaze, man to man. "She needs someone to take care of."

"I don't know. Your mom is pretty tough. She has to be to take care of you, right?" That didn't stop Jeff aching from wanting to be the one Beth counted on.

The one she took care of.

Danny dropped his head and studied the ground beneath his feet. "All I wanted to say is that if you wanted to take her out on a date I'd be cool with it."

Jeff smiled.

Hallelujah! Just the words he'd been longing to hear.

****

Beth's nerves jumped and skittered around as she waited for Jeff to bring Danny home from practice. She'd put the meatloaf she'd just pulled out of the oven into the freezer and a tray of ice cubes into the microwave. She was losing her ever lovin' mind.

Danny would want Jeff to stay for dinner and Beth agreed with him, so she'd made man food. Meatloaf with mashed potatoes and gravy along with frozen peas. If there was one thing she knew about man food, it meant meat, mashed potatoes and gravy.

Lots of gravy. Boatloads of it. Enough gravy to sink the Spanish Armada. The frozen peas? Not so much, at least in Danny's case.

Damn. She didn't even know if Jeff liked peas, never mind frozen ones. They'd created a child but still had so much to learn about each other. She fretted over the table settings, wondering if her choice of the good dishes and silver was too much. Maybe more casual would be better.

Especially if she was wrong about that kiss last weekend.

She'd replayed every minute, every second of those kisses, of the thrilling ways he'd touched her, right up to the point when Danny had gotten sick.

Pursing her lips, she lightly touched them with her fingertips. Maybe she should put some lipstick on.

She looked down at her plain pink cotton button-down blouse. Maybe she should change into something a little tighter. Did she own anything tighter? Too late! She heard Danny's typical clatter up the front stairs.

"Mom! Can Dad stay for dinner?" Danny did his usual fling the backpack onto the sofa, drop his jacket where he stood, and rush into the kitchen.

"Hi, buddy." Beth returned Danny's quick hug and looked over his head to see Jeff standing in the doorway.

He gave her a little lopsided smile. "Hi."

"Hi." Her heart thumped a little at the sight of him. "Do you want to stay for dinner?"

He glanced at the table, saw the three table settings and chairs. "Are you sure I'm not imposing?"

Her mouth went dry. "Absolutely not. "Not imposing I mean. I made meatloaf."

"Smells great. Can I help?"

"Nope, I've got it all covered. Danny?" She rubbed the hair on top of his head. "Why don't you take Jeff's coat and then go wash up."

"'Kay." He grabbed Jeff's hand. "Let's go."

Beth felt weightless as she made quick work of getting the food onto the table and was pouring Danny a glass of milk when he dragged Jeff back in. "You're right on time."

"Dad, you can sit right there, 'cause Mom sits there and I sit here."

"I'll wait until your mom sits, champ."

Oh, the thrill. "What can I get you to drink? I've got milk, juice, or water."

"Water sounds great." She moved to the fridge to pull out the pitcher.

He took it from her. "For you, too?"

"Please."

Oh, she could hardly grab a breath. He'd eaten with them before, but they'd been at odds.

What a difference one kiss made.

****

"This is really good, Beth." Jeff forked up some potatoes drenched in gravy. "I don't cook, so most nights I'm grabbing takeout from Maggie's."

"He could come here every night for dinner, couldn't he, Mom?" Danny said around a bite of meatloaf.

"He might have plans for other nights, buddy."

Jeff tried to catch Beth's gaze as she looked at Danny. He couldn't quite make it. "And I eat a lot, champ. Let's just see how it goes."

Beth glanced at him then. "You're welcome anytime," she said, her mouth curved in a warm smile.

Danny wiped his mouth with his napkin. The kid managed to smear most of the food across his face anyway. "Now'd be a good time to ask Mom on a date."

Jeff coughed.

"Danny!" Beth's face turned a very pretty shade of pink.

"Well, he asked if he could take you on dates and I said yes. So…" Danny nudged Jeff with his elbow. "Go ahead."

Jeff cleared his throat. "I think I can handle that on my own."

He rolled his eyes. "Okay. Can I be excused,

Mom?"

"Yes, go ahead. Take your plate to the sink and rinse it, then go practice piano."

"Do I have to?"

"What do you think?" Beth tilted her head and gave him one of those faces moms made when you didn't stand a chance getting out of what they wanted you to do.

"Dad?" He turned those big puppy dog eyes at him.

"Outta luck, kid. Go tickle the ivories."

Danny slinked out of the kitchen, the entire weight of the world on his over-burdened shoulders.

"Can I get you anything else? Some coffee or something?" Beth winced as Danny attacked the piano. "He's still playing everything wrong on purpose." She sighed. "I hope this phase passes soon. So, coffee?"

"No thanks. I'll help you clean up though." He had so much work to get done tonight, but he didn't want to leave yet. "I haven't asked you about that date yet."

She blushed. "You don't have to do that. I'm sorry Danny put you on the spot like that."

"He didn't. When I asked about dating you, ,he gave me a checklist."

"A checklist?" She squeaked. "Oh, God." Her face turned an even brighter shade of red.

"Didn't you have a good time when we went to the Cliffside?"

"I had a wonderful time." Her eyes turned dreamy. It got him all jazzed up.

"I'm going to make sure you have a lot of wonderful times." He would do his damnedest to make it so. "What do you want to do?"

"Oh, I don't know." She tilted her head to one side.

"Surprise me."

"Surprise you, eh? Are you sure you trust me?"

Her face turned somber. "I think I do."

Something loosened inside him. He stood, crossed to her chair, pulled her up, and banded his arms lightly around her. "I won't hurt you ever again, Bethy. I promise it." He bent his head and kissed her.

"Ewww! Yuck!" Danny sounded truly disgusted.

They broke apart. Beth stepped away, her color in the neighborhood of hot pink. "What's up?" Beth ran her hand through her hair.

"I'm done practicing. Can I go read now?"

"That was no half hour, but never mind this time. What's for homework?"

He grimaced. "Math."

"Better get at it. Help me clear the table and you can do it in here."

"It's hard." He wrinkled his nose.

"How about this?" Jeff just couldn't tear himself away. "I'll help your mom clean up and if you get stuck, I'll help you out."

"I guess." Danny tromped out to get his homework.

"You don't have to do this. It's common core and all. It makes zero sense to me."

"I want to. He's a great kid and I look forward to every second I get to spend with him." With you, too, he added mentally. "I also happen to be a math whiz." He kissed her again.

"Ugh! Are you going to be doing that all the time now?"

Jeff smiled down at his son. "Better get used to it, kid."

"Totally barfalicious!"

Jeff noticed that Danny didn't look as disgusted as he let on.

Good kid.

Chapter Thirty

"So, you'll do a guy a favor, please, Evelyn, and set me up with all of that?" If Jeff needed to drop down on both knees and beg, he would.

Evelyn ran a gourmet take out business in Bar Harbor. Jeff was her biggest fan. Her food made world famous master chef Lucien Durand's food look like McDonalds.

"For you sweetie? Anything."

He wanted to give Beth the perfect evening and a moonlit picnic sounded like just the thing. Yeah, it was October and getting a little cold at night, but he could work around that. He'd take her to his condo, but apart from the fact that his place was furniture challenged, the idea was to go out.

Like on a date.

Their love had always been cloaked in secret. He wanted, needed it to fly out into the open.

No more backseats in Volvos because of psychotic fathers. Or jealous best friends who called the cops on them.

So while he wanted to take her back to his cave and have his way with her, she needed some romance. Only sunshine from here on in. He smiled at the thought of it.

Sunshine. His sunshine, bringing warmth and light into his life.

Well, shit. How sappy could he be?

When it came to Beth? As sappy as he had to be. Back in the day, he could have gotten a girl like Beth with a snap of his fingers. Back in the day, Beth hadn't been a jock groupie. She'd been all about the music. But he'd missed the part of her life when her father jerked all that away from her. He'd missed how brave she was to stand up to her father to be a mother to Danny. She'd raised him on her own with no help.

Well, she had help now.

"Hello, Coach? You in there?"

Evelyn stood there looking at him. "I'm sorry. What did you say?"

"When do you want to pick this up?"

"Saturday? Around four?"

"Saturday at four." She pulled out a pencil and jotted that down on a piece of her restaurant's stationery. "You got it."

"Thanks, Evelyn! You're a lifesaver."

"No problem. The Sharks going to win on Friday night?"

"We'll give it our best shot." He grinned at her.

With the luck he was having lately, how could they lose?

****

Beth stared at her reflection in her bathroom mirror and fussed with her hair. Should she leave it down or put it up? Curl it?

Arrrgghhh! She tortured it into a French braid.

Jeff had said to dress warmly, so she had on her favorite pair of jeans and an azure colored angora sweater over a white T-shirt. On a whim, she'd splurged on some lace and silk lingerie. It was the first time she'd worn something like that, ever.

And it was about damn time.

The doorbell rang. She opened it to find Jeff smiling at her and, just like that, every cell in her brain short-circuited. "Hi," she said.

"Hi," he said, his eyes warm and avid. "You ready to go?"

Dear Lord, the man had everything going on. Sandy hair, those eyes holding all those flecks of green, blue and gray, those shoulders filling out his jacket. Who could resist him?

Beth couldn't. "Yes. Just let me get my jacket."

He stepped over the threshold, took the coat from her, and held it for her to slip into. "Let me help you."

A first. No one had ever helped her into her coat. "Thank you." She slipped a glance at him under her eyelashes.

"Let's go." He took hold of her elbow and started to lead her out of the house.

"Let me get my purse and my keys."

He chuckled. "Of course. I guess I'm too excited about getting you all to myself."

So was she.

Her legs only kinda, sorta worked. She managed to find her purse, looked in and was delighted to see her keys in there. She put on a brilliant smile, held up and jingled her keys. "All set!"

"Let's go, then." He grabbed the hand not holding the purse and keys and pulled her to him.

He kissed her. Her legs got a bit more rubbery. If this kept up she was never going to survive this night.

"I feel like I've waited a lifetime to be with you again," he murmured against her lips.

Well, if she didn't survive, at least she'd die happy.

Chapter Thirty-One

"Where are we going?" Beth lounged in the passenger seat of Jeff's truck, seat belt in place, hands clasped in her lap.

"You'll know when we get there."

"No fair. I want to know."

"Bethy." He reached his right hand over and squeezed her arm. "Curiosity killed the cat."

She blew out a breath. "I'm sorry. I'm just intrigued." Turning her head to look at him, she pushed a strand of hair that had escaped her braid out of her eyes. "I know Danny-World. Date-World doesn't exist in my universe."

"It's time to change that." And wasn't he ridiculously happy that she hadn't been on a date for the past ten years?

It really wasn't right. A fog of guilt descended on his head. He hadn't been a monk. She should have had the same opportunities. She should have dated and been with men other than him. All the same, he felt, well, relieved about it. It was incredibly selfish, he knew.

He would do his best tonight to honor that and give her as much pleasure as she could stand.

More than what she could stand. She would be a very well-loved woman when she left his bed tomorrow morning.

He desired her, man did he desire her, but taking

care of Beth and making sure she shared his desire was the most important thing. Tonight was for her. Okay. Not all for her. He intended to have some fun himself. If it meant giving her so much pleasure she lost her mind, oh well.

He felt his lips curl into a very wicked smile. He'd take one for the team.

He'd learned a technique or two or three in the ten years they'd been apart. He couldn't wait to show them to her. But right now he had to make sure she knew he wanted her, Beth. No one else. Just Beth.

Always Beth.

A little gourmet picnic, courtesy of Evelyn, then back to his condo to warm up in front of his fireplace and enjoy dessert.

Evelyn had made an espresso chocolate mousse. She told him to serve it in martini glasses. He might ignore that, even though he'd bought two glasses for that purpose.

The taste of chocolate espresso mousse satisfied his desire for something sweet. Licking it off his lover's stomach?

Orgasmic.

Beyond orgasmic.

The thought of the taste of the chocolate combined with the taste of Beth's scrumptious skin had him shifting in his seat to make room for his growing hard-on. Damn.

He looked at her out of the corners of his eyes. She moistened her top lip with the pink tip of her tongue.

He had plans for that tongue tonight. He smiled.

He'd kiss her all over and satisfy every craving she'd ever had.

****

"You never told me where we're going," Beth pointed out.

"Didn't I?"

"No, you didn't." Beth watched as Jeff maneuvered his way through Lobster Cove's streets to the cliffs just north of town. He pulled up to a little area with benches that overlooked the cove. "Here we are." He leaned over and gave her a soft peck on her mouth. "Wait right there."

A couple of seconds later and he opened her door and reached in to help her out.

"Thank—"

He gathered her in his strong muscular arms and kissed her again, making her acutely aware that it was a man kissing her, not a boy. Draping her arms around his waist, she opened up and poured all the passion she felt for this man, all the longing that plagued her for the past ten years. To show him a woman, not a girl, kissed him back.

The kiss spun down into soft gentle brushes of their lips, little sips that sizzled. He pulled his mouth away and rested his forehead against hers. "I need to get our dinner all set up here, but now that I've got you in my arms again I don't want to let you go." His voice rasped along her skin, making her shiver.

He did let her go, but only to open the back of his truck and pull out a blanket. He handed it to her. "Here. Can you carry this for me?"

"Yes." She took it from him as he drew out an enormous picnic basket.

Jeff grinned. "I know just the spot where we can watch the sun set over the water."

Delighted, she gaped at him. "I can't remember the last time I went on a picnic."

He motioned with his head for her to follow. "You and Danny don't go on picnics?"

"Not like this!" Beth smoothed the soft blanket over her arm as she walked along with him. "We made a tent in the kitchen when there were thunderstorms and ate hotdogs." She scrunched her nose. "Danny used to get really scared of the thunder and lightning. It took away the fear and turned it into fun."

He smiled at her, his eyes bright. "You're a really good mom, Beth. I know I accused you of a lot of things in the past and I'm not proud of that."

Her eyes misted over. "Thank you. It's been an adventure. I love Danny more than I could have ever imagined."

"I know your father made your life a living hell. I wish I could have saved you—"

"Shhhhh. It's done and gone. No use thinking about it any more." She hugged the blanket to her chest. "I'm looking ahead these days."

"Me, too," he said. "Me, too."

Their eyes met and held. Beth's heart skittered hither and yon. At that moment, she believed wishes could come true. Dreams, hopes, prayers, all of them could absolutely come true.

The air became too precious to breathe. Here it was, all she had ever wanted, a perfect life close enough to grasp it. She went on tiptoes and cupped her hand to caress his cheek, to touch the elusive part of her dreams.

The moment spun on and on, suspended in a pool of longing that they floated in. Finally he took her hand, brought it to his lips and pressed a kiss into her palm. "Maybe I should feed you before it gets too cold. Are you hungry?"

"For what?" She spoke before she thought.

He chuckled. "I've got a picnic basket full of food. Let me feed you before I love you." He bent to kiss her one more time.

He broke the kiss. "That's dessert, sunshine. Right now, let me feed you."

"Dinner before dessert?" She cocked her head to one side.

"I'm a very good dad, so dinner always before dessert." He wagged his eyebrows up and down.

She laughed then took a deep breath. No guts, no glory. "I'm a big girl and I can eat dessert whenever I want to." She wagged her eyebrows back at him.

He shook his head at her then blew out a huge breath. "Oh, Bethy. You have no idea about what I'm thinking about for dessert." He licked his lips. "We're going back to my apartment when it comes to the dessert course."

She shivered, hoping to *be* dessert.

****

He managed to keep his hands off her as he spread the blanket. As he set out the candles and lit them, the love of his life fussed with arranging silverware. Usually he couldn't have cared less about freaking place settings. But Beth did.

And because Beth cared, Jeff cared.

She put stock in those kinds of things, which was the whole, total reason he'd packed real dishes and silverware instead of paper plates and plastic forks.

Still he worked like hell to keep his hands to

himself. So he kept lighting candles. So beautiful before, but now, in flickering candlelight, in the brilliant tones of the sunset, Beth's beauty outshone them all.

Okay. He was a jock not a poet. Still, those were the words he used to describe her.

So shoot him.

He just breathed in the sight of her lovely face. Unlined of course, yet life had taken its toll in other ways. He'd loved the girl with all his teenage heart. Now he quite believed he'd come to adore the woman.

Her presence in his life had become essential.

Essential for his ability to breathe, for his ability to put one foot in front of the other.

He pulled a chilled bottle of Breakwater Vineyard's 2012 Riesling, which Evelyn had told him to get, popped the cork and poured a tiny bit in one wineglass. He swirled the liquid around and sniffed it. Taking a tiny sip, he checked out the wine.

He didn't know one end of a Riesling to another. So wanting to impress Beth, he followed Evelyn's instructions to the letter. He poured some wine into Beth's glass and added some more into his own. "Cheers!"

She clinked her glass against his. "I can't believe you put this all together for me." Beth sat on the blanket.

"I did it for me, too. Are you warm enough? I know October is a little on the chilly side for a picnic, but after hiding back in high school, I wanted to bring our relationship out in the open. Literally."

"I think it's really romantic."

He had to kiss the tip of her nose for that. "I hope

you're hungry." He knelt by the basket and pulled out a thermos and a couple of other containers.

"I am."

"Good." He unscrewed the thermos and poured creamy clam chowder into two bowls the topped each serving with a dollop of butter. "There." He sat after he handed Beth hers. "*Bon appetit.*"

She spooned up some soup. She closed her eyes as she swallowed. "Mmmmm." The tip of her tongue peeked out of her mouth to catch some of the creamy broth that lingered there and he salivated.

Opening her eyes, she said, "This is delicious. Did you make this?"

"Are you kidding? I don't cook, ever." He chuckled. "However I do know a very good caterer, named Evelyn, in Bar Harbor. She also runs the kitchen at the Spinnaker Yacht and Sail Club."

"This is sinful." She took another taste.

"You think that is sinful? You ain't seen nothing yet."

Beth's mouth parted and under her jacket he could see her chest rise and fall rabbit quick. "I'm looking forward to that."

If he hadn't been holding a bowl of hot chowder he would have pulled her into his lap and kissed her silly. They were in public, though, and while there was taking their relationship out into the open it was a little different taking their relationship out into the open and putting on a show.

He knew she wouldn't feel comfortable with that. Plus the waiting would make their coming together all the sweeter.

She slid her gaze away from his and turned her

attention back to their meal, her cheeks beautifully flushed. Done with the soup, he took the bowl and set it aside. "Are you ready for the second course?"

"Yes!" She craned her neck to peek into the picnic basket.

"I've just got to do a couple of things." He moved the basket out of the way then opened the cooler. Evelyn had given him specific instructions on how to serve the entree.

"You look like you know what you're doing. I don't believe that you can't cook."

He snorted. "I'm just following directions." He shook a glass jar to mix the contents. Once satisfied he'd gotten it right, he poured it over a plate of green beans and tossed them together. Done to what he hoped was up to Evelyn's standards, he put a plate holding a lobster salad croissant and a chilled green bean salad in front of Beth. "*Voila!*"

"It looks delicious! What are they?"

He put his own plate down and reached for the wine bottle in its terra cotta holder then topped up Beth's glass. He donned his best fake French accent. "For tonight we have steamed lobster salad dressed with *crème fraîche*, a champagne mayonnaise, fresh tarragon and fennel served on a croissant alongside blanched green beans with a Dijon mustard, fresh dill and caper vinaigrette." He held his fingers up and air kissed them. "*Magnifique!*"

"You sound like Pepé La Pew," she laughed.

"You wound me, *madame!*" He faked outrage then grinned. "I guess I should stick to English." Motioning to her plate, he said, "Dig in! Let me know what you think." He topped off his own wine.

She cut the croissant in half. "It's so big, I don't know if I can eat it all."

He couldn't help himself. "Maybe you'll repeat those words later on back at my condo."

Blinking furiously, she picked up the half sandwich. "What?"

He barked a laugh.

Then dawn broke at Marblehead. "Oh." She shook her head and smiled. "You're so bad." She shrugged. "We'll just have to see about that." She took a bite and sighed. "So good."

"Yeah?"

"Your friend Evelyn is a food genius." She frowned. "Just how a good a friend is this Evelyn?"

"Only as much as I found about her and fell in love with her food. Besides," he told her, "she's in her sixties and has been very happily married for about forty years."

"Oh. That's good then."

"Try the green beans." She forked up a couple, popped them into her mouth, chewed and swallowed. Jeff watched every motion, every movement of her mouth and throat. "Good, yes?"

There she went licking those gorgeous lips of hers again. "Very good."

They ate in silence though the air around them snapped, crackled and okay, popped—electric, and potent.

Intimate.

He put his arm around her while they watched the sky turn from pink and orange fire into deep, dark blue velvet. As the stars winked on, when the candles he had lit began to flicker, he felt her shiver.

"Getting a little chilly out here," he said. "Why don't I pack this up and we go to my place for dessert?"

She took a very deep breath. "I'll help. We can get there faster." She picked up a candle, pursed her lips and blew it out.

"You look like you're in a hurry," he murmured, wishing to laying his lips over hers. Desire for her raced through his blood.

She tossed her head back. "What do you think?"

"That I better get with the program. After all," he kissed her, "my mother told me to never leave a lady waiting."

Not that he intended to. He and Beth had already waited too long.

****

Beth walked around Jeff's small living room, marveling at the sparseness of it. Eggshell colored walls held no paintings, but it did sport a large, flat screen TV. Very few books sat on the black book case in one corner. A small stone fireplace took up part of the room. A large framed photo of Cookie, obviously a school photo, held the place of honor, along with a smaller picture of Nancy and Cookie on the mantelpiece. He'd framed the baby picture of Danny he'd stolen and put it up next to the other ones.

A small brown plaid covered couch took up space against another wall. The battered maple coffee table in front of it was covered in *Sports Illustrated* magazines. She winced when she saw a battered floral covered recliner next to a small table that was home to a lamp made out of a chianti bottle, and the remote control for the television. She didn't think that *Better Homes and Gardens* would show up to do an article on his decorating prowess.

Venetian blinds shaded the windows, but no curtains draped them. Either he hadn't gotten any or he hadn't had time to put them up. This was just a place to sleep, hardly anything around to turn it into a home.

If she'd learned anything about Jeff since he'd dropped back into her life, she knew he wanted a family. He needed to be a father, an active hands-on one. She wouldn't have been embarrassed about the well-worn condition of her own furniture if she had known how sad his living space was.

She pulled up the dream she'd been having so often lately, Jeff, Danny and her living in her tiny house as a family. Moving to a bigger house when they had a baby on the way. She touched her stomach imagining that baby inside her.

Whoa! She was getting way ahead of herself. Danny had another sibling to get used to before that. But if she wasn't misreading him, Jeff wanted to be a family with her and Danny as much as she wanted it.

A constant worry nibbled on the edge of her mind. What if she was wrong? Her experience with Y chromosome challenged humans involved her father, Jeff, and Danny. Not a whole lot to go on.

He came out of his kitchen with a bottle of champagne and two glasses. He looked at her with a half-smile on his face and heat in his eyes.

Desire streaked through her.

He swept a pile of *Sports Illustrated*s off the coffee table and set the champagne bottle and glasses on it. She was about to pick up the magazines but he said, "Don't worry about it. I'll pick them up later." He smiled and kissed the tip of her nose.

He tore open the foil and wire cage surrounding the cork and twisted the cork and the bottle, one to the left, the other to the right. The cork popped out with a fizzy *thip*. "Well, look at this," he gloated, triumph in his tone. "Didn't lose a drop."

He poured the effervescent liquid. Both glasses hissed and foamed up as he filled them. He added more when the bubbles subsided. He held out a glass. "Try it."

She took the glass, his fingers brushing over hers before he relinquished the drink. "Be careful, sunshine. Those bubbles are pretty potent."

Something was pretty potent, but she didn't think it had much to do with the bubbles. She conjured up her inner sassy. "Doesn't champagne demand a toast?"

His eyes lit brighter as he grinned. "I do believe it does. What do you want to toast?"

In for a penny, in for a pound. She'd put on Sassy Beth for a reason. Might as well own it. "How about you and me?"

He cleared his throat. "Just you and me?"

"Yes." Beth couldn't believe what she was about to say. "I love my son, our son, but he has no place in this room right now."

He held her gaze for several atomic-powered moments, his eyes searching hers. "I guess you're right. Danny's not here right now. It's just you and me. No kids or ex-wives or crazy fathers between us."

Oh, she ached for this with all her soul. "I hope I don't disappoint you. I haven't been with anyone since you."

"You can't know how much that turns me on. Just let me love you." He dragged her down onto his ugly couch. "I'll be with you every step of the way."

He put his glass of champagne on the coffee table then stole hers and set it right next to his. "We deserve this, Beth. You and me." He pointed to her then to him then to her again. His face had a fierce look to it.

"Do you really think we can make it work?"

He smiled a very wicked smile. "I know it. Just let me prove it to you."

She shivered in anticipation. "I just want to please you."

He put a finger on her lips. "Shhhh. You worry too much, y'know. Nothing pleases me more than being here with you right now. Kissing you." He replaced his finger with his mouth, spreading a soft, achingly sweet kiss across her mouth. He cupped her face in his warm, rough hands. "Right now it's just us, no past, our whole future ahead of us." He brushed his lips over hers, once, twice, three times. "Please. Let me make love to you." He pressed his lips to her forehead. "One night at a time."

"But…"

He put two fingers against her lips. "No buts. Just let me love you tonight."

Just tonight. After all the lonely days and the lonely nights, she had the promise of this night. Her heart lurched and she trembled. "Jeff."

He gathered her into his arms, he pulled out the hair tie holding her braid and ran his fingers through her hair.

She moaned as he gently massaged her scalp.

He nuzzled her hair and whispered, "It's going to be so good, Bethy."

She climbed into his lap and straddled him, placing

her head so that her mouth hovered over his, so she could kiss him the exact way she wanted to be kissed.

Like a woman in love.

Chapter Thirty-Two

She'd never kissed him before. She'd responded to his kisses, but hadn't made a move on her own.

Ever.

So he let her have her way with him.

Who was he to deny a lady what she wanted?

Not him.

Her soft lips parted over his, inviting him in. Jeff slid his tongue against hers, his head spinning with the force of their kiss. He sank into her, each kiss hotter, more avid and greedy than the one before. He felt her heart trip against his chest, could hear the soft moans she made in her throat.

He pulled his mouth from hers. "I need more." Without waiting another beat, he gathered her into his arms, managed to stand and carried her into his bedroom. He made it to the bed and laid her on it. Damn, she looked amazing, clothes rumpled by his hands, hair mussed by his fingers, lips swollen by his kisses.

He had to have her. He toed off his shoes and stretched on his side next to her. Stroking her hair away from her face, he spread it on his pillow. "You're so beautiful." He dropped a kiss on her forehead. "You can't begin to imagine how many times I dreamt of seeing you right here, in my bed."

"Jeff," she whispered, the desperate sound making

him hard and aching to bury himself in her body.

"I'm going to touch you now, I can't wait another minute."

Sitting up, she licked her lips. "Please."

"Oh, baby. I was hoping you'd say that."

He nearly swallowed his tongue when she pulled her sweater and tee over her head, leaving just a pretty sheer peach colored bra trimmed with pale pink lace and a tiny darker pink bow nestled between her breasts. He cupped one breast with his hand while he pressed his mouth against the other one, tonguing her nipple through the delicate fabric of her bra.

"Oh, God, yes!" She threaded her hands into his hair and brought his head closer to her breasts and held him there. Hooking his fingers in the cups of her bra, he slipped them down so he could feast on her bare flesh.

She gasped. "They're a little bigger than they were."

"They're gorgeous." He tweaked one long pink nipple as he scraped his teeth along the other.

She undulated underneath him, her pelvis arching up and down, begging for his touch. He ran his hand down the soft skin of her stomach to where she churned. "Shhhh, darlin'. We've got all night."

She worked at the buttons on his shirt, her fingers clumsy.

"Let me take care of this." Jeff reluctantly maneuvered onto his knees. He pulled his shirt out of his pants and jerked it over his head just like she had done with her own.

Beth rose to her knees keeping her eyes locked with his. She reached behind her and slowly unhooked her bra. After letting it slide between them, she took his hand and guided it to cup one breast.

Jeff sucked in sharp breath as he touched her soft smooth skin. Her breasts were round, pale, and crowned with rosy stems surrounded by puffy areolas, so much more beautiful than he remembered. Needing to taste her, he guided her back down on the bed and stretched out next to her. He teased one nipple with his tongue while molding the other with his hand.

"Mmmmmm." She leaned into his touch. "So good."

"I can make you feel better," he murmured against her skin.

"Please—"

He didn't need to be asked twice. He went, stripped her out of her jeans, desperate to see all of her. "You are even more lovely than I remember."

He scraped his teeth against each of her nipples then ran his mouth down her torso, licking here, nipping there. He settled her legs over his shoulders and cupped her sweet, soft bottom. He lifted her, nuzzled his face in her soft curls and used his thumbs to open her up to him.

Wet. She was so wet and ready. Using the tip of his tongue, he laved and teased the hard little button of her clitoris. She nearly flew off the bed and he was glad he had a good grip on her ass. "Do you like that?"

"Eep!" She squeaked, the sound startled and helpless.

"What about this?" He smiled against her soft flesh and fluttered his tongue over her sensitive bud. "Like that, too?"

"Yesssssss."

He lapped and lapped at her, reveling in the spicy

scent and taste of her while she trembled.

So responsive, his Beth. So damn responsive to his touch.

"Oh, oh, ohhhhhhh," Beth panted. He felt her start to shiver violently as she lifted her hips up into his mouth and his cock ached, eager to be inside her.

He feasted on her soft, wet flesh as he took her closer to the edge. One more pass of his tongue, then another, then a slight scrape of his teeth and she fell apart.

She screamed as she came and he chased every last tremor, every last sensation, fluttering his tongue over her exploding bud. When she finally relaxed, he moved up alongside her to hold her close.

"You okay, baby?" He kissed the top of her head and rolled one hard, pebbled nipple between his thumb and forefinger.

"I didn't think it could be like that," she said, her voice shaky.

"Did you like it? 'Cause I gotta tell you there's a lot more where that came from."

"Any more might kill me."

"Nope, not gonna let that happen." If he didn't get inside her soon, he was the one who might die. "Are you ready for your second trip to heaven?"

"Oh, God."

He hopped off the bed and took care of taking off the rest of his clothes, easing them gently over his massive erection.

"Yikes." Her blue eyes grew round as licked her lips.

"It's all for you, darlin'." He liberated his painfully erect penis, desperation riding him to thrust into her hot, slick sheath. "All for you."

****

Beth's heart thudded as she tried to catch her breath. She couldn't tear her eyes away from watching him free his shaft from his clothes. She didn't remember him being that big.

And what had happened right before that? The thing with his mouth? She'd heard of it, of course, but never thought the pleasure would be that intense. She'd certainly never had an orgasm like that before.

Actually, she'd never had an orgasm with someone else in the room. It was a revelation.

Jeff fished around in the nightstand, flinging things out of it in his haste. "Gotcha." He pulled out several little foil packets and tossed all but one on the bed.

He ripped that one open and rolled it down the hard length of him. "I need to be inside you, Bethy. I can't wait any more."

Her inner muscles spasmed in anticipation. "Me neither."

He lowered himself between her legs and covered her gently. "I'll try to go slow, but I can't promise anything. I've waited so long to be inside you again."

"I can't wait, either." She trembled. "Come inside me now."

He kissed her hard on the mouth, wrapped her legs around his lower back, and guided his erection into her soft, welcoming heat. She gasped when he pushed all the way inside. Oh, this. This was what she had longed for, that moment when he burrowed deep inside her all the way to her womb.

"Damn. You are so tight," he rasped, his voice grating against her skin. "So damn tight. Am I hurting you?"

Tears welled behind her eyelids as she stretched to accept all of him, but not because he hurt her. She blinked them back. "No, you're not hurting me. I love how you fill me."

"Thank God." He started to move in slow shallow thrusts at first, gradually picking up speed and going deeper. She arched her pelvis, meeting him stroke for stroke. Every time he moved inside her, that wonderful long, hard column of his rubbed against a sensitive spot high inside her. Little whimpers escaped her throat with every pass.

Those whimpers turned into full-blown screams as he moved faster and harder. His breathing was harsh and ragged as he drove them higher and higher. Every relentless thrust of Jeff's sent her up, up, up and then finally over the breaking point. She shattered into million pieces, convulsing in wave after wave of excruciating pleasure.

"Me, too, baby," Jeff groaned as he pushed into her deep, so deep. "Me, too." One last amazing thrust and he came, groaning as he filled her.

The sound of their hoarse, ragged breathing filled the room. Her inner muscles kept clutching and releasing him, the aftershocks, she guessed, of incredible loving. He groaned before he braced a forearm on each side of her head. His head bowed and he claimed her mouth in one incredible, kiss.

"I'll get off you in a minute," he murmured.

"No hurry," she assured him. "I love being with you like this."

"I'm heavy." He rolled over next to her, took care of the condom, gathered her into his arms and held her tight. "That was amazing. You," he dropped a kiss onto the top of her head, "are amazing."

"I had no idea it could be like that." Beth shivered in his arms. "It never was before."

He frowned. "What?"

She sighed. "Those were the first orgasms I've ever had that I didn't give myself." She felt her color rise. So humiliating to admit.

He went absolutely still. "Man, I'm sorry. I had no idea." His voice turned gruff and sounded like a rusty gear trying to work itself free. "What a stupid jerk I was. Why didn't you say something?"

Levering herself up so she could look into his eyes. "I didn't know any better. And I was so shy, even if I had known what I was missing, I wouldn't have been able to tell you. I just liked being with you. Holding you. Kissing you." She pressed a warm kiss onto his lips.

"I'm glad you weren't too shy tonight." He grinned. "I may have picked up some skills I didn't have back then in my mom's Volvo."

She snorted. "I guess you have. I've got some catching up to do."

Laughing, he gave her a squeeze. "Well, there it is. We'd better get working on that. You are so beautiful. I hate repeating myself but you just are." He ran his hand up her body to cradle her hypersensitive breast and rub his thumb over its still hard, pebbly rose stem.

She held her breath as both peaks of her breasts, even the one he wasn't stroking, hardened and lengthened. "Oh, God."

"You like that?"

She could only nod.

"I love how your body responds to my touch." He stole a kiss. "I just really love you."

"I love you," Beth whispered.

"Then I am the luckiest of mortals." He rolled over onto his back, dragged her with him and draped her body over his. "Kiss me again."

She did and they let the kiss spin on and on, the stuff of dreams.

"Hey, Bethy." He smiled at her so sweetly.

"Hey, Jeff." That smile bathed her in its warmth.

"I'm putting you in charge."

She blinked. "What do you mean?"

"It's another one of those tricks I learned about. You're in charge." He reached to the side and pulled up one of those square foil packages he'd thrown on the bed. "Ride me." After handing her the condom, his big warm hands claimed her breasts and his fingers tweaked her achy nipples.

She felt his penis harden again. "I think I'm going to like this." She ripped open the foil square and shifted so she could roll it on him.

He hissed as her hands caressed him. Feeling powerful, she grabbed and lowered herself down the solid, stiff length of him. Once she had completely covered him, once he had filled her to the brim, she swiveled her hips in small teasing circles.

"Oh, baby, you ride me so good."

She chuckled. "Let me show you how good."

No doubt about it. Being in charge ruled.

Chapter Thirty-Three

Jeff lay on his back, Beth wrapped around him, sleeping deeply. Poor thing. He'd worn her out.

He had a lot to think about, the first being all the regret he had about how he had treated her back in the day.

He'd been so clueless.

Selfish.

How generous of her not to blame him. Truth to tell, he was pretty ignorant about giving a woman pleasure then. He'd just assumed because he'd gotten off, she had.

Holding her in his arms while she slept brought him back to that one night they'd had when they tried to elope.

Beth shifted against him and he adjusted his position. Beyond his misgivings about the past, this was the absolute best night of his life.

****

Beth woke to the feel of Jeff's lips nibbling at the sensitive hollow behind her earlobe. The stubble covering his jaw scraped deliciously against the side of her neck and his gentle fingers plucked her diamond hard nipples.

Spooned against her back, he grumbled, "'Bout time you woke up."

She hummed. "I thought I was having a good

dream."

He chuckled. "I can make it a better dream. I can make it an amazing reality." Keeping one hand on her breast, he ran the other one down her body to cup her mound.

Beth wiggled and undulated against his questing fingers. He parted the soft pillowy folds to tease the achy bud hidden there. She moaned.

"You're already wet for me, darlin'." He nipped her earlobe and softly pinched the ruched peak of the nearest breast. "I want you to come for me. I want to feel you fall apart in my arms."

He alternated rubbing that needy little button up and down then traced circles around it. "Come for me, Beth. I need you to come for me."

Pleasure spiraled within her with every pass of his fingertip. She couldn't contain the helpless mewls of excitement that escaped her throat.

So close, she was so close, only one pass more over her clit—

She exploded with a scream of ecstasy, bucking against his wicked hand, shuddering in wave after wave of pleasure. Coming back to herself as he chased every last wave of her release, she panted harshly, desperate for air.

"Good morning." He flipped her onto her back and smiled Satan's very own grin. "Think you could get used to waking up that way every day?"

He parted her thighs and rubbed his rock hard penis against her cleft and managed to arouse her again. Unable to keep still, she wiggled against his erection. He began to breathe heavily as he hardened even more. "I've got to love you now." He placed one leg over each of his shoulders and claimed her in one sure, smooth thrust.

He held onto her thighs as he moved deeply within her, smoothly gliding in and out. Still over stimulated from her first orgasm, the waves of desire built inside her again as she raced with him to go over the hot edge of fulfillment. Their mouths fused together, desperate for the taste of each other.

Their climaxes destroyed them, her first, him following right after.

When he could move, he fell next to her and pulled her into his arms, settling her head over his heart. It thumped heavily beneath her ear.

Had she ever felt so safe? So warm? So loved?

Neither said anything for a while. Beth closed her eyes and absorbed the feeling of being pressed close to the strong masculine warmth of him.

He pushed her hair out of her eyes and kissed the top of her head. "What are you thinking?"

"I'm thinking that I've got a lot of catching up to do." She smiled. "I'm thinking I'm going to keep you pretty busy making it up to me."

He chuckled. "It's a dirty job, but somebody's got to do it."

"I never knew what all the fuss about sex was. I mean, I loved being held by you and kissing you, but I never got the whole fireworks thing. Okay, I knew about the urges and figured out how to take care of them but it was no big whoop." She grinned. "What we just did was huge whoop, the hugest whoop ever. I had no idea."

"You have no idea how sorry I am about that I disappointed you back then."

She sat up and grinned. "I'll just have to let you make it up to me." She pressed her lips to his. "Over and over and over again. Until you get it right."

"I think I better get started."

"Good plan."

He kissed his way down her body and proceeded to make good on his promise.

Chapter Thirty-Four

Jeff watched his second string players run passing drills when his phone buzzed in his pocket. He checked the caller I.D. Nate Cavanaugh, his lawyer. He handed one of his assistants his clipboard. "Can you watch them for a minute? Make Brendan and Sully run that combination again. I've got to take this call."

"Of course."

Jeff nodded and stepped away. "Nate. What's up?"

"Good news this time. The family court judge ruled in favor of your petition to have Cookie visit you in Maine without Katie tagging along."

"Yes!" Jeff's heart leapt. "That's fantastic!"

"There's more. He also ruled that Katie has to split the travelling expenses with you."

Jeff shook his head to clear it. "Come again?"

"Katie's got to share the cost of getting Cookie to and from Lobster Cove."

"I bet she's not too happy about that."

"Neither Katie nor her father liked the ruling. I'd prepare myself for a very angry phone call from your ex-wife if I were you."

"Thanks for the heads-up. I'm really grateful you pulled this off. I'll have a crate of your favorite wine sent to you right away."

"I'll look forward to that."

Jeff wanted to call Beth right away to let her know

the good news, but he decided to wait until he took Danny home later on.

Maybe he could wrangle an invitation to dinner and steal a couple of sweet, steamy kisses from the cook.

He glanced back at the field and sighed. If only he could get Brendan and Sully to perfect the play he needed them to by Friday night.

****

Beth smiled as Danny barreled his way into the kitchen dragging Jeff behind him. "Hi Mom! Dad can stay for dinner, okay?"

She caught Jeff's gaze and noted his sheepish grin. "Please?"

"My astounding psychic abilities told me you would ask if Jeff would stay for dinner, so I made enough. Go ahead and put away your backpack, then clean up." "Do you have a lot of homework?"

"I gotta finish my book report and some math." He grimaced.

"Why don't you get a head start on it while I finish making dinner and after you wash up."

"'Kay." He raced off.

"Smells good in here. Can I help?" Jeff sauntered over to her, a sexy look simmering in his eyes.

"I've got it under control." She checked the elbow macaroni boiling on the stove.

"Is this," he sniffed and peeked over her shoulder, "American chop suey?"

"Sure is." She gave the tomato and beef mixture a stir. "With my secret ingredient."

"Man, I haven't had American chop suey in forever. I mean, since I moved away from home to go

260

to school." He licked his chops. "My mother's recipe is killer."

"Mine's better." She scooped a sample in a spoon and held it up for his inspection. "Taste. Be careful, though. It's hot."

"Thanks for the warning." He lightly blew over the top of it his eyes never leaving hers then slipped the spoon into his mouth and swallowed. "It's very good."

"And better than your mother's?"

"Yes, but don't tell her I said so. I'll deny it to my last breath."

"Your secret's safe with me. Now, shoo, out of my way. I'll never get this food on the table with you standing so close to me."

"Really?" He drew the word out long. "I like the sound of that." He leaned in like he was going to kiss her when his pocket buzzed.

"I've got to take this call. Be right back."

He walked out to her back steps and put his phone to his ear. She watched him as he leaned against the wall, his shoulders looking so broad in the long-sleeved slate gray waffle weave Henley shirt he wore. His faded jeans clung to his amazingly round, hard butt.

She swallowed as she turned her attention back to the boiling pasta and drained it in the sink. Glancing back Jeff's way, she wondered when the call would be done and should she put dinner on hold.

He came back into the kitchen just as she was mixing the elbow macaroni into the tomato and beef sauce. A huge smile stretched across his face. "This smells awesome."

"I take it your call was about good news?" She poured the contents of the pan into a huge blue serving bowl.

"Oh, yeah. I'll tell you later." He bent and kissed the tip of her nose. "Want me to go get Danny?"

"Sure. Thanks." Curiosity nibbled at the edge of her brain.

Danny and Jeff came into the kitchen. Danny sat immediately, but Jeff went and held Beth's chair out for. "Hey champ. Back it up. Remember you don't sit down until the lady in the room is seated."

Danny popped out of his chair. "Can you hurry it up? I'm really hungry."

"Thank you," Beth murmured to Jeff. "It's so nice to have a gentleman in the house."

"My pleasure," Jeff said as Danny rolled his eyes.

Beth looked around the table thrilled beyond belief that this was now her new life.

****

"So, Danny's gone and is working on his homework. Can you tell me the good news?" Beth poured boiling water into a teapot.

Jeff grinned. He knew she'd been going crazy all through dinner wondering what was up. He leaned against the kitchen counter. "I got a call from Nate Cavanaugh today."

Her eyes widened. "Oh, really? About the adoption?"

"No, something else. The family court judge in Massachusetts ruled in favor of me being able to bring Cookie, without Katie, to Lobster Cove for visits."

Beth gave a little hop and clapped her hands. "Jeff, that's wonderful!" She gave him a quick kiss on his mouth. "I'm so happy for you!"

"It gets better. She has to pay for half of the travel

expenses."

"Wow! That's pretty generous of the judge."

"You ain't kidding me." He sat on a chair and pulled her into his lap. "We've scheduled a visit for the Harvest of the Sea Festival next weekend. We're meeting halfway, in Portland, to hand her off." He couldn't help but smile. "I'm really jazzed about this, but I'll need your help."

"Whatever you need."

Another reason, as if he needed one, to fall in love with Beth all over again. "I don't think the *décor* in my spare bedroom is something a six-year-old girl will appreciate."

"You want me to decorate a room for a girl? Oh my God! I've dreamed of the room I'd put together for a girl." She practically jumped up and down. "I'd be happy to! I love Danny with all my heart and soul but I've always wanted to have a girl so dolls could balance the plastic dinosaurs."

He nuzzled the top of her head. "You know what she likes; anything shiny, sparkly and pink. Throw a Barbie or two in there and she'll be fine."

Beth's eyes gleamed. "This is going to be so much fun! What's my budget?"

"Um, I hadn't thought that far. My condo can't compare with the house in Addington." He realized he didn't care about budget. And Beth probably wouldn't throw caution to the wind and spend his money without caring about it anyway. She knew how hard it was to make a dollar. "Make it a room for a princess. I trust you to not break the bank."

"Of course I'll mind the spending. Jenna's got some adorable fabric that'll make the room special. I can make everything there."

Whoa! "You're going to make everything?"

She laughed. "Why not? That way we'll get exactly what we want. Oooh. Well, not everything. I don't have that much time." She nearly jumped up and down. "I have an idea. I have several ideas."

"Okay." He remembered his mother mending but he had never seen her sewing anything for fun.

"I'm going to take her to Happy Thoughts and let her pick out the material for her curtains and some stencils to paint as a border. We can sew and paint together!" She nodded. "You and Danny can help her paint the stencil border and I can teach her how to sew. A family project!" Her brows knit. "Unless she already knows how to sew."

Katie? Sew? "I'm pretty sure Cookie doesn't know one end of a sewing machine from the other."

"Does that idea work for you? I mean it does give her a sense of ownership of her space here, so hopefully she'll feel more comfortable."

"I think it's a great idea." He nipped at her earlobe. "How did you get so smart?"

"I eat a lot of fish. It's brain food, I've been told."

"God, you're precious." She was a miracle to him.

Katie would never have even considered coming up with a plan to make Danny feel welcome.

Case in point, that terrible weekend in Addington.

Beth had grown up in a nightmare, yet she only wanted the best for everyone. Katie had grown up with every advantage, yet if you looked up entitled in the dictionary, Katie's picture would be right there.

Beth humbled him.

She also turned him on beyond belief.

And, on that note, he needed to go before he did something he didn't want Danny to witness.

"I've got to go, darlin.' I've got a ton of work to do."

"I understand. I have to put the hammer down and get Danny in bed."

She slid off his lap and he stood in front of her. "Thank you for him."

Her face flushed a pretty shade of pink. "I was confused until the first time I felt him move inside me. That's when I fell totally in love with him. I did whatever I had to do to keep him." She looked him right smack dab square in the eyes. "He's my everything."

Jeff felt a little tinge of green at that. He wanted to be her everything.

Jesus. He was jealous of his own son. Someone needed to give him a solid slap upside his head.

He had to get out of there. "I'll see you tomorrow when I bring Danny home."

"Are tacos okay for dinner tomorrow night?"

He threw his head back and laughed. "Anything you make is light years beyond okay."

She gave him a half smile and shook her head. "Tacos it is."

Jeff stroked her cheek. "See you tomorrow." He stepped into the living room. "Danny," he bellowed. "I'm going."

"'Kay!"

"He's a man of few words," Beth told him as she handed him his jacket.

"I can see that." Jeff reached out and flipped the end of her ponytail. "I'll see you tomorrow."

"I'll be here."

And, he realized, she would. He'd never have to wonder about where she was ever again.

Totally made of win.

Chapter Thirty-Five

"Jenna, I think it's going to work out," Beth rhapsodized when she floated into work the next day.

"I hope for your sake that's true. From what you've told me, Skankarella sounds like a piece of work."

Beth squeezed the skeins of yarn she held in each hand. "I honestly don't know why she's like she is. The girl I remember was a really good friend."

"Who knows what lies underneath?" Jenna put on her best *Twilight Zone* narrator impression.

Beth shoved the yarn into a diamond shaped cubby holding its brethren. "I guess you're right, Jenna, she was my best friend. She knew all my secrets."

"I hate to say this, but sometimes teen girls are like that. Honestly," Jenna moved some red embroidery floss from the green bin to the red bin, "I think all we need to do to conquer Al Quaeda is to unleash twenty middle school popular girls on them."

Beth snorted. "They'd run into the hills and hide in the caves crying like babies. But here's the thing." She picked up a couple other skeins to re-file. "Katie wasn't that popular. I mean if she was part of the inner circle, she never would have given me the time of day. But she was my best damn friend."

"Maybe she was threatened by your relationship with Jeff. If you got popular by dating him, she'd be left in the cold," Jenna said.

"I don't know. I never could have dated Jeff out in the open anyway." Beth grimaced. "Katie knew that." She rearranged more of the yarn. "I remember being pregnant and sitting in my bedroom on the night of the prom. I fantasized about being there with Jeff, with my real body, not my fat pregnant one, dancing around in a beautiful princess gown with Jeff so handsome in his tux."

Jenna didn't say anything for a long time. "Sorry kid. But look on the bright side. Things are finally going your way." Jenna ran her hand through her blonde pixie-do.

"I hope so," Beth prayed. "I sure do hope so."

****

"We're going to have so much fun, princess!" Jeff had just picked Cookie up in Portland to take her for the weekend in Lobster Cove. He'd left right after school on Friday to get her and to get back to Lobster Cove for the Sharks' pre-game warm up.

He smiled at her in the rearview mirror. She sat there all safely buckled in her booster seat brushing her Barbie's pink and white hair. "The whole town is having a great big Harvest of the Sea Festival. I hear it's lots of fun."

"Do they have things for girls?"

"Of course they do. You know there are girls your age in Lobster Cove."

"Okay." She frowned while tugging the tiny brush through some snarls in her doll's tangled mess of hair.

"And you'll get to see my new team play tonight! Maybe you'll be our good luck charm and help us win the game!"

She made a raspberry. "Silly Daddy. I don't play

football."

"I know that princess, but you can sit with Beth and Danny and watch the game and cheer us on."

She glanced up. "Do they live at your house?"

"No." Though he'd been thinking along those lines for a while now. Maybe he should check with Jessica Martin, a local realtor, to see what kind of houses she had listed. "Danny and Beth live in their own house."

She nodded. "That's good. I don't like boys. They're too noisy and rough."

"Not always." He hit his blinker and moved into the passing lane. "But don't worry. You've got your own room and Beth is going to help you pick out cloth to make your own curtains."

"I don't know how to sew."

"That's why she's going to teach you. You'll see. It'll all be fun!"

Or at least that was the plan.

****

Jeff looked up into the bleachers to see where Beth, Danny and Cookie were. Tonight's game was a make or break game for the Sharks. Win this one and they would place second in the league.

And he wanted to win it for Cookie.

Danny stood up and waved. Jeff laughed and waved back. The three of them looked great up there, bundled up in their Sharks hoodies.

They looked like a family.

His family.

He couldn't help but grin like an idiot.

He and Beth hadn't talked marriage, but he wanted to marry her.

But first he had a football game to win.

Chapter Thirty-Six

"Way to go, Dad! You clobbered 'em!" Danny danced in circles around Jeff when he got to Lobster Lanes to join Beth, Cookie and Danny for some ice cream.

Jeff grinned. "The team did a good job."

"Are you kidding? Max and Simon totally nailed that new pass play!" Danny bounced from one foot to the other.

Jeff grinned and enjoyed his son. Six weeks ago the kid had never even been to a football game. Now he lived for it.

Jeff slid behind the hard plastic booth. Danny followed him. "Hey, princess!" Jeff turned his attention to his daughter. "What did you think of the game?"

Cookie slid a glance to the ever-exuberant Danny then looked at Jeff. "I liked the cheerleaders."

"Maybe we can find you a cheerleader camp this summer. You're a great dancer. You would make an awesome cheerleader."

Cookie beamed. "I've got a solo in the next dance concert."

"You do? I'm so proud of you! When is it?" Jeff realized he needed to check-in with Cookie's schedule more. Now that he could bring her to Lobster Cove to visit he'd fix that.

"I can't remember. Mommy knows."

"Remind her to tell me."

Beth stood. "Who wants ice cream?" She put her hand on Jeff's shoulder. "We've been waiting for you."

Danny didn't hesitate. "Chocolate in a cup with rainbow jimmies."

"Of course. I never would have ever guessed." Beth winked at Danny. "What about you, Cookie? What do you want?"

"Just vanilla in a cup."

"You don't want jimmies or strawberries or anything?" Beth coaxed.

"Maybe rainbow jimmies."

"You got 'em." Beth turned warm eyes to Jeff. "What about you, Coach? Want some ice cream?"

Jeff's stomach growled. "Actually, I was thinking of begging Sal for a couple of slices with pepperoni, extra cheese, and olives."

"I can take care of that." Beth said. "You just sit here with the kids and bask in the well-deserved glory of beating the other team."

"First year here, second in the league, baby." He sat back and clasped his hands behind his head. "I am the man."

Danny hooted. "Who da man?"

"Me da man!" Jeff and Danny fist bumped.

Beth stood. "Let me go get you some food." Beth looked at Cookie, her eyes filled with worry.

What was that about?

****

Beth had noticed Cookie didn't seem very happy about Danny grabbing Jeff's attention again. "Danny. I need you to help me with the ice cream."

"Just get a tray from Sal."

"Danny." Jeff gave the kid a nudge out of the booth. "Help your mother."

"'Kay." Danny sighed then stood.

Beth smiled her thanks to Jeff over Danny's head. Jeff's smile was warm, maybe overly warm, in return. Maybe hot, in return. Inappropriately hot because there were children there.

She had trouble swallowing. "Danny, you go get the ice cream. She pulled her wallet out of her purse, liberated a twenty-dollar bill from it and gave it to Danny. "I'll go talk to Sal about your dad's pizza."

"'Kay." He ran off.

"He never does anything at normal speed," Jeff commented.

"He never has." Danny scrambled through the crowd of teens. She always held her breath until she saw him arrive unscathed. "I'll get you your pizza."

He grabbed her hand, turned it over, and pressed a kiss into her palm. "Thank you."

"It's my pleasure." Right about now she needed a fan. Flashes of Jeff's mouth against other parts of her body popped across her mind.

"Hmmmmm." He'd made that noise as well when she'd put her mouth on parts of *his* naked body.

And she had no business fantasying about Jeff naked when his daughter was sitting across from him.

"Daddy, why are you always kissing Danny's mommy?"

Jeff froze. "Why are you asking that?"

Beth put a hand on the back of the booth to steady herself.

"You kiss her," Cookie pointed to Beth with her finger. "All the time and you never kiss my mommy any more. It makes me sad."

Jeff glanced at Beth before turning all his attention to Cookie. "First, it's not polite to point. Please say you're sorry to Beth."

"Sorry," she muttered without looking up.

"It's okay." Beth sat on the bench again.

"Now second, you know your mom and I got a divorce. Do you remember what that is?"

"It means you're not married any more and you don't live with Mommy and me. But I want you to live with me and Mommy again! I want you to kiss my mommy."

Beth had to tell herself to breathe. Given how smoothly the evening had gone so far, this came way out of left field.

Jeff stroked a hand over his daughter's hair. "I'm sorry but that's just not going to happen. I have to live here in Lobster Cove now because this is where my job is. Do you understand?"

She sighed. "I guess so. I still don't like it when you kiss Danny's mommy."

Jeff looked at Beth, his gaze filled with chagrin. "I'm sorry that you don't like it, but I'm still going to kiss Beth."

Cookie turned to face Beth, her face filled with anger.

Time to get out of Dodge. "I'll be right back with your pizza."

****

Beth had just settled herself into bed with a cup of chamomile tea and Scarlette LaFlamme's latest, when the phone rang.

Jeff. "Hi."

"Hi," he said. "I'm sorry about Cookie tonight."

"You can't control her feelings. I think it's natural for her to resent me and Danny. It's going to take some time for her to come around."

"I know. I just hope it's sooner rather than later." He coughed. "I don't think Katie is helping matters. Cookie spent a lot of time on the phone with her tonight before she went to bed, but I don't know."

"It'll get better the more she gets used to me and Danny."

"What are you up to?"

Smiling, she said, "Are you changing the subject?"

"Maybe. So what're you doing there, Bethy?"

"I'm in bed with a book and a cup of tea."

"Wish I was there with you." His voice got low and husky. "I think I'd try to make you lose interest in that book."

"Oh really?" She leaned back against the pile of pillows behind her.

"What are you wearing?"

She looked down at her usual bedtime ensemble, an extra large Maggie's Diner tee shirt, a pair of blue pajama pants with small red flowers on them and a thick, soft pair of socks. "Let me see. A very skimpy black silk and lace teddy and a very, very skimpy black lace thong," she purred.

She'd never worn a thong in her life, but he didn't have to know that.

"Hmmmmm. I wish I was there to see you."

"Me too."

"You know what I'd do?"

She swallowed. "Why don't you tell me?"

"I'd slip that teddy off you and kiss your breasts.

I'd tease your nipples until they turned into tight little points. Think you'd like that?"

"Eep!"

He chuckled. "Then I'd kiss my way down your body and use my lips and tongue, my teeth maybe, to make you so crazy for me you'll beg."

She licked her lips, her skin quivering as she imagined him pleasuring her with his lips, tongue and teeth. Her breath hitched in her lungs.

"After I'd made you come at least a couple of times I'd thrust deep inside you and make us both very happy."

Oh, boy. And she thought Scarlette LaFlamme was steamy!

"What do you think of that?"

"Um, I'm pretty much in favor of it all." Her mouth went dry. "I need a glass of water to cool down."

He chuckled. "And I think I need a cold shower. Will you dream about me tonight?"

"You know I will."

"Good because I'm going to be dreaming about you."

"Oh, Jeff."

"Gotta go. See you in the morning. Sweet dreams."

"Sweet dreams."

After they hung up Beth stared at the cover of *The Duke's Desire*. Maybe Jeff should be writing these books. There had to be some men who wrote romance novels.

Right?

Chapter Thirty-Seven

"I don't think I've ever seen so much food," Jeff said as he walked along with Beth and the kids through downtown Lobster Cove. "Do they do this every year?"

"The Harvest of the Sea just gets bigger every year." Beth waved to her friend Anita, the one who used to drop Danny off and pick him up before Jeff knew the kid was his son.

Speaking of Danny

"Mom! Can I go jigging for tinker mackerel with Ben?"

"Not right now. You need to stay with us and keep Cookie company. You're the only kid here she knows."

Cookie, ever the drama queen, sniffed noisily. Danny's chin jutted out. "But the contest will be over!"

"You don't even have your fishing pole and mackerel lure," Beth pointed out.

"But Mom—"

"Don't 'but mom' me. We're going to the lobster boil for supper after we check out all the other contests."

Sliding his gaze to Jeff, Danny opened his mouth. "Don't even think of asking me to contradict your mother," Jeff warned.

Danny glared at Cookie. He muttered something under his breath and Jeff was pretty sure the word stupid figured large in it.

"I don't like lobster," Cookie said.

"I'm sure they'll have something you like."

"They always do." Beth smiled at Cookie who didn't return the favor.

Great. Just great.

What happened to the civil child he'd picked up yesterday?

They wandered through the crowd checking out all the exhibits lining the street. He bought a stuffed Lionel Lobster for Cookie, bright red with big black bugged out eyes. Danny proclaimed it was for babies, but Beth shut that down right away.

They tasted clam chowder, cranberry relish, beach plum jam, chowed down on lobster shaped cookies from Sweet Bea's, sampled blueberry pie and enjoyed the street performers.

At least, Jeff thought, he and Beth did all that. Danny sulked and kept sending meaningful glances toward the pier where the tinker mackerel derby was happening. Cookie apparently had lost all interest in food, but she did want to get her face painted.

"This is the last year for the beach plum jam contest." Beth turned, a jar of the stuff in her hand. "It's an endangered plant species in Maine. Only in Maine." She shrugged. "Who knows?"

"I didn't know that." Jeff watched Cookie getting a rainbow painted on her face.

"Mom, please let me go to the tinker mackerel derby! Just for a minute. I'll come right back, I promise!"

"Danny." She took her son's hands. "You're the big brother. You need to get to know Cookie."

He pulled his hands out of hers. "Whatever." He

jammed his hands into the front pouch of his Sharks hoodie and slinnked off.

Jeff decided to intervene. "Beth, I think it'll be okay if we cut him loose for a little bit."

"But Cookie won't have anyone to play with."

"Do you see the two of them doing any playing?"

"I don't want him going off and deliberately lose track of time."

"Good point." Light bulb moment! "I'll go with him. That way I can keep him on track and you can have some alone time with Cookie so she can get to know you."

"I don't think that's such a good idea, Jeff. She already resents me. She's here to visit with you."

Jeff frowned. He'd wanted to hold her hand all day long, kiss her every once in a while, but had refrained because of Cookie. "She needs to get used to you. Spending time with her is the best way to fix that."

"I don't know. She seems to get more hostile by the minute."

"Come on. It'll be fine. It'll be beyond fine. It'll be awesome." He put on his best 'you know you want to' smile.

She huffed. "Okay, I suppose. Don't let him stay too long."

He gave in to the urge to kiss her. "Be right back. Danny! Cookie!"

The kids turned at the sound of his voice. "Danny, I'm taking you to the mackerel derby. Cookie, you're with Beth. Be good!"

Danny cheered and ran in the direction of Pier Two. Cookie stood frozen on the spot.

Beth could bring her around, like she did when she

helped her make chocolate milk back at his mother's house. Cookie'd come around that time. Beth had a knack.

Right now he had to catch up with the blur that was his son.

****

Cookie stood in front of the face-painting booth like she'd grown roots into the pavement that went all the way to China. The bright rainbow on the side of her face became more obvious as she grew paler and paler.

Beth cringed. This kid did not want to like her.

There was very little of Jeff in her. She was all Katie. Memories of Katie when she'd been Cookie's age, when she'd been Beth's best friend flooded her memory. She shoved back the pangs of regret and loss. "So Cookie, where do you want to go next?"

"Where did Daddy go?"

"He's taking Danny to watch his friend Ben compete in the tinker mackerel derby, so we girls are on our own. What do you want to do next?"

She hitched up one shoulder. "Dunno."

Beth looked around. Ah ha! "Let's go get you a balloon hat."

Cookie blinked at her then shrugged one shoulder again. The other one. So the girl was an ambidextrous shoulder-shrugger. Cool. We all had our talents.

Dealing with a sullen six years old diva was not one of Beth's, yet here she was.

"I bet we can get the guy to make you a pink balloon swan. I'll get one, too."

"Swans aren't pink."

"I imagine he'll make you a swan in any color you want."

Both shoulders went up. Would wonders ever cease?

She had to stop it. Cookie was confused and upset and it was no joke. "He has some balloons that are iridescent. Those would make a magnificent swan."

Cookie gave her the stink eye. "What's iridescent?"

"The balloon is clear but it has hints of color in it." You're talking to a six-year-old Beth. Get a grip. "Like when you blow soap bubbles."

More silence. The back of Beth's head started to itch.

"I guess that would make a beautiful swan." A wistfulness came into Cookie's eyes. "I think it would." Beth made a decision. "Swan Lake was your mother's favorite ballet."

"I know. It's my favorite too."

Now we're cooking with gas. "She'd play the record and make me dance around with her, even though I didn't have an ounce of grace. Still don't." Beth had an acute sense of rhythm. Too bad her feet decided not to share it.

"She dances with me. I like it."

She thought about playing piano duets with Danny, the kid hell-bent on never touching a piano again. "I bet. I bet your mom is really proud of you.

"She is. She tells me all the time. Everyone is proud of me." Cookie had a very smug smile on her face.

"I know your dad is proud of you too."

Clouds descended onto Cookie's expression again. "Then why did he go with Danny and not me?"

"He's proud of both of you." Beth stopped in her

tracks, knelt in front of her and put her hands on Cookie's upper arms. "Your father adores you. He loves you very much."

"I know."

Good-bye clouds. Hello Rainbow Bright. Cookie lit up.

Beth stood. "So let's go get you a swan hat."

Cookie peered at her. "Can we get one for my mommy too?"

"Of course. Whatever you want." Beth doubted Katie would wear an iridescent balloon hat that had been twisted to represent a swan. "It'll be a nice present to take back to her."

Cookie tossed the stuffed Lionel the Lobster they'd bought her earlier into the most nearby trashcan.

"Cookie!"

"I don't want it any more."

Beth leaned against the trashcan. "Your dad bought you that stuffed animal because you begged him for it."

"Danny made fun of it so I don't want it any more." Her smile now stretched across her face, probably because she thought she was getting Danny in trouble. "He's mean to me."

Danny was jealous but not jealous enough to torture Cookie. "You two just have to get to know each other. I know you're used to having your father to yourself. I understand that you don't want to share him." Beth stopped. Cookie grudgingly stopped with her. "Your father is going to be very hurt to learn you threw away Lionel."

"He loves me more than the boy." Cookie nodded. "My mommy told me so. She said he loves me and her way more than he ever loved you. Someday he'll make you and Danny go away."

Oh, holy crap! This was a situation Jeff had to deal with, pronto. She seriously didn't know what to say. Still she had to try. "How about this? Let's go get you a balloon hat and then you can do something by yourself with your dad." She reached in the trashcan and pulled out the stuffed lobster.

After brushing it off, Beth handed it back to her. "There you go. Good as new."

Cookie relented and took back the toy.

Baby steps, Beth thought. Baby steps.

Chapter Thirty-Eight

Beth stowed her wallet back in her purse and picked up the bag holding the shirts she'd just bought for Cookie and Danny. "Hey, Cookie! Let's go find your dad and Danny and—"

Where was she? She wasn't standing where she was supposed to be. She craned her neck to look around. "Cookie?"

The world spun around her for a minute in dizzying loops. "Cookie?"

No sign of her.

"Have you seen the little girl who was standing here just a minute ago?" She grabbed the arm of a woman with several kids who stood nearby.

"Blonde? Pink jacket? She was here." The woman turned around.

"I've got to find her!" Nearly hyperventilating, Beth dropped the bag with the shirts and slapped her hand against her chest. "What if someone took her?"

"She ran off that way." One of the kids pointed in the direction of the waterfront.

"Toward the piers?"

The kid nodded.

"I've got to find her! She doesn't know anybody or anything! She doesn't live here!" Little spots marched across Beth's eyes.

"Go to the public safety booth. They'll be able to

help you. In the meantime I'll keep my eye out and spread the word."

"Oh, thank you!" She started to run to the booth and nearly collided with Jeff and Danny.

"Beth?" Jeff steadied her. "What's wrong?" He looked over her shoulder. "Where's Cookie?"

"I don't know! One minute she was standing here and the next she was gone. One of those kids said she ran away to the piers." Beth started to tremble.

"You lost my daughter?"

"I'm sorry! I stopped to get the kids some T-shirts and while I was paying for them she disappeared."

"We've got to find her!" Air rasped in and out of Jeff's lungs.

"I was on my way to the security station when I ran into you."

"You do that. I'm going down to the pier and look." His hands fisted by his sides and his voice was rough and staccato. "I can't believe you lost her! I trusted you to take care of her, keep an eye on her at the very least. Danny, stay with your mother and I mean it. I don't want to worry about her losing you like she did the night you sneaked out and she didn't know about it. Jesus." He ran a hand over his head. "What kind of mother are you?" He sprinted down to the docks.

Beth swayed with horror as Jeff's angry words filtered through. No time for her hurt feelings. She grabbed Danny's hand. "Let's get going. The sooner we find her, the better."

****

Jeff couldn't hear anything over the roaring in his ears. "Cookie! Cookie!" He rushed around, legs unsteady, desperation riding him hard.

She was so little! She could be anywhere. Someone could have taken her!

He couldn't think about that. She was around here. She had to be.

Beth, Danny and a couple of rent-a-cops caught up with him and joined the search. Some of his players on the football team were there and they pitched in right away.

Everyone was calling her name, combing every inch of the festival space for her.

He could lose any visitation rights to her because of this!

Starting to shake, he kept forcing himself to breathe and calling her name. "Cookie!"

If he didn't find her, he would never forgive Beth. Ever.

Chapter Thirty-Nine

The wind started to whip around; the temperature dropped. Fat drops of rain plunked down on the harbor, causing circles in the water. Cookie only had on a lightweight jacket. She was bound to be so cold. His world narrowed around him as he searched every place he could think of to find his little girl.

"Hey! I found her!"

Jeff's head swiveled to see Danny holding on to Cookie. He sprinted in their direction, hardly noticing that Beth got there first.

He lifted his daughter and held on tight. She sniffled against his shoulder

"She's been hiding under this table the whole time, listening to all of us trying to find her." Danny's voice dripped disgust.

"Did not," Cookie murmured into his ear.

"You're such a liar." Danny nodded emphatically. "You told me you heard everybody calling for you and hid under the table anyway!"

"Why, Cookie girl?" He couldn't wrap his head around her pulling something like this. The crowd had dispersed and the four of them, Beth, Danny, Jeff and Cookie, had made a little circle.

Cookie wouldn't meet his gaze and she'd clamped her mouth shut so tightly her lips turned white.

Beth stood next to Danny, her hands stuffed into

her jacket pocket. Her eyes were very solemn and sad.

"You're right." He nodded. "Let's all go back to my place."

"I don't think so, Jeff. Danny and I would like it if you dropped us off at our house."

His stomach dropped. He had a lot of apologizing to do. "I'm really sorry, Beth. I said some things in the heat of the moment I didn't mean. I was just so panicked about Cookie going missing."

"Okay. Danny and I still want to go home."

"Let's get going." He reached down and grabbed Cookie. He made a sweeping gesture, inviting Beth and Danny to walk ahead of him.

What a mess. The understatement of the century. He'd get to the bottom of it no matter what.

****

Beth stared straight ahead as Jeff drove. She had a lot to think about. More than anything, she had to step up and protect Danny from Katie's lies. How could Katie have become so bitter?

Better question. How could she manipulate her daughter like that? Cookie's mother was a total stranger to Beth. Not that Beth could criticize her for lying, not with the lies she'd told.

It still didn't excuse Jeff's cruel words to her. She'd told him … never mind. Just never mind. The damage was done.

Jeff pulled into her driveway and turned off the engine. "I'll walk you to the door."

"There's no need to do that."

"There's every need."

Beth and Danny were both out of the car before Jeff could even round the car to help them.

Beth fumbled with her house keys while Jeff talked to Danny.

"Sorry things didn't work out the way they were supposed to today."

"S'all right. I had fun with you on the pier at the derby."

"I didn't know you liked to fish. I'll have to take you sometime and you can teach me how to, what do you call it?"

Danny grinned. "Jig for mackerel."

Jeff crouched in front of Danny and gave him a hug. Tears sprang in Beth's eyes but no, she would not cry in front of this man. No chance in hell.

Never again.

"Okay, champ. Looks like your mom's got the door open. Go on in while I talk to your mom out here a little bit."

Danny nodded. He started to walk into the house then turned around and hugged Jeff around his waist. "I love you, Dad!"

Jeff closed his eyes. "I love you too, son."

Danny left Beth standing in front of Jeff.

"Again, I'm so sorry for what happened today. I'm sorry for what I said and I apologize on Cookie's behalf. I'll make sure I get to the bottom of this and make her apologize to you."

Beth felt like she was a hundred years old. "That's fine." She licked her suddenly very dry lips. "You should know that Katie is filling her head with some revisionist history, and it's pretty serious. You need to set them straight." She shrugged. "I need to get in. Danny's hungry and you don't want to leave Cookie alone in the car for too long. Who knows what she'll do."

"I think she knows to stay belted up in her car booster." He reached out to touch Beth's cheek and she flinched.

"Cookie has a problem with you showing me any affection. You need to go and deal with her."

Jeff froze. "I guess I do. I'll call you later."

Beth remembered last night's phone call and wanted to weep. Last night she'd thought she'd hit the jackpot and was on the verge of getting everything she'd ever dreamed of. Today reality conked her in the face with a frying pan.

"Please don't. You've said enough to me today. I'm not up for another round. Good night, Jeff. Go take care of your daughter."

His eyes smoked as he stared at her. After a long moment he said, "Yeah, okay. But I am going to call you later and we are going to deal with this."

"Good night, Jeff. Please go home."

"Good night, sunshine. I'll talk to you later."

"Don't call me that ever again." She let herself in her house and closed the door firmly behind her.

"Mom! Can I have a hotdog for dinner."

Beth closed her eyes. She'd only bought some recently because Danny had begged her to. "Absolutely. How many do you want?"

Chapter Forty

Jeff stared at his phone, dreading the call he had to make to Katie, but it had to be done.

After he'd talked to Cookie and rocked her in his arms as she cried herself to sleep, he'd nearly wept himself. How could Katie fill her head with all those hurtful lies?

Manipulate her own daughter as a weapon against Beth?

The headache brewing behind his eyes didn't show any sign of going away, so he might as well get it over with. He punched the screen over Katie's contact picture. Instead of an actual picture of Katie, he'd uploaded a photo of Jessica Rabbit.

Katie wasn't wrong. She was just written that way.

Give him a break.

She picked it up on the third ring. "Jeff. Why are you calling? Did something happen to Cookie?"

"You might say that." He told her what had happened at the festival.

"She ran away and hid?" Indignation bounced from satellite to satellite. "What did Beth do to her?"

He caught himself grinding his teeth. "Stop right there. Beth didn't do or say anything to upset Cookie. You, however, have been telling her a lot of, shall we say, lies."

"I don't know what you're talking about."

Of course not. "Knock it off. Cookie told me everything you've been telling her. You've been feeding her a pack of lies, Katie. You may have even orchestrated today's little event and I want to know why."

"She's very troubled about Beth's son. I can't help it if she makes things up and acts out."

"I know Cookie and I can tell when she's making things up or telling fibs. She's not lying." He took a moment to let that sink in. "You are."

"You're confusing me with Beth. She's the one who's been lying to people for years."

He wished she were there so he could shake the truth out of her. It was probably better that they were on the phone. "Beth owned up to the lies she told about Danny being my son. If *she* could admit the lies that she'd told, for Danny's sake, then you can do the same for Cookie. Jesus, Katie. I had to hold her while she cried until she fell asleep. A damn hour, Katie. She cried herself until she fell asleep for a whole damn hour and it's all because of the lies you fed to her."

Katie gasped. "You bastard! I'm done with this conversation."

"Not hardly. When I drive Cookie home tomorrow the two of us are going to sit down with her and set the record straight. It's not negotiable. You'll either have to accuse her of being a liar to her face or admit that you lied to her. Choose wisely," he warned.

He could hear her breathing heavily. "Then you drive all the way here. I won't have any conversation about this in public."

Finally! "That's no problem. It's actually what I had in mind."

"When do you think you'll get here?"

"Early afternoon. And I warn you," he said. "I don't trust you as far as I can throw you. We *will* fix this issue and set her straight."

Katie just clicked off. He should be offended but he just felt relieved.

His next phone call was to Beth and he had a lot to make right.

He remembered the devastated look on her face and the resigned tone of her voice and hoped with all his might that it wasn't too late.

****

Beth felt her phone vibrate on the nightstand next to her bed. Tempted not to answer, she could tell Jeff tomorrow that she'd already been asleep. What was one more lie onto the heaping pile of them?

Might as well get this over with. She picked up her phone. "Hello, Jeff."

"Beth, hey. Is this a good time to talk or is Danny still up?"

"Danny fell asleep reading the latest installment of *Adventures of The Refractor*, so yeah, I can talk freely."

"Good. I really can't tell you enough how sorry I am for the things I said to you when Cookie went missing. Some of them were unforgiveable but I hope you'll find it in you to forgive me. I went a little crazy."

No kidding. "What's done is done. No need to hold a grudge. And you forgave me, or at least I thought you did, when you found out I lied about Danny. I just didn't expect to have Danny sneaking out thrown in my face and be accused of being negligent. I told you I wouldn't allow you to talk to me that way and I won't." She cleared her throat to get rid of the misery threatening to choke her.

"I know and I regret saying those things more than I can say. I was totally out of line. I, uh, would like to bring Cookie over tomorrow morning before I take her back to Addington so she can apologize to you."

"There's no need."

"She has to apologize, Bethy. I can't let her get away with that kind of hurtful behavior." He coughed. "I know it won't make a difference to you, but I'm going to make sure Katie stops telling her stories. This has to stop."

"I agree. She's a very confused little girl."

"Can we talk on Monday night when I bring Danny home from practice?"

"I don't think so. I won't stand in the way of your relationship with Danny, I'll still let the adoption happen, but I won't spend any time with someone who accuses me of being irresponsible and calls me a bad mother."

Damn. Unshed tears gathered and welled in her eyes. She swallowed.

"Please, Beth, I don't think that. I didn't know what I was saying."

She sniffled but would not give him the satisfaction of hearing her cry. "I need some space. I don't think we should see each other for a while, except for when it involves Danny."

"Beth."

"I mean it, Jeff. It doesn't matter if I have feelings for you. I can't be with you if you're not good for me. I can't live in fear that the next time you get angry you'll hurl unfounded accusations at me." She swiped at her eyes. "I lived that way for too long. I won't do it again."

She could hear him breathe. "We'll talk about this in person. I promise I'll make it up to you."

"Jeff, please, just...just...don't. Okay? I can't take it right now."

He made a choking sound. "Okay. I'll bring Cookie around eleven o'clock if that's good for you."

"I'll be playing at mass then, so it has to be before or after."

"Is nine okay then?"

"Sure. As long as it doesn't take too long."

"We'll see you at nine, Bethy. I will make this up to you. I promise."

"Good night, Jeff." Please just let him say good night and not make her hang up on him.

"Good night."

Thank God. She hung up and threw her phone back on the nightstand.

When she got a call from Jeff last night she'd been in heaven. Tonight he called and she was in hell. What a difference twenty-four hours made. She noticed her copy of *The Duke's Desire*. From now on she'd count on the dashing hero, Rolf, for all her romance.

Chapter Forty-One

"Mom, can Dad stay for dinner?"

Beth perched on the arm of the couch. "I'm afraid not. Dad told me he has things to do tonight."

She dared him to contradict her.

"That's right, champ. Another night."

Over her dead body.

"Go on and grab a shower. We'll eat once you're done."

Jeff studied her face while Danny hurtled out of the room.

"Can we find some time to talk, Beth? I really want to make it up to you."

"Is this your definition of giving me space?"

He ran his fingers through his hair. "I made Katie make things right for Cookie. She won't ever bad mouth you or Danny again."

She raised an eyebrow. "Thank you."

He reached out like he wanted to touch her. She moved so he couldn't. "Please, Jeff. I don't want to deal with this right now."

"Does this mean you are willing to deal with it some time in the future?"

Throwing her hands in the air, she raised her voice. "God, you don't give up!"

"No, I don't. I've waited to long to be with you," he said.

"Jeff, please. Not now." She hugged herself and rubbed her hands up and down her arms.

He gave a very curt nod. "Tell Danny I said good night and I'll see him tomorrow." Turning on his heel, he left.

Somehow all the air in the room left with him.

****

"Please, Jenna, you've got to help me." Jeff said.

A couple of weeks had passed. Beth still wouldn't talk to him about anything except Danny's schedule. She'd let him take Danny out trick-or-treating, but refused to come with them. There was so much sadness in her eyes and it killed him to know he put it there.

Jenna, on the other hand, looked mad. She had a pair of sharp, knitting needles in her hands and it was clear she knew how to use them.

Ouch.

"Why? You broke her heart."

"I'm going crazy. She's got to give me a second chance."

"I think you're on your third or fourth chance."

"Haven't you ever done or said something that hurt someone you love? Something you wish with all your heart you could take back?"

She frowned. "Good point." She aimed those knitting needles, those weapons of mass destruction, the business ends in his direction, at his chest. "If I help you and you hurt her again, I'm going to stake you through the heart with these."

"I won't, I promise."

She held up one of the needles of doom. "First you're going to grovel like it's your job. Second." She held up the other one. "You're going to take her to the

Fall Formal."

"What? Why would I take Beth to a high school dance?"

Jenna shook her head at him. "Think about it. Given her father and his oh-so-enlightened views on dating, do you remember ever seeing her at a dance?"

"No, I guess not." His brow furrowed. "Do you really think taking her to a dance in a high school gym, surrounded by hormonally charged teenagers dressed in tacky polyester, is the right thing to do?"

Jenna put the needles of mass destruction on the counter. "Yes. We were talking about it one day and she told me how when she was pregnant with Danny how she dreamed of dressing up in a beautiful gown and dancing with you at the prom. So you're going to give her that."

His heart constricted into a tight ball. He'd gone by himself to prom and dreamed of Beth being with him. "I would never have thought of that in a million years."

Jenna rolled her eyes much more expertly than Danny did. "Of course not. That's why you needed me." She nodded. "And not just taking her to the dance. She deserves the whole nine yards, to put it in terms you understand. I'm talking tuxedo, limo, corsage, making out somewhere you shouldn't, all that good stuff she missed out on. Since I don't trust you to pick out the dress, I'll do it. Can you handle the limo and corsage? I know you can manage the whole making out somewhere you shouldn't. Danny's the proof of that."

That was a low blow, but well deserved. Jenna didn't pull her punches. "Do you think this prom thing will work?"

She rolled her eyes, again taking the gold in the eye

rolling Olympics. "Would I have told you to do it if I didn't think it would work?"

"Um, you might if you secretly want to sabotage me."

Jenna held her hands up, palms facing out. "Good point but no sabotage here."

"How am I going to get her there?"

"Do I have to do everything for you?" Jenna sputtered. "Man up and figure it out."

"Yes, ma'am."

He had a lot of work to do in just a week, but if it got him Beth back, it'd be worth it.

Chapter Forty-Two

"Whoa! That's a lot of sequins." Beth touched the sparkliest dress she had ever seen. "I need to get my sunglasses."

Jenna beamed as she held it up. "Isn't it? I copied it from a picture of a Jenny Packham dress Kate Middleton wore once. I saw it on the Fug girls website. I think it came out okay but you have to try it on."

"I do?"

"Yes."

"Why?"

"Just humor me and try it on, okay?" Jenna shoved the silver dress at her. "And damn if you don't look like Kate Middleton sometimes."

"I don't look like Kate Middleton. I could never pull off one of those ridiculous hats she has to wear." Beth grabbed the magnificent creation before Jenna dropped it on the floor.

Oh my God, how many pounds could one dress weigh? If she'd known she was going to wear this silver sequined work of art, she'd have eaten Wheaties for breakfast.

"Actually, when you wear your hair down, you really do. Well, Kate Middleton disguised as a harried, single soccer mom. Please go try on the dress."

This was so not Jenna, but hey! What would it hurt to put this glitzy frock on? "I'll be right back."

"Let me know if you need help with the zipper," Jenna called.

"Will do."

After closing the door to the break room and hanging the dress on a hook on the wall, Beth took off her khaki skirt and pink button down blouse. When she looked in the mirror she didn't see Kate Middleton. She saw plain Beth Pritchard, clad only in a plain Playtex white cotton bra and bikini panties. Her choice of underwear did not deserve this gown.

It deserved the underwear she'd conjured up when Jeff called her and she'd had her first, and likely only, phone sex. Lingerie she'd only seen in her fantasies. Fantasies of Jeff taking that teddy and thong off and kissing her in all kinds of places she hadn't known about back in the day.

Maybe it had been better if she'd never had an orgasm brought on by someone else and not her battery operated boyfriend, because that way she wouldn't crave one now at just the thought of him.

She'd better buy a whole bunch of Evereadys. No, she would not think of that. She could not think of that. Hating that she still loved him, that she still longed for him, Beth renewed her vow to get over him for once and for all. He was Danny's father. No more, no less.

No matter what, he would never be more than that. She couldn't afford that kind of pain, the kind that kept you awake at night trying not to bawl your eyes out under your covers so your son doesn't hear you and get scared.

She loved Jeff, dear God how she loved Jeff. She'd never love anyone else. But it could never work, not if she couldn't trust him to hold her past against her. Her life had run along without stress and drama before she'd seen him again. It could be that way again.

She prayed to every deity in the cosmos, just to cover all her bases, to make her life smooth again.

She pulled the dress off its hanger and held it up in front of her. Another kind of longing came, so innocent and, well, childish.

She wanted to enter the ballroom, or a church aisle, a princess-bride in a gorgeous dress, dripping with jewelry and a diamond crown on her head, and have every man fall at her feet.

Just like every princess-bride in the world. Who was she kidding? She was no princess and certainly not a bride. Though she had desperately wanted to be one ten years ago.

Taking a big breath, Beth soldiered on. It was a dress, right? Not a lifetime commitment. Then she saw herself in the mirror. The woman looking at her bore no resemblance to the woman she usually saw. She might have worn a dress like this to play the piano in concert, right in front of the orchestra.

Her hand rose to cover her mouth. Her hands, her fingers didn't work. Her fingers! She should have been a concert pianist. Her fingers always worked.

Not today.

The dress was not skimpy and revealing. Rather it was modest, a classic sheath with not a bit of sexy about it except for the sparkle quotient. And what it hid while it suggested.

Her perfect dress.

Too bad she'd never have an occasion to wear a dress like this, because she loved the way she felt in it. She looked awesome. Drop dead gorgeous awesome. It was like Jenna had made it just for her.

Oh, no fair. How could Jenna do this to her? Jenna knew she hadn't ever worn anything special, had never been to an occasion where she would worn something like this, even if she could have gotten her hands on it. She closed her eyes and gave herself a moment, imagining wearing this fairy tale dress, living in a fairy tale story in which Jeff held her in his arms while they danced.

Oh, how she craved it.

"How are you doing in there?"

Beth's eyes flew open. She opened the door. "I need help with the zipper," Beth said.

"Hold on." Jenna bustled in and took a gander at Beth in the mirror. She put a hand over her mouth. "Oh my. I knew it would be perfect." She pulled up the zipper.

"What do you mean you knew it would be perfect?"

"What if I asked you to be prepared for surprises tonight and just go with the flow?"

"I can't go with the flow. Going with the flow doesn't exist in my life. I've got a kid and I have to keep to the schedule. I have a kid and I just can't leave him alone while I go skipping out willy nilly."

"Promise not to yell at me."

"No."

"You are so mean." Jenna looked full of regret. "What if I told you that I made arrangements for Danny to have a sleepover with Ben tonight at Anita's?"

Go to holy hell and back again! "You can't do that? How dare you make arrangements for my child without consulting me?" Beth's pulse raced as she tried to process what Jenna was telling her.

"Listen to me." Jenna grabbed Beth firmly by the shoulders. "You know I am your biggest cheerleader." Jenna shook her hands.

Consider me your fairy Godmother. The first wish I grant you is that you're going to Hair's The Thing and you're going to get the whole enchilada, hair, nails, makeup."

"What?" Had she stepped into an alternate universe populated by the likes of The Refractor and Mega Mole? "Jenna this is—"

"Right and overdue." Jenna pulled Beth in for a hug then let her go. "Way overdue. Just let this happen, girlfriend. If at any point you need to run away, you've got my cell number. I'll come and get you right away."

"This is insane! What are you doing?" Beth couldn't get her bearings. This was the opposite of everything she'd struggled so hard to acquire and achieve.

Jenna gave her gentle shake. "Beth, nothing's going to happen that you don't want to happen. You've got to trust me." Jenna gave her a quick hug and spun her around to look in the mirror. "Who do you see?"

"I see me playing in Kate Middleton's clothes."

"I made this dress just for you so it doesn't belong to anyone else but you."

"Why?"

"It's part of the surprise. It's all arranged. Like I said, you're going to go to Hair's the Thing and get the whole enchilada, hair, nails, makeup." Jenna poked her in the shoulder. And don't you dare take off the makeup. After that, you're going home and Bran will be there."

"What?" This got worse and worse with every word Jenna said. Her ears started buzzing. "Why?"

"Let's just say that you're going to the prom."

"Are you two out of your minds? I can't go to the prom. What prom?"

Jenna smiled. "You keep asking me that. I assure you my mind works just fine. Bran's going to be there to make the experience complete." She smirked.

Beth couldn't see straight what with all the swooping around her brain was doing. "Bran? What experience?" She squeaked louder than Ernie's rubber ducky as she reached for someplace to sit before she fell down.

Jenna pushed her into a chair. With a vice grip worthy of a WWE champion on her neck, she pushed Beth's head between her knees. "Don't you dare get sick on my masterpiece. I'll never forgive you."

"I'm okay, unless I die from you choking me to death."

Jenna relaxed her hold and rubbed Beth's back. "It'll be okay, sweetie. When push comes to shove tonight," Jenna snorted in a way that made Beth think she was laughing, "all the choices will be yours. Nothing will happen if you put the kibosh on it. Now stand up and let me see this brilliant piece of work I sewed."

Beth's body went into mannequin mode, but her mind was racing a mile a minute.

Jenna arranged the dress, pulled the pony tail holder out of Beth's hair and fluffed said hair up and around Beth's face and settled the longer curled ends around her shoulders.

Finally happy with her handiwork, she took a step

back. She smiled so beatifically she could have been the Lady of Fatima handing out 'You're saved, go sit on the right hand' cards to all and sundry like they were Pez candies. Clapping her hands together she said, "This turned out better than I ever could have predicted. Look at yourself, Beth. Really. Take a good look at yourself."

Beth did, not expecting to see anything different from what she always saw. Plain, simple, perpetually single mother Beth.

"Go ahead, look," Jenna said. "Take a good look and see what everyone else sees."

So Beth did. Her eyes flicked to the dress first, which was pretty damn awesome and fit like a glove, outlining curves while preserving modesty. She slid her eyes up to check out her reflection and gasped. Everything looked brighter, more vital, more alive. "How?"

"And this is without makeup. Once we get you the whole shebang you'll be deadly." She rubbed her hands together like Danny's favorite villain Time Bomb did. "Let's get you back into your clothes and over to Hair's The Thing."

"I still don't get it."

"Okay. Jeff is desperate to get you back. He says he knows he screwed up and he really loves you and won't be an insensitive lout ever again."

"Jeff would never say insensitive lout."

"The thing is, sweetie, I believe him. He screwed up bad, he knows it and he just wants to make it up to you, to show you how sorry he is and how much he loves you. The prom was my idea, but was more than happy to go and run with it."

"I don't have to go if I don't want to?"

"Of course not." Jenna smiled. "But my money's on him. Give him a chance." She put her hands on Beth's upper arms and squeezed. "Give yourself a chance."

Beth sighed and rolled all this over in her mind. Did she really want to give Jeff another chance? Could she believe in him? Jenna had already gone to a lot of trouble and she guessed she was going to find out. It was only polite. "Okay. Let's go get my hair and makeup done.

****

"So, what do you think?" Marge, the owner of Hair's The Thing, spun Beth's chair around so Beth could see what she'd done.

Her jaw dropped. "Oh, my."

The woman staring back at her had long, soft curls the color of mink. Smudges of gilded eye shadow turned her blue eyes into a sultry shade of violet. Her eyelashes were outrageously long and thick. Lipstick the color of a dusky rose slicked her lips. "I don't know what to say."

"You are gorgeous, girl! You've been hiding one crazy-hot MILF in there."

"MILF?" Beth let out a strangled squeak. Even she knew what that stood for.

"She's right," Jenna said with a wide smile. "You ready to blow this Popsicle stand and go home to put on the finishing touches?"

Beth could only nod. She truly had no words.

Chapter Forty-Three

"Would you please stop pacing? You're making me nervous," Jenna's fiancé Bran grumbled

"Why are you here again?" Beth stopped in her tracks to turn and face him.

"I'm the overprotective father. I'm here to threaten him with death if he hurts you." He grimaced. "It might not be hypothetical. I might rip his guts out through his mouth if he manages to do more damage."

"Dear Lord." Beth turned away from the couch where Jenna and Bran lounged together. "I've got to practice walking in these shoes so I don't fall flat on my face."

Jenna grinned. "They are killer."

"And I'm the one they're going to kill," Beth muttered.

A marvel of modern engineering, the four-inch platform stiletto sandals glittered with rhinestone-encrusted straps.

"You're doing fine." Jenna laughed as she pulled her legs up on the sofa.

"I don't know about that." She pressed her hands against her stomach, where a battalion of butterflies fluttered around. Not butterflies. Worse than butterflies. Bumblebees. "What if I can't do this? What if I can't forgive him?"

The doorbell rang and Beth yelped. Bran jumped

up. "I'll get it." He opened the door and there stood Jeff. "Come on in, young man," Bran said.

"Thank you, Mr. Cudahy." He stepped over the threshold. "Hi, Beth."

Oh they were playing their parts like Broadway stars. But all she could see was her date.

"Jeff," she barely breathed.

Dear lord. He wore a black formal tuxedo over a snowy white dress shirt and a black silk bow tie. He carried a clear plastic box with flowers in it.

He strode to her. He swallowed and looked really uncertain. "You look exquisite."

"Thank you." She rubbed her damp palms on her dress.

Jenna groaned. "Don't rub—"

"Shhhh," Bran told her.

"I've got something for you." After opening the box he pulled out a breathtaking wrist corsage made of an elegant white gardenia on a bed of shiny dark green leaves. "Give me your wrist."

Beth held her breath as he slipped the flower on her arm. "There. Do you like it?"

She brought the fragrant flower to her nose and inhaled. It smelled exotic and seductive. "It's lovely."

Jenna came up to them and handed Beth a barely open white rose boutonniere. "You need this."

Beth stopped herself from biting her lower lip because she didn't want to get lipstick on her teeth. She managed to get the boutonniere on him without sticking him with the pin, but it was a near miss.

"Are you ready to go?" Jeff offered his arm.

"Just a second." Bran stopped Jeff from leading her out. "Hurt her and I'll hunt you down, find you and gut you with a dull butter knife and use your pitiful entrails to make a sausage no one will ever eat. Got that?" Beth was startled to see a real threat on Bran's face.

"Just one more sec!" Jenna pulled out a camera. "Let's get some pictures."

So they posed in typical pre-prom poses while she clicked away. "Now you can go." She put down the camera and handed Beth a small, beaded evening bag. "Have fun!"

"Are we really going to the prom or is that code for something?""

"Sunshine? I hope you have your dancing shoes on." Jeff escorted her out of her house. "We are most definitely going to the prom."

****

Jeff had always thought Beth was pretty in the girl-next-door kind of way. It was one of the things that attracted him to her.

The woman he had on his arm was no girl-next-door. This woman defined glamour and style and drop dead sexiness. His fingers itched to touch her, to kiss her and claim her. Amazingly aroused, he felt his penis harden. But then he always had that reaction to her, everyday Beth and glammed-up Beth.

"Oh my God, it that a limo?"

"Of course it's a limo. You're getting the whole prom experience." He opened the door and offered his hand. "Let me help you in."

"I can't believe this," she said, her amazement plain to see.

He slid in next to her, his skin tingling at being so close to her. "I have never, in my whole life, seen a more beautiful woman. You are stunning."

"It's the dress." She ran her hands over the skirt.

"It's not the dress." He picked up her hand and kissed her knuckles. "It's all you." He held on to her hand.

"Are we really going to a prom?"

"Not exactly." He cleared his throat. "We're really going to Lobster Cove High School's Fall Formal. I didn't want to wait until spring for the prom. I hope that's okay with you."

She sighed. "You and Jenna went to all kinds of trouble to make this happen."

"I do have to caution you that the dance is in the high school gym. Only the prom gets a special location. The other school dances get the gym." He snapped his fingers. "Maybe you'll chaperone the prom with me."

She ran a fingertip over the gardenia he'd given her. "I wouldn't know the difference."

"I've got to say this now, Beth. I am sorry from the bottom of my soul about what I said to you the day Cookie caused all that trouble. If I had been seeing clearly, I would have seen you turning over every rock and stone to find her." Searching her eyes, hoping for some sign of what he wanted from her, he went on. "You're an amazing mother. Danny is the proof of that. Teaching Cookie how to fix her own glass of chocolate milk is the proof of that. I was totally out of line and though I was panicking, I shouldn't have come down on you. I promise you I will never, ever treat you like that again."

Beth sat so still, so silent, he thought he might have lost this chance with her.

"Your mother is a wise woman," she finally said. "I didn't grow up in a house where there was any forgiveness. I kept a huge secret and told a huge lie to you about Danny. Your son. I think that in the end forgiveness is all that matters. You forgave me, so I can forgive you."

Closing his eyes, the sweet rush of relief ran through him. "Oh, sunshine. You don't know how happy I am to hear that." He grinned and rubbed his thumb over the top of the hand he held. Such a small hand, cold and trembling in his palm. Her scent wrapped around him, delicate, floral and fresh.

Pure, sweet Beth. Nothing, no one else ever smelled as good.

"I went to what should have been our prom alone, since no other girl was you. I danced a couple of times, but I pretended those girls were you. That I was dancing with you." He licked his lips and tightened his grip on her hand. Damn, those deep blue eyes of hers always got to him. "I didn't slow dance with anyone."

Those violet eyes widened. "Oh, Jeff." Her rose painted mouth quivered ever so slightly. "I knew when the prom was. I was so pregnant with Danny and spent the night dreaming that I was in Addington, slow dancing with you."

"Sunshine." His chest constricted, thinking of her alone and pregnant while he went to the prom. Thankfully he hadn't taken a date. He just couldn't see himself with another girl.

"Tonight is about you, Bethy. As far as I'm concerned, we're back at Addington High, hip-deep in first love, in each other's arms and swaying on the dance floor."

Her eyes shimmered, another assault on his heart.

She had it already. She'd always had his heart right

311

in the palm of her hand, a cliché he knew, but true.

The limo slowed, so they must be near their destination. "You ready for this?"

"I don't know. Right now, I'm feeling so many things I can't tell them apart."

"Only good feelings, I hope." He prayed that forgiveness and trust were part of the mix.

She opened her mouth to say something, but the driver of the limo let down the barrier separating him from them. "We're here, Jeff. You're good to go."

He couldn't take his eyes off Beth. "Thanks, Tony." He lifted her hand and kissed it again. "Let's go."

As he helped her out of the limo, he couldn't help but marvel at the softness of her skin, the sweetness of her smile, the delicate spill of her glossy hair down to her shoulders.

He got her to trust him again, to believe that he really and truly loved her. He was both amazed and humbled by his luck in getting this second chance. He wasn't going to blow it, not ever again.

They got to the door to the gym. "Stop," Beth said, her voice a little shaky. "Please. I just need a second." She took a deep breath.

"Take whatever you need. I'm right here with you."

She turned those big blue peepers up to look at him. "Yes. I think you are. Okay. I'm ready."

He pulled open the door and ushered her inside.

****

"Oh," Beth put her hand over her mouth. Jeff had told her the gym would be decorated but she thought it would be black, silver and purple crepe paper streamers, a couple of tables covered with plastic tablecloths and only the bleachers out for people to sit on.

Instead they had re-created a Paris outdoor bistro on a starlit night. Murals depicting Paris streets in the evening covered the walls of bleachers. Round café tables covered with butcher paper were scattered around the room. A red pillar candle flickered on each table. Tiny white fairy lights that blinked on and off had been strung from the ceiling and the baskets to make the illusion of stars. Some genius figured out how to rig a huge orange harvest moon to glow and used it to disguise the scoreboard.

Most of the students stood around or boogied to Beyonce, Kanye, and Lady GaGa on a dance floor beside a small stage where a deejay spun the tunes. Dressed to the nines, the kids looked impossibly young, she thought with dismay.

Jeff leaned his head down and whispered in her ear, "You don't look a day older than any of them."

How'd he know what she was thinking? Beth turned her gaze from the party to meet his. Though the lights had been turned low to get the effect of evening, she could still see the green and gray flecks in his hazel eyes. Her heart skipped a beat as she saw the desire reflected there. He shouldn't look at her like that, not with all these teenagers there.

But she couldn't look away.

"We need to dance. This way," he told her.

As he guided her across the gym different kids came up to him and said hello or shared a joke or just traded a simple smile with him. He touched these kids. He made a difference in their lives, just like Mike Kelly had done for him.

Like Andi Kelly had done for her.

Pride in the man he'd become blossomed within her. "They like you."

"I like them." He shrugged then pulled her closer to his side. "I never thought I'd love teaching and coaching like I do." He blushed. "You know my dream was to play for the NFL. I wouldn't trade this job to play for any pro team."

She remembered. "So if Tom Brady retired tomorrow and the Patriots came knocking on your door, you'd say no?" She nudged him in the ribs with her elbow.

"I'd stay here. Every kid has brilliance inside them. I like helping them unlock that brilliance and set it free." He shrugged. "Maybe that's hokey or something, but it's how I feel."

"It's not hokey. It's beautiful." If Beth hadn't fallen in love with him ten years ago, she'd have fallen in love with him for sure now.

He cleared his throat. "I'm sorry you didn't get a shot at your dream."

"My dream?"

"You were going to be a world famous concert pianist. You didn't even get to college, all because I got you pregnant."

She stopped and moved to stand in front of him. "I got Danny, which is so much more precious than any career playing the piano could ever be."

"So, I guess we're on the same page."

Beth nodded. "I think we've always been on the same page."

"I'd love to kiss you, but the chaperones—" He

shook his head. "We might get detention."

Detention? Dear Lord. She knew it existed but, what? "What's detention? I've never been there."

He grinned. "Detention equals annoying misery. The chaperones will write us up for P.D.A. You know, public display of affection."

If arousal hadn't drenched her before, it ran through her body and zapped every single nerve ending she had. Dying for him to kiss her, aching for him to kiss her, she decided to get into the game. "I can't go to detention. My father, Mr. Cudahy, will blame you and who knows what he'll do then?"

He chuckled. "Then we'll save the PDA for later. I don't want to get on Bran Cudahy's bad side. Want to dance?"

"To this music? Not a chance." Adele was singing about not having it all and rolling in the deep.

"No worries. I've got this all worked out." He tugged her hand and pulled her to the dance floor.

"Wait right here," he told her once they got there. "I have to go talk to the deejay."

"Okay."

Beth watched him go up on to the platform, lean toward the deejay. They both laughed, then looked at her and the deejay winked. Jeff shook his head as he walked off the stage back to her then got waylaid by some kids from the football team.

"Mrs. Rawson, is that you?"

"Hannah?" One of Beth's piano students along with three of her friends stood in front of her. "You look so pretty!"

"Well, you look amazing!" Hannah goggled at her. "That dress is totally sick."

"Thank you." Beth felt her face flush. "Are you having a good time?"

Hannah nodded. "Seriously, you are totally gorgeous!"

"She is, isn't she?"

Beth jumped when Jeff put his hands on her arms.

"Hi, Coach." Disbelief and awe coated Hannah's face. Her eyes bugged out of her face, like a Chihuahua on crack.

"I'm going to steal Mrs. Rawson away from you, okay?" He took Beth's hand. "I requested a song and I want to dance with you."

"Of course. It was good to see you."

Jeff tugged on her hand. "Enjoy the rest of your evening, girls." He pulled a little harder. "Let's go."

Beth heard the girls giggle and whisper as Jeff guided her to the dance floor. "I should warn you that I don't know how to dance."

"Don't worry. You don't have to know much for what I have in mind."

When they got to the floor, Jeff caught the deejay's gaze and nodded.

"Got a request," the deejay said into the mic, "for a trip in the Wayback Machine, back to 2004, to the Addington High School prom. So to Beth from Jeff." The beginning quiet guitar intro to Maroon 5's *She Will Be Loved* filled the gym.

"Come on. They're playing our song." He held his hand out to her, palm up, beckoning her.

She took his hand and her skin sizzled at the innocent touch. He gave her the most wonderful smile she'd ever seen. The next thing she knew she was in his arms and they were shuffling to the music.

"Since we are at a dance full of impressionable minors, I can't hold you as close as I'd like to," he murmured just loud enough for only her to hear.

She stared up at him unable to look away from the love in his gaze. She was pretty sure she had stars in her own eyes. Jeff sang along about the girl with a broken smile who will be loved, just so she could hear. He had a beautiful singing voice. She just moved with him to the music. What else could she do?

Applause, hoots, whoops, and whistles erupted around them. Pulled out of their bubble, they finally noticed they were the only ones on the dance floor and that the song was over.

"Oh, God," Beth breathed, totally embarrassed.

Jeff, however, grinned like an idiot. "How about we go somewhere so I can kiss you the way I need to?"

"I like the way you think." And she really did.

He grabbed her hand and they practically ran as they left. Once safely away from the building, out of sight impressionable eyes, Jeff banded his arms around her and gave her an open mouthed kiss full of passion and promise.

He dragged her out to the park right behind the school and took her to the Sharks' end zone.

"I love you," he told her.

"I love you so much!" The words bubbled out, propelled by all the elation inside her.

"It's going to be good, Bethy, I promise. I'm going to kiss you now." And he did, right underneath the home team goal posts. "I'm going to make you so happy."

"Jeff. I don't have enough words to tell you how happy I am right now. Please kiss me."

"Wait just a second more. Do you want to marry me, be the family we always should have been? You, me, Danny and add in Cookie?"

"Oh Jeff. Yes! Of course I'll marry you!"

He closed his eyes. "These last weeks when you wouldn't talk to me were the worst of my life. I couldn't stand to lose you again."

Reaching into his pocket, he pulled out a small, velvet box. She put her hand over her heart to keep it from beating out of her chest and watched him open the box.

"This is the ring my father gave my mother. After the weekend from hell, my mother gave it to me to give to you."

"Oh, my!"

"Breathe, sunshine. This ring is her blessing. Please put me out of my misery and say yes."

He lifted the old-fashioned diamond solitaire, set in white gold, and took her hand. "You better be sure, because once I put it on your finger, I'm not letting you take it off ever. Just say yes. I've never, ever wanted to hear that word so much in my life."

"Yes." She was so, so sure.

He closed his eyes, relief and joy etched on his face. "Thank God."

He slid the ring on her finger then held it up to admire it. "It looks perfect there on your finger."

"It's so beautiful."

"Not nearly as beautiful as the woman wearing it. Tell me yes again."

"Yes, yes, yes, a million times yes!"

"Shall we seal the deal with a kiss?"

"Please."

And so they did.

"Think Danny will be happy?"

"He'll be over the moon," Beth knew that better than her own name.

"Let's go tell him."

"It'll have to wait until tomorrow, since he's sleeping over at Ben's. Of course, that does mean we'll have the house all to ourselves until tomorrow morning." She ran a finger down his lapel.

"Really alone or will Bran Cudahy be standing on the porch with a shotgun?" He shuddered. "Or a really big knife with the threat of castration in his eyes?"

"I can guarantee Bran Cudahy will be nowhere in sight."

"In that case, what are we waiting for? Let's go home."

That was the best idea Beth had heard in a very long time. "Yes. Let's go home," she repeated. "It's way past time."

"I feel like all my life I've been working my way back to you. Glad I finally made it." He took her by the hand.

"Me, too. Let's get out of here."

"I'm right there with you, sunshine, every step of the way."

A word about the author...

Doreen has wanted to be a writer her whole life but took a detour into being an opera singer and choral conductor. She realized that maybe she should spend more time writing when creating the back stories was more fun than actually singing them. Plus her romance-lovin' heart couldn't take all the dead bodies littering the stage at the end of the performance. She is still an active conductor and is regularly found waving her arms around in front of singers.

www.doreenalsen.com